A WINTER IN CHINA

Also by Douglas Galbraith

The Rising Sun

A WINTER IN CHINA

Douglas Galbraith

Secker & Warburg
London

Published by Secker & Warburg 2005

2 4 6 8 10 9 7 5 3 1

Copyright © Douglas Galbraith 2005

Douglas Galbraith has asserted his right under the Copyright, Designs
and Patents Act 1988 to be identified as the author of this work

First published in Great Britain in 2005 by
Secker & Warburg
Random House, 20 Vauxhall Bridge Road,
London SW1V 2SA

Random House Australia (Pty) Limited
20 Alfred Street, Milsons Point, Sydney,
New South Wales 2061, Australia

Random House New Zealand Limited
18 Poland Road, Glenfield,
Auckland 10, New Zealand

Random House (Pty) Limited
Endulini, 5A Jubilee Road, Parktown 2193, South Africa

The Random House Group Limited Reg. No. 954009
www.randomhouse.co.uk

A CIP catalogue record for this book
is available from the British Library

ISBN 0436206269 (hbk)
ISBN 0436205912 (trade pbk)

Papers used by Random House are natural,
recyclable products made from wood grown in sustainable forests;
the manufacturing processes conform to the environmental
regulations of the country of origin

Typeset in Bembo by Palimpsest Book Production Limited,
Polmont, Stirlingshire

Printed and bound in Great Britain by
Mackays of Chatham plc, Chatham, Kent

A WINTER IN CHINA

1

Hugh was waiting in the hall, hat in hand. Outside, a pair of black Humber Pullmans exhaled thickly into the cold morning air. Figures in bulky coats were sitting in the back, already half obscured by the mist on the windows. The engines' heavy breaths clouded around the cars like a stage effect preparing for a magical disappearance. Fumes began to seep into the embassy porch. Hugh looked again at his watch and shouted up the stairs.

'Oh, come on, darling. Peter's waiting at the hotel.'

Sally Marsden shouted back – she was coming and he should not be so impatient. Two floors up and at the end of the corridor in the second guest bedroom she could feel the cold from the open hall door. It stirred the cornflower curtains, made the fine hairs on the back of her neck ripple upwards. The travelling set her mother had given her lay disarranged about the dressing table – silver-topped bottles, tiny scissors, a nail file and a surplus of tortoiseshell brushes each supposed, according to the manufacturer, to have a specific function in the *toilette* of the modern adventuress. She chose one carelessly and applied it to her hair with punitive energy before throwing it in the half-packed suitcase on the floor.

Sally leaned closer to the hinged triptych of mirrors and silently questioned her own image. She strained her neck to get a better view of her second reflection, that half-strange version of one's features that was all the outside world could see. She ran a curious finger along the high-angled line of dark eyebrows and then around her startling, pale hazel eyes themselves. She pushed her nose about critically without finding any improvement. It was this paternal trait, along with the strongly incised lines of mouth and chin that had caused her several times to be mistaken for a boy around the age of fourteen. She straightened again and watched the little crinkle of her nose that signalled the ambiguous regret she always experienced on catching sight of her own features. Well, at least they weren't ordinary.

Three minutes later she appeared, fixing the angle of her bottle-green Tyrolean hat and bounding down the stairs two at a time.

'Sorry! Just a tick.'

The future Mrs Hugh Jerrold – the announcement was just a formality – paused before the hall mirror. She pulled down the hem of her check riding jacket, wriggled her fingers into new gloves, replaced a lock of black hair under the brim of her hat.

'Are you sure it's all right?'

'It's perfect,' said Hugh, 'as ever.'

'You know very well what I mean. We'd all look so silly if there was trouble.'

'It's fine – they're all miles away. Anyway, look.'

Sally took down her Burberry from the stand and let Hugh lead her out on to the step. He pointed to the new, enlarged Union Jacks on the front wings of the two cars before helping her in.

'I'd better keep Brindle company, all right? He gets positively twitchy if he has to go an hour without talking about ball bearings. See you at the other end.'

Hugh closed the door on his near fiancée and got into the other car. The Ambassador smiled at Sally and brandished his guidebook.

'All ready? Off we go.'

He tapped the glass. The chauffeur set the car in motion and the journey began.

The cars crept out of the driveway and turned left. Sally wiped a porthole of clarity in the middle of the misted window. China dropped down around her, as sudden and bizarre as the backcloth of a Savoy opera.

The cars moved slowly, waiting for walkers, cyclists and straining rickshaw coolies to get out of their way. Only a skeletal, waspish motorcycle, its goggled rider completing the insect, and the Japanese attaché's car returning from the station shared the motorised world. On either side of the road, low wooden buildings filed by. Neat rows of shoes waited by sliding doors. Beside them stood innumerable pots with green, branchless stumps that would speckle the city with geranium red throughout the distant summer. Sir Harold leaned forward and signalled through the window with his guidebook.

'Ah, my good friend Mr Fukuda. We will be dining with him on Thursday – Hugh and I only, I'm afraid. It seems he has something to tell us. You must hear him speaking English before you go – it's quite the funniest thing.'

The Ambassador rapped the partition sharply with the handle of his umbrella.

'Heat up! Heat up! Oh God! Why don't they ever send

me anywhere warm? Mind you, Miss Marsden, the summer here is quite awful.'

The car accelerated as it turned into the main street. Modernity appeared in discrete concrete intrusions, the first footsteps of a giant that would trample over the entire city. There was the International Club, the grimy offices of the Transoceania News Agency, the Metropolitan Hotel and in the distance the pale blocks of the university and the government ministries that gave substance to China's future. There was the odd compromise – villas from that same design sold in Cheam or Chorleywood, but with alien roofs of semi-cylindrical tiles and upward-curving, horned eaves sitting awkwardly over central doors and square-set windows of hinged iron frames. Sally had long known these structures were to be despised. At home, to her father, they were 'blight', 'sarcoma'. Their functionless chimneys could be seen from the upper windows, an advancing skirmish line of vulgarity from which the Marsden stock had been too recently extracted. Her father's greatest fear was that he would one day be recognised by someone who lived in one of these houses. How odd that they should be here too, a version of them at any rate, still recognisable under their heavy, oriental maquillage. She had mentioned them in a letter a week or so back, describing them with acceptable rudeness and reassurance too. They meekly proclaimed their transitional status – unsuccessful answers to a question no one had yet understood, they too would be stamped on and replaced by concrete. Sally's style had come a long way since handkerchiefs had been waved at Southampton. She was more conscious too of her new worldliness and thought long about her final image before putting it down on paper. She contrived a letter addressed only to her father and was sure he would be pleasantly shocked to learn that such houses were like the ailments left in the wake of a travelling army – they too would pass.

The cars had stopped and were waiting for an opportunity to U-turn through the flow of traffic. Crouching by the side of one of these mongrel houses was a wooden shed with an economical wisp of smoke drifting from a tin stack into the still air. Its double doors were wide open to advertise the business within. Rows of tools hung from the insides of the doors and the cobbler himself knelt on the ground just in front of them, hammering at something held tightly between his thighs. His customer sat on a chair alongside, his white-stockinged feet on a small wooden stool. From above the open doorway a cloth hung down with three complicated characters painted in black. Still labouring under what she had been told by one of the 'old hands' she had met in Shanghai, Sally stared hard at the scene, moving her eyes constantly between the two men and the characters like an artist preparing for a sketch.

'They're all just pictures, really,' a woman with a martini and a black cigarette in an amber holder had told her one evening. 'Not really writing at all. All you have to do is let your eyes go out of focus and use a bit of imagination.'

She had described in the air with her cigarette the symbol for 'tree' and explained that three of them together meant 'forest'. The point was followed immediately by an outburst of laughter as if she had just delivered the punchline to a paralysingly funny joke.

Sally tried to find the shape of a kneeling cobbler and his seated customer in the tangle of black brush strokes on the cloth. In focus, out of focus, sideways – nothing. But she supposed it was beautiful. This too she had heard many times since arriving in China and she had begun to conform to this aesthetic of the incomprehensible. Where one knew

5

nothing at all, there could at least be no objection to a polite and general praise. The important thing, as she had quickly learned, was not to be thought a dull person without opinions.

The chauffeur sounded the car's horn and gestured to a small, muffled figure struggling with a handcart. Sally turned back to Sir Harold. She had been aware of his gaze all the time she was looking at the cobbler and now that their eyes met he almost embarrassed her by holding the stare for several seconds. She broke the moment with a smile and looked across to the other side of the street. She shifted her position on the seat, though not too discouragingly. She had become entirely used to such scrutiny over the last two months and had decided that it would be pointlessly selfish to reject it, not to mention old-fashioned. She coolly envisaged the casual generosity of giving herself to the Ambassador. The image must have been in his mind too. It made her smile – how disgusting life was, how absurd, and how wonderful that she should know it.

She had been confused by these attentions at first, though only for a very short while, and then conventionally disquieted – not her own emotion, she had to admit, just a courtesy to the expectations of her absent mother, so worried as she was about the whole foolish notion, the new scheme of her husband, determined, as he had always been, to turn his daughter into a boy. But now here she was – desired, reassured and managing rather well.

'Do you read Chinese?'

'Good heavens, no,' said Sir Harold. 'No one bothers with language in the diplomatic service. No point – you've only just mastered "Have my boots ready in the morning" and they post you to Turkey.'

The sentence had an elaborate, well-turned intonation that suggested a lengthy process of perfection in many parts of the world. He laughed and Sally laughed too.

'Still,' he added, 'I can't help thinking it's rather beautiful.'

'Yes, I suppose it is. Oh, look. There he is.'

The cars were on the move again, turning slowly round, the polished baffle of an enormous valve shutting off for their own convenience the flow of a quarter of the city's traffic before sidling up to the steps of the Metropolitan Hotel. Peter Moss stood at the top, hailing them with two bottles sheathed in straw. The Leica, which he was never without, hung at his side from a thin leather strap that ran across his chest like a toy version of something military. He came down the steps and leaned towards the window of the first car to have a word with Hugh.

'Ah', said Sir Harold, 'now there is a decision to be made. Will he travel with Hugh and Mr Brindle, do you think? Or will he find our company more attractive? I believe I already know.'

Peter straightened up and began to come towards the second car.

'There you are! Diplomats – what a sinister lot we are.'

Sir Harold laid an innocent hand on Sally's knee, treating himself to a last indulgence before they were no longer alone. He continued in a confidential tone.

'There is a contract for ball bearings in Tientsin we would rather the Americans didn't know about. For Hugh, you see, it is partly a working trip.'

'Morning! I'm with you it seems.'

Peter had opened the door and stood for a moment, smiling awkwardly with rosy cheeks and steaming breath.

'Red or white?' demanded Sir Harold.

Peter presented his bottles.

'Barsac.'

'Be a good chap and put it in the boot, will you?'

Peter did as he was asked and fairly ran back into the car,

perching on one of the facing seats, rubbing his gloved hands and coddling them between his knees. The Humbers crept back into motion, adding a little strength to the feeble draught of heated air that rose from an invisible vent. Peter declared it was so cold they could be in Illinois and then apologised to the Ambassador for the wine.

'I thought something sweet would be good for this weather – keep us going. But they didn't have any Sauternes left.'

Sir Harold threw up his hands.

'The horrors of war!'

The cars turned into the relative calm of Fukien Street and picked up speed. Husbanding their conversational resources for the three-quarter-hour drive to the temple, Sally, Peter and Sir Harold looked out on the passing scene. Skullcaps and trilbys mingled on the heads of the people, pigtails and short bobs on the younger women. Confucius rubbing shoulders with Charlie Chan. Children were swaddled thickly against the cold. The youngest were tied to their mothers' backs. Their faces, the colour and roundness of peaches, turned to watch the strangeness of this little motorcade, the bright flags, the people behind glass like the good things in a shop. Small groups of soldiers in their quilted blue smoked cigarettes and kept close to braziers. A sign caught Sally's eye – 'Marx! Marx! Marx!' Men were tacking boards to the windows of a small picture house and another was up a ladder, leaning to one side to balance against the weight of a large 'S'. She could still read 'A Day at the Race'.

'You seen it?' asked Peter.

Sally shook her head, the Ambassador looked mournful.

'No time for films, I'm afraid. Do you think I should? Is it good?'

Peter reddened a little and got halfway to saying he had been asking Sally really before tailing off. Sir Harold had always been admired in the service for his skilful handling of embarrassment.

The cars turned to the left and Sally looked up at the oppressive city walls and the thick buttresses of the Tai Ping Gate. Sandbagged machine-gun nests now flanked the tunnel running through it. A soldier was coming from one with a kettle in his hand, suddenly the focus of a dozen of his comrades. A barrier was moved out of the way and after a second or two of darkness they emerged into the country-side of Kiangsu.

Sir Harold turned abruptly away from the window as if a thought had just occurred to him.

'Tell me, Mr Moss, you must have many American friends in Shanghai, yes?'

'Quite a few, I suppose.'

'And you are in touch? How are they faring?'

'They all seem to be fine, thank you – last time I heard, anyway. The Metropolitan can't get their telephones to work since yesterday, but they seem OK. The rest of the city is in a mess but the Settlement is being respected. I got a telegram Tuesday from a newspaperman I know. He thought things were quietening down.'

'You don't know any casualties, then?'

'No.'

'I'm thankful. I don't know any either, I'm pleased to say.' He turned to Sally.

'The timing will work out well, I think. Even if it's awkward here, you'll be able to return to a peaceful Shanghai. Say what you like about the Japanese, but they're an efficient lot. It's not like being occupied by – I don't know – Italians or something. God forbid! Do you know Mr Fukuda?'

Peter said he did not.

'Decent chap. Bit comical, but decent.'

The morning mist was beginning to clear. The sun became visible – a pale heatless disc one could look at directly without discomfort. Purple Mountain, at first an ink-wash hint at distant solidity, darkened and then became suddenly clear as the cars climbed into lighter air. The brilliant white tomb of Sun Yat-sen was set like a lighthouse in the middle of the dark scrubland.

'They say he's just asleep up there,' said Peter. 'Waiting until China needs him again.'

'A Chinese King Arthur,' observed Sally.

Sir Harold considered the analogy with a show of concentration.

'It's remarkable how many cultures have them, these sleeping heroes. I knew a Frenchman once who thought it blasphemy to say Charlemagne was dead. What about America, Mr Moss? Will we have the chance to speak again with Washington, do you think? Will Lincoln stir to the sound of the trumpet?'

'Not our style, sir.'

'No?'

Peter Moss looked at Sally with a slightly complicit smile as he made his answer.

'We're too prosaic for that.'

'Ah, well – it's for the best, I suppose. There's only disappointment otherwise. I'll say one thing, though. If Dr Sun were to come walking down that hill again, I can't see the Little Marshal being very pleased. Perhaps he has sent some agents to slip a few sleeping pills into his coffin – what do you think?'

'I think,' said Peter, 'that Sun Yat-sen would be well advised to swallow them just at the moment.'

The conversation bored Sally. She looked out the window, paying little attention to Peter as he went on, describing to the Ambassador his recent visit to the mausoleum, the sight of it covered in bamboo scaffolding and sheets of hessian, the memorial park full of vacant Chinese army trucks, each one with a driver dozing behind the wheel.

The two cars moved through an almost deserted countryside. Frost melted off empty fields only a few weeks from midwinter. There was the occasional figure, straightening from where they worked on small patches of vegetables to check on the sound of approaching engines, relax and then puzzle at the strange sight of two black Humbers and their fresh, outsized flags. The only greater concentration of humanity was to be found clustered around a bridge – mounds of cut branches lay by the road and were being hauled up on ropes piece by piece and tied to the concrete. The bridge had been almost entirely wrapped in green fir when they passed underneath it. Sir Harold turned for another look through the back window, but said nothing.

A half-hour of the journey remained and passed with little of note. There was agreement on the peculiarity of Chinese hills – how they rose sheer from the plain without preamble. Sir Harold and Peter competed briefly with unamusing attempts to link landscape to national character. A nip of brandy was passed round from a pewter hip flask, the two men drinking from the flask and Sally passing her test by gulping down a tiny sample from the upturned cap. For several hundred yards the cars had been running beside a high wall and Peter was beginning to wonder aloud whether 'this was it' just as they entered a wide clear space and came to a halt in front of the sweeping façade of Qixia Temple.

The cars emptied, save for the two drivers who remained immobile behind their wheels. Five figures gathered together before the wide granite steps and the wooden pillars of the great entrance. A conversation between Hugh and Mr Brindle on machine tools and discretion tailed off as they joined Sally, Peter and the Ambassador and turned as one to the display of elegantly curving roofs, a pleasingly typical pagoda and the soft cliffs behind pitted with caves and innumerable carved buddhas.

'Hold on,' said Peter. 'Group photo. This'll look good.'

Brindle had a confidential word in Sir Harold's ear.

'Not for the papers, I assume, Mr Moss?' asked the Ambassador.

'Souvenir, that's all. Over there a bit. Good. Bunch up. That's it.'

Peter uncovered the lens of his camera and began to compose the shot while someone said something about the last day of school.

'But you won't be in it,' said Sally. 'That's not fair.'

'Never am — ready?'

'Hold on a minute.'

Sir Harold spoke in pidgin to one of the drivers. The man got out of his car and went to stand beside Peter.

'Now you can be. Come on, Mr Moss, join the line.'

Peter looked reluctant but accepted that he had no option. He gave over-elaborate instructions to the chauffeur and finally surrendered his precious camera with an almost maternal anxiety. He took his place by Hugh's shoulder, looking just a little sour in the shadow of his friend's superior height.

So there they were on that cool, clear morning against the Morning of Birds Temple — the American journalist, the young English diplomat, the intrepid Miss Marsden of the society pages, the Ambassador and the arms manufacturer, all surprised and laughing at the moment their Chinese photographer demanded 'Say cheese!' and froze them with a tiny, anti-climactic click.

The group broke into motion at once — Peter sprinting forward to retrieve his camera, the chauffeur going back to his post without another word, Sir Harold fishing for his guidebook, Sally and Hugh keeping together, disengaging one hand, reconnecting with the other as they turned to look at the temple, and Mr Brindle, rubbing and clapping his hands, stamping his feet, looking about himself with the abruptness of a cockerel and wondering aloud where this famous picnic was to be.

'Let's see the sights first, shall we?' suggested Sir Harold.

'Righto – art first. Always makes me hungry anyway.'

Brindle advanced with a will towards the temple, now the only obstruction between him and food and drink. He paused by a braided, coloured rope hanging down from the roof timbers of the portal with what appeared to be an enormous, closed cowbell attached to it three-quarters of the way up. He tugged at it vigorously and then, dissatisfied by its toneless clatter, shouted 'Ding ding!' and marched in, startling a passing novice with a breezy 'Morning!' The Ambassador followed his lead, and then Peter, looking upwards and almost tripping over the threshold.

'Is it all right?' Sally asked Hugh.

'I expect so – Eastern hospitality and all that. Anyway, they won't have a telephone. They must be used to people dropping in all the time.'

Inside, the five visitors formed a group in the middle of an acre and a half of courtyard. Brindle's entrance had scared up a flight of pigeons. He followed them with an imaginary shotgun and then planted his fists on his hips and glared at the temple. Blue-grey wisps of smoke rose from bronze urns on either side of the entrance to the main building. From its darkness dim lights could just be seen. The sounds of a thin, high bell and organised voices drifted across.

'Is there a show on? Perhaps it's their Sunday. Come on Harold, tell us what that book of yours says.'

13

Sir Harold began to read the relevant paragraph. Everyone dutifully noted the caves in the soft cliffs behind, the stone pagoda to one side, the snarling chimeras so alarming to ill-intentioned spirits.

'What!' exclaimed Brindle. 'Rebuilt in 1908? It's a bloody film set. I'm older than this temple and no one comes to see me – well, not as a tourist anyway.'

'The pagoda's original.'

'Do you know Kew, Miss Marsden?'

'Yes.'

'Nice pagoda in Kew. I feel I should brush up on my pagodas. Sir Harold and I will go and have a look at this one – we'll be about half an hour.'

The Ambassador was dragged off across the courtyard. Brindle's earthy talk of 'transport problems' and 'bit too greedy for my liking' could be heard before they were out of earshot.

'Well, then,' said Hugh.

The three of them looked with some trepidation towards the temple.

'Shall we have a look?'

They had set foot on the topmost step when a monk appeared and padded up to them. He looked down at his bare feet. Sally, Peter and Hugh took off their shoes and stepped on to the polished boards. To their surprise they were ushered immediately into the central chamber and shown a place where they could sit cross-legged on the floor at the back of some fifty or more shaven heads and backs clothed in various shades from russet brown through brick red to orange and yellow. Their attention centred on a gilded buddha glinting dimly in the lamplight and on an elderly monk seated just before the statue in a similar attitude and rocking slowly with the rhythm of the text he was reciting. In the smoky dimness Sally felt across the matting, encountering Hugh's hand and squeezing it tightly. Thrilled by this first close brush with something unquestionably separate from her own culture, she leaned close to her future husband's ear and quietly whispered, 'Wow!' Hugh squeezed back, shifted to relieve a growing cramp in his leg and looked straight ahead.

Peter, unhappy about the lack of light and sure in any case that it would hardly be acceptable for him to take a photograph, made his excuses after a few minutes and declared that he would go outside for a little walk around. In his thick winter socks he could practically skate on the wide, smooth walkways that surrounded every building in the temple complex. Increasingly confident that the place was deserted apart from in the main hall, he began to peer into doorways, to explore the narrower, less frequented passages. He came upon a tiny courtyard garden. A small but seemingly ancient tree emerged from raked gravel. Water trickled slowly through a mossy cascade of brimming stone basins still edged with ice. Peter mimed the exaggerated actions of an ice-skater only to be caught out as a monk came round the corner. He straightened sharply and apologised for his irreverence. The monk smiled and walked on.

Peter went back to the front of the temple, leaned on the railing and watched the Ambassador and Mr Brindle as they talked by the foot of the pagoda. Sir Harold noticed him and gave a brief and none too encouraging wave. Brindle looked round and offered a broad, commercial smile before guiding the Ambassador to the other side of the building, perhaps to observe the carvings recommended in the guide-book. Peter watched them carefully and for a moment even considered taking an interest in the pagoda himself, perhaps overhearing the odd word. Professional habits had caused him to calculate the usefulness of a story about clandestine British arms in China and he knew it would do him no harm at all. Thought of his friendship with Hugh and something less defined about Sally, a vague sense of his standing with her, kept him where he was.

He crossed to the other side and went down a walkway he couldn't remember exploring before. A couple more turns and the discovery of another intimate courtyard garden revealed that Sally and Hugh had also abandoned the ceremony in the main hall. Peter stopped where he was, embarrassed that they hadn't noticed him. He knew he should have said something, but watched them instead for several seconds, framed in winter sunlight, against miniature pines and two large spirit-inhabited rocks. Hugh's arms were around her waist, the fingers of his broad hands splayed wide against her back. He pulled her in more tightly, she stretched up on the tip of her toes and they kissed. A betraying floorboard creaked and caused them both to turn in Peter's direction.

'Sorry,' said Peter, and then, in fear of the silence that threatened, 'Take your picture, ma'am?'

'Go on then,' said Sally, 'but you must promise not to say "cheese".'

They posed, Hugh's left hand curving proprietorially around Sally's arm. The railing behind them and the wooden boards beneath their feet might easily have suggested an English seaside pier. Only the proportions reliably marked the place, an invisible eloquence, enduring from the maker's hand and eye and surrounding these dominant figures in their magazine advertisement clothes ensuring that years later, yellowed in an album with only an unhelpful date written on the back, it would still, and quite unmistakably, be a picture of China.

Sally said she was hungry and all three of them went to find the Ambassador and Mr Brindle. They were standing in the middle of the courtyard, Brindle having gone back to stamping his feet. He waved at them cheerily and demanded that they should hurry up. Hugh paused at the bottom of the steps, selected a stone and left ten Chinese dollars underneath it.

They made their way back to the cars, listening to Brindle in full flow.

'I suppose it's a sort of rank thing – a different colour for, oh I don't know, different ages or holiness or something?'

'I don't think so,' said Sir Harold.

'Well, it must mean something. You can't have an army walking around with everyone dressed differently and it not meaning something, surely?'

'Hugh, do the different colours of the monks' robes mean anything?'

'As far as I know they just buy their cloth from different dyers.'

'Well, that's just shabby,' said Brindle, indignant at the very idea. 'If they're all the same they should look the same. But it's a thought, isn't it? Three or four yards a monk and – well, how many monks are there in China? That's quite a market, I'd say. I don't suppose the boss man's about?'

'Who?'

'The eh – what do you call him?'

'The abbot?'

'That's him. I could have a word.'

'Would he understand you?' asked Peter.

'It would save him money – what's to understand?'

'The language, I mean. Would he speak your language?'

Brindle rubbed his chin but couldn't find a solution.

'It's a pity. There's a man I know in Canton with a textile factory and it would be just the trick for him. Get people all wanting the same thing, then make that thing. One colour for the lot of them, sort of official. Always good business.'

Mr Brindle caught sight of the picnic and was immediately cheered.

'Well, now. Dandy!'

The chauffeurs had not been idle. Folding tables had been set up beside the cars. On a covering of stiff, white cloths stood slices of bread from the German bakery, quails' eggs drained of their brine and glistening in a porcelain soup plate, gherkins, a dish of chrome-yellow piccalilli, apples past their best, two tin-shaped blocks of Fortnum's foie gras, the opened bottles of Barsac and five good crystal glasses. Sir Harold was most apologetic.

'It's not exactly Ascot, I'm afraid.'

'Not at all! Initiative – that's what I call it. This picnic . . .'

Brindle stood by the tables and held his arms wide like an impresario introducing a new star.

'This picnic has Britain written all over it, that's what I say. Allow me . . .'

The two Chinese drivers stood impassively by their cars as Brindle filled the five glasses and handed them round.

'Sir Harold?'

'Well, eh – to China, I suppose.'

'Hear, hear.'

'China!'

Glasses were held high. The heavy, sweet yellow wine slipped down and was soon tingling in the tips of chilled fingers, toes and ears.

The diners set to, Peter rolling the crinkling shell from a quail's egg on the hard rim of the plate, Brindle setting his companions' teeth on edge with the way he crunched off the end of a gherkin and dipped the remainder in the lurid piccalilli. He waved these violent colours about as he spoke.

'God, how this takes me back! I used to live on stuff like this when I was a child. Pickled anything. My mother even took me to the doctor once, but it never did me any harm. Oh, here – Mr Moss, you must try some of this.'

Peter barely hesitated when he had a slice of bread and foie gras thrust under his nose and was told it was all right for 'his lot'. Sir Harold was already doing the rounds with the second bottle when Sally, reading the Ambassador's guide-book, tried to raise some enthusiasm for the caves.

'They've got sculptures in them. Some are over a thousand years old.'

'Past their best, I expect,' offered Brindle.

'I like caves,' Sally persisted.

Peter was keen but Hugh said they had to watch the time and the matter was left for consideration while attention turned to a tray of petits fours and coffee steaming from two large vacuum flasks. Conversation thinned as the visitors turned away from each other to look at the pitted faces of the cliffs, the hills in the distance, the incomprehensible film-set temple and to savour the sweet cakes and the warming hot bitterness of the coffee as the chauffeurs began to clear away the tables.

Both cars were hit. They were perhaps ten kilometres from the city, on a stretch of road darkened by tall trees on either side. Brindle and the Ambassador were ahead. Hugh, Peter and Sally followed in the second car. Sally had been drows-ing, her head on Hugh's shoulder, and at first the new engines vibrating in the air around her seemed to be nothing more than a confused dream, or perhaps a simple change of gear. Then, without yet understanding why, she was horri-fyingly awake, trembling in the superconsciousness of fear, demanding to know 'What? What is it?'

The car rattled violently as if someone had thrown a handful of stones. From a bridge perhaps? Sally looked up. She could see the light of the sky through a small hole in the roof and in front of her a large white star of shattered glass in the middle of the windscreen. The road erupted, stitched with plumes of earth and stones. Two black blades flickered over them and the roar of aero engines set everything shuddering as the planes pulled up and began to bank for a second run. The car in front veered to the right and came to a jarring halt as one of its wheels sank into a ditch. For the rest of her life it was the flash-seared image of that motionless car in Sally's mind that would stand at the gateway to all other nightmares – canted over at an angle as if already derelict, the back window shattered and the body work dented and holed in a dozen places, the clean metal showing around the wounds where the paint had been blasted off. There was a moment of appalling stillness, but then a door was kicked open on the left-hand side and there was Brindle, briefcase welded to his right hand, clutching his thick houndstooth coat about himself with the other as he stumbled frantically across the road and into the trees.

'Get out! Get out! Get out!'

Brindle knew what guns could do. In the car he left behind there was no sign of the driver, but in the back the unmoving head and shoulders of the Ambassador were still clear.

In the second car, the door by Sally's elbow had opened and someone was grabbing her arm.

'Time to go. Quick, Miss. Quickly quick!'

The Chinese chauffeur pulled her out and began to drag her into the trees. Hugh followed immediately after. Sally was never really sure, but she seemed to hear him saying, 'Leave her alone. Take your hand away!' In any case, it was Hugh beside her, thirty yards into the gloom of the forest as Peter ran towards them from the brightness of the roadway and the climbing pitch of engines grew louder. They crouched behind a fallen trunk and put their hands over their heads as the quick double shriek of fighters swept over the trees. There was no firing this time and within a few seconds the sound had diminished to silence.

'The Ambassador? Where's Sir Harold?'

Hugh began to shout the question into the trees.

Brindle called from where he had taken cover on the other side of the road.

'It's all right. I'm not hit.'

'He's still in the car,' said Sally. 'He never got out.'

Hugh ran through the trees towards the ditched car.

'Sir Harold? Sir Harold? Oh, God!'

Sally and Peter were fifteen yards behind him when he reached the car. He just had time to say that it was all right before realising the truth. Sir Harold sat in the back seat, pale and rigid. He tried to speak, but couldn't form a word. Beside him a tuft of white hair had been plucked out of the backrest of the seat where another bullet had gone through. Hugh slipped his hand behind Sir Harold's back and brought it out again, scarlet with blood.

For a few seconds this was his private shock while behind him Sally and Peter were transfixed by another story. The driver, the man who had taken their photograph in front of the temple, lay with his body on the ground and his legs still up in the car. Half the windscreen was red and it was clear that a bullet had entered the back of his head, tumbled through his skull and exited again, taking with it everything from the bridge of his nose to the hairline, leaving an open, half-empty bowl of bone. Steaming water from the pierced radiator mingled on the ground with blood.

Hugh moved back from his examination of the Ambassador, showing his bloodied hand, only to find the greater horror lying on the ground. He took hold of Sally with his clean hand and tried to guide her away.

'No! Don't look at it, Sally. Peter, help me. Don't let her see this.'

But it was Hugh who had to break away with a cry and take a few steps into the trees to retch up his meal. Sally and Peter stood together by the corpse of the Chinese driver. Their eyes locked together for a moment, and though Sally never suspected it, it was only that contact that prevented Peter from reaching instinctively for his camera.

On the road the other driver was taking charge. He had seen the water from the useless radiator and his dead colleague and was now busy with his own survival. In emphatic Mandarin he ordered Brindle into the front seat of the remaining car. He plucked the bright flags from their sockets and threw them in after him. With the bread knife from the picnic basket he cut small branches from the nearest trees and inserted these where the flags had been and into the new bullet holes at the back. Other larger branches he tried to tie on to the roof with a length of rope from the boot.

Hugh and Peter had understood and were already struggling towards the camouflaged car with the stricken Ambassador between them, his head lolling sideways in merciful unconsciousness.

'Keep his back straight,' Hugh kept saying. 'For Christ's sake, Peter, keep him straight.'

'I'm trying, I'm trying!'

But in the end, in frustration and panic, they pushed Sir Harold roughly into the back the only way they could, propping him up in a corner. Hugh, Sally and Peter squeezed in behind him.

Still outside the car, the driver froze and listened to the sky. For ten seconds there was a paralysed silence. He got behind the wheel and fired up the engine. With a roar and a slewing spin of the wheels, they fled back to the city.

2

The International Club had never quite got going in Nanking. Early ambitions were represented by a deep chesterfield armchair, the large fireplace and its velvet upholstered club fender. The rest was gimcrack, folding. There was something ineradicably temporary about it, something of the military camp as if, under all the denials, members had always felt it wise to be ready for an emergency departure. Reproductions of Western pictures and an English railway advertisement for the benefits of a week in Cromer were on the walls. Sally let their colours swim vaguely across her vision. They all began to seem like steamer tickets and perhaps had always been versions of those pictures in children's stories which you could enter and be transported to the real place just by wishing hard enough. She tapped her heels together three times and quietly recited, 'There's no place like home.'

Just at that moment, and probably for the first time in her life, the embroidered cliché of that phrase was a real and intense sentiment. She had never felt it while actually at home, or for that matter when anywhere in England. There had only been a secure familiarity, inseparable from the sense that the unknown, the elsewhere must, by definition, be part of what was meant by 'life'. Things moved on to a sense of uniform dullness as she herself moved from child to young woman. Last of all was the overwrought, inexpressible revulsion that had possessed her last summer, the sense of falling back into dangerous comforts, of having a clear view from there to the grave and doubting very much that there was anything to please or excite beyond the ordinary in that whole bleak, safe scene of English female life.

She had known Hugh since her last years at school. He had come to the house with his parents one weekend in the summer of 1932. His father was in the Foreign Office, Sally's in the Treasury. They had a common past in Westminster and Balliol. She could not recall a single word that passed between them over those two days. Even the excruciating tennis match Hugh and she had to play before their four parents had become a silent movie, none the less painful for that. Later, there had been a series of occasional meetings, walks in the garden or during a holiday in Scotland without any other company. There was the shared memory of Hugh's mother's funeral, the first such event Sally had ever attended. The odd inter-university opportunity and sightings during the London season caused others to speak of them at the same time. An acquiescence set in – a slow, passionless gravity against which neither Hugh nor Sally could find any very compelling objection. More attractive alternatives never presented themselves. In time, they began deliberately to keep their distance, obedient to the assumption that something had been settled and that it was too late for anyone decently to intervene. Separations began to seem temporary. Even Hugh's rapid progress in the Foreign Office had been arranged to conform with the accepted inevitability. With his father's help he had been assured a home posting and would be back in London early in the New Year. No one doubted that Hugh and Sally would end 1938 as well-suited man and wife.

So there, in the high, hot, English summer, sitting by the lawn and with Girton only a few weeks behind her and her father across the table hiding behind *The Times*, she sighed long and deeply for no particular reason. As the wide wings of the paper were turned and refolded Sally vacantly absorbed the offers of a savourless, disengaged world – FURS OF AUTHORITY; BARRIE THE MAN – MEMORIAL SERVICE; GET YOUR WIFE A GAS REFRIGERATOR; AMBASSADORS – BATS IN THE BELFRY – 'MAKES YOU LAUGH QUITE IRRESPONSIBLY'; SLENDERISE!; INSURGENTS ADVANCE ON SANTANDER; WHAT DO YOU KNOW OF CZECHOSLOVAKIA? MODERN HOTELS WITH ALL CONVENIENCES.

Geoffrey Marsden put down his paper, took a handkerchief to his perspiring and increasingly hairless head and made an observation about the weather. Sally said nothing. She closed her eyes and turned her face to the sun. Geoffrey regarded his daughter with his usual sense of mystification and grateful amazement. Here was the one unalloyed and effortless triumph in his life, the product of nature's virtuosity. She almost embarrassed him – like the mediocre sportsman's hole-in-one she was an achievement to which he had no right, an occasion, on his part, for self-deprecation and apology. Everyone said she was so like him – in appearance at least – and here even Mrs Marsden agreed. Ordinarily, Geoffrey himself could not see it, but on that summer afternoon with the brilliant sunlight straight on her face it was quite clear. Sally was the exquisite female perfection of himself. Put her in khaki and she would be hard to distinguish from his own photographic portrait as second lieutenant taken over twenty years before. Geoffrey prodded the newspaper.

'Do you have any idealistic young friends out there?'

'Mm?'

'Spain.'

'No. Well, I don't think so.'

'I shouldn't think it would do any good.'

'I suppose not.'

Silence stretched again. The telephone rang in the house and the parlourmaid was heard taking a message for Sally's mother. Sally writhed with frustration in her chair. She couldn't stand it much longer and was already preparing excuses for going into town.

'Look at this,' said her father.

He read out an advertisement from the front page – *Young gentlewoman (now in Japan) wishes post Hong Kong October: Nursery College trained; French; piano.*

'I didn't go to Nursery College.'

'Well, of course. I just mean there are people out there.'

Sally opened her eyes and raised her head out of the sun's glare.

'What do you mean – "people out there"?'

'When's Hugh coming back?'

'End of March.'

'That's what I thought.'

Sally sat up straight and looked her father in the eye. They had both heard the car in the driveway and knew they would soon be interrupted by Mrs Marsden.

'I had a word with Hugh's father the other day,' he went on. 'I don't know how we got on to it – I think I just said you were a bit bored. Anyway, it all seemed surprisingly easy and as he assured me it was quiet out there at the moment, in all the big towns at least, and I wondered if –'

They were being hailed cheerily from the side of the lawn. Sybil Marsden began to bear down on them. Sally's father leaned forward over the glass-topped table, highly excited by the prospect of a conspiracy against his wife.

'We'll have to be clever with this, Sally – she'll think we're completely mad.'

Sally waited until the heat from the fire burned sharply against her thigh before she moved. She picked her feet off the floor and tried to curl into the enormous chair, searching hopelessly for sleep. She opened her eyes fully at the sound of Peter's voice. He was talking to one of the waiters and then coming towards her, taking off his overcoat. A wave of reassurance swept through her, and a leap of emotion that made it impossible for her to speak for several seconds.

'I'm sorry,' Peter said.

He leaned towards her, covered her hand with his, the cold shock of the outside over her feverish heat startling them both.

'It's all right, really.'

'It's not. It was rotten of me. I'm sorry. How are you?'

'I don't know.'

Peter sat down opposite her. He leaned forward on the edge of the chair, held his clasped hands tightly between his legs. He struggled to relax, but the concentration required was too much and every few seconds he began to tremble again like a swimmer who had just stumbled out of a dangerously cold sea. Sally began to feel stronger as she watched him.

'You're cold,' she said. 'Did you wire your paper?'

'Yes – I had to. If they found I'd known about this and not told them . . .' He tailed off, all too aware of how unimpressive this excuse sounded.

'It's all right, I understand,' said Sally. 'It's a scoop. After all, it's an ill wind . . .'

'Please.'

'Sorry. Stupid thing to say.'

They were both silent for a while, watching the fire, trying perhaps to extract some primitive charm from its warmth that might protect them from what they had just seen, intercede somehow between raw, outraged consciousness and images they both knew they would never be free of. The waiter arrived and began to transfer cups, two white metal coffee pots and two large glasses of brandy from his tray to the table. Peter poured thick, sweet hot chocolate into the cups as Sally made an appreciative exclamation.

'It's from their secret hoard. You have to know something compromising about the major-domo to get at it. I'm told this is the last, but I shouldn't think that's true either. Stores are disappearing pretty quickly at the moment. Here – chocolate first, then brandy.'

The prescription did its work – a little sensual pleasure and a little intoxication posing so easily as moral goods and making the world seem not quite so bad as it had been a moment before. Sally drank down the chocolate as fast as she could, clattering the thick cup on its saucer. She sent a full mouthful of the brandy down after it. It burned through the heat and sent a heavy shudder up her spine, shaking her head and shoulders. She tried to curl more tightly into the chair.

'Better?'

She nodded.

'Have you heard anything?'

'Hugh called from the hospital half an hour ago. He was still alive then – that's all he would say. I've been too frightened to call back. Such a coward, I'm afraid. He told me to stay here "come hell or high water" until he came for me. He's cabling London.'

The windows darkened as the afternoon wore on. Peter told Sally about Illinois, answering all her questions, pretending not to notice when she repeated herself or struggled to keep her eyes open as he spoke. He told her about

London too, or his London – the fringes of Fleet Street, semi-invitations to functions at embassies, the reported indiscretions of some enticingly disreputable names, the photographs he took in his own time of the more interesting (as he claimed) nameless people. She exhausted him at last, and when forced to speak herself could only say: I don't know anything really. Just books. *The Seafarer* to Shelley, you could ask me about that – or you could have done three months ago. And boredom. I know a lot about boredom.'

'Are you bored now?'

'No. I'm frightened now. But it's not half as bad as being bored. They don't call it "deadly" for nothing – it can be literally true, you know?'

'Is that why you came to China?'

'I was in a garden in Hertfordshire and I was asked. Who wouldn't say yes?'

'I can think of a few people.'

'And Hugh, of course. A last chance to see the world and then back together in March. That was the idea. But now . . .'

The four reedy notes of a noodle seller drifted by in the road outside. The lights guttered and dimmed as the evening voltage reduction began. A waiter began to place oil lamps on the tables. Trucks rumbled by, clearing the way with their horns, a long, regularly spaced line of twelve or fifteen that set a thin membrane of glass buzzing in its frame. Two men beside the window looked out then sat down again without speaking. Their attention turned to a new entrant. It was the man Sally had seen that morning on the steps of the hotel. He took off his hat and polished the mist from his spectacles with a handkerchief. He declined an offer to help him off with his coat and made a brisk round of the room, talking briefly to half a dozen people and noting the response of each on a piece of paper. Only when about to leave did he notice Peter by the fire. He went over at once.

'Mr Moss! I heard only an hour ago. Deplorable. An outrage. You are hurt? Not at all?'

Peter reassured this neat, middle-aged German with his energetic, penetrating eyes and his patriotic moustache that he was quite unharmed. The news was received with extravagant, hand-on-heart relief. Peter introduced Sally. The little German held her hand and bowed.

'Rabe, Siemens China,' he said. 'You were there? You are all right? Thank God! A driver was killed, is that right? Awful for you. Awful. I'm so sorry.'

He turned back to Peter.

'And the Ambassador — there is not bad news, I hope?'

'He's at the hospital. We haven't heard since about two.'

Here Rabe lowered his voice and leaned down to ask Peter a more confidential question.

'You have made your arrangements, Mr Moss? You are ready for tomorrow morning?'

Peter seemed to know what he was referring to, but was reluctant to answer. Sally sensed that she was the cause of his reticence.

'Well — we're not quite sure yet. We'll see.'

'Forgive me,' said Herr Rabe. 'I must run. I have everything to do.'

He repossessed his hat and made to go but stopped suddenly on the threshold of the room.

'I almost forgot. I've just passed Mr Jerrold. He is coming here, I think — and one of yours, Mr Moss. They will tell you everything. You must not delay.'

John Rabe literally ran from the room and could be heard clattering down the stairs and flaying the engine of his car as it shrieked away in first gear.

'He was on the steps with you this morning,' said Sally.

'The Siemens representative. Been here for years apparently. Pillar of the local community. He's a useful man to know – pretty thick with the Chinese authorities. He's staying – trying to organise something.'

'Staying?'

Peter hesitated.

'Don't condescend to me, Peter.'

'I picked up a fair bit when I was at the news agency. Things seem to have moved rather fast. If what I heard is –'

'Hugh!'

Peter turned to see Hugh coming through the doorway from the landing. Sally was instantly on her feet. She embraced him, rubbed his back vigorously, said how cold he was. An American Embassy official had come in just behind him. This man went straight to Peter and handed him a piece of paper.

'Here, Moss – we got room even for you.'

He moved on into the room.

'American citizens? American citizens to me, please.'

Hugh sat down, looking grey and utterly exhausted. Peter signalled urgently for another glass of brandy. They both held off asking the question. Hugh drank, then covered his eyes with his hand and seemed to deflate into the back of his chair.

'Well, he's gone.'

There was nothing but a miserable, drained silence from Peter and Sally. One of them began to speak but was interrupted as Hugh resumed his explanation.

'The doctors said it was his only chance.'

'What?'

'To Shanghai. Only the hospitals in the Settlement can get the bullet out safely.'

'He's alive?'

Hugh looked surprised.

'Yes – of course. It seems to have missed everything vital and there's still feeling in his legs, but they have to get the bullet out. Han says he knows a way through by the back roads. He left an hour ago with one of the other house-boys. Sir Harold's had a little morphine, but they couldn't spare much. Han will telegraph if they get through, if the lines are still working.'

Hugh gulped down the rest of the brandy. The American official had finished his business and was buttoning up his coat and preparing to leave. Hugh stopped him with a hand on his arm as he was passing – two shepherds exchanged favours.

'Look out for any of ours, will you?' said Hugh.

'Sure.'

'I'll be back in the embassy in twenty minutes. Tell them to go there if they need anything. Hsiakwan tomorrow morning otherwise – queue by alpha for HMS *Bee*. I'll be there.'

'I'll tell 'em. Do the same for any of my strays.'

'Goes without saying.'

Hugh looked into the space between Sally and Peter and asked them dully: 'Do you know what's going on?'

Peter said he had been at the news agency and picked up most of it there.

'But that was four hours ago now.'

'Am I the last person in Nanking to be told?' demanded Sally.

'Well,' said Hugh, 'I'm very sorry, but we've all rather miscalculated. It seems the Japanese are no more than two days away. General Tang has been given orders to defend the city – it's absurd of course, there'll only be a bloodbath and then they'll lose it anyway. It's too late to go south. If Sir Harold makes it he'll probably be the last person to get out that way. We have to go upriver. Boarding tomorrow morning. Christ! It's all so bloody incompetent.'

Hugh summoned the waiter and asked him to bring three boxes of matches. He gave him a coin and slipped them into his pocket. The mantel clock chimed six high, thin notes and the waiter, as if part of its mechanism, moved to the wireless set as he had done every evening at that time for the last ten years and turned it on so that members could hear the news in English from Shanghai. A strange, peculiarly accented voice emerged, as noticeable and offensive as the intrusion of a non-member.

'The forces of progress advance. The enemies of the future melt away before the new warmth of Sino-Japanese friendship. Japan, a loving father to the Asian family, chastises the unruly so that harmony and happiness may be more quickly restored. The enemies of happiness deserve no mercy in this heroic work. The following units have been mentioned to the Emperor . . .'

A half American, half German voice spoke loudly out of the gloom.

'Give us a rest, will you?'

The wireless was turned down and retuned to another, less objectionable station. The waiter, in the midst of profuse apologies was waved away. The Andrews Sisters emerged from the crackle.

'Well,' said Hugh, 'I think we should go.'

There were not many lights outside, but no blackout as yet. The air was thick with smoke from stoves and the smell of food. There were perhaps a few more people in the streets than usual, but nothing a stranger new to the city would remark on.

'Shall we see you tomorrow morning?' Sally asked Peter.

'I'll be in Hsiakwan, that's for sure – different boats of course.'

Hugh was no more encouraging.

'It'll be total chaos.'

'I'll wear my green hat,' said Sally. 'You can look out for it.'

'See you in Hankow, maybe. Or if we all get back to Shanghai I'll stay at the Imperial and make sure they have my address if I move on. I'll give it to the embassy there, too.'

Sally stepped forward and kissed Peter on the cheek.

'Good luck.'

Peter waved and walked away in the direction of his hotel. Sally and Hugh took the other way along Chung Shan Street towards the British Embassy. They were discussing where they might obtain another car when the air-raid warning began to sound.

'False alarm,' said Hugh.

They walked on slowly, hand in hand. Sally reviewed the day with astonishment. Would anything so awful ever happen again? Could there be another story to her life more stark, or had the matter been fixed that morning, the moment when the planes opened fire? Perhaps that would be her anecdote of anecdotes, to be recounted again and again and with a sense of occasion, a rehearsed supremacy however long she lived. She would trot it out unfeelingly, having quite outlived the horror, and vainly too, demanding the tributes of the less experienced – 'Really?' 'My goodness!' 'You were there?' But why was she so unchanged? Some part of her mind delivered a distasteful surprise when it skipped to the idea of losing her virginity. Was there anything that would ever really make a difference? The planes weren't shooting at her – just at the cars. The incident was already beginning

34

to seem meaningless. There was a flicker in the air, like distant lightning. Pillars of light appeared and began to search the sky. It seemed for a moment as if a movie was about to begin. Sally and Hugh stopped to watch. A steady hum of engines began to make itself heard over the background noise of the city. Suddenly there was a glimmer in the sky, something like the evasive flash of a trout in a river as one of the lights found a target and a reflection was sent shooting back to earth, and into the eyes of the AA crews who began to send up streams of flak. High up, the shells exploded at their predetermined height in little flashes of orange, or sudden puffs of black smoke when caught in the lights. The aircraft banked, but was followed across the sky by the deadly glare. The spectators stepped back at the sound of a car being driven at reckless speed. The brakes were applied sharply and the driver leaned over to the open window, though without entirely stopping. In the gloom, Sally could see the large swastika on the door and the edge of another painted on the roof. It was John Rabe waving at them and shouting excitedly. He pointed up to the sky.

'Siemens searchlights. The best!'

He killed his own headlights and accelerated into the darkness.

3

Sally sat on the back porch of the British Embassy, looking down on its small walled garden. The clouds that had earlier glimmered in the searchlights had cleared and the temperature was dropping fast. On the wooden steps and on the handrails the first crystals of frost were growing. It was 2 a.m. Since they had parted from Peter the last cables to London had been sent. The lines failed shortly afterwards and the hoped-for instructions had not come through. The remaining domestic staff had been dismissed with a month's pay and advised to make their way north-west as fast as possible.

'No,' Hugh had been forced to say to one of them as he took his leave at the front gate. 'You are not a British citizen – the consul at Hankow will not be able to help you.'

Just as in the International Club earlier that evening, the nations were dividing, running away from each other in all directions. The next day the Americans and associated passport holders would queue for one ship, British subjects and citizens of the Commonwealth, Colonies and dependent territories would queue for another. The

Chinese would stevedore their baggage for them and then go home to Nanking.

Hugh came past her with another armful of papers and threw them on the fire. A few sheets fluttered away to safety but were carefully gathered up and fed back into the flames.

'Oh, God,' groaned Hugh, mostly to himself. 'I don't even know if they are the right ones.'

'Can't you burn them all?'

'Too many.'

'You could burn down the whole embassy.'

'Is that supposed to be a helpful suggestion?'

'Well, it would be effective. But then, what if the Japs just stop, or decide to go somewhere else? London would send a new ambassador out, or perhaps Sir Harold would come back from Shanghai with a walking stick and you'd have to say, "Sorry, Sir Harold, I seem to have burned down your embassy. Jumped the gun, I'm afraid." That wouldn't be good.'

She regretted it instantly as Hugh strode up to her, on the last thin edge of his self-control.

'For Christ's sake! Don't you know what's going on? Don't you understand? This is a real crisis.'

'But we're leaving.'

He seemed not to have heard her properly.

'Well, if this isn't a bloody crisis, I don't know what is.'

He went back in to get another heap of files, shouting to Sally as he went: 'This is the sort of thing that can ruin a career before it's even started.'

Then he was standing beside her again, just his shoes and the spattered turn-ups of his trousers visible. Sally felt a sharp cut of disappointment as she heard him say, 'So you needn't think it won't affect you.'

After a few more loads of paper they apologised to each

37

other and stood together close to the high blaze of files. An iron kettle now sat in the middle of the flames and on the steps, waiting for the water to boil, a pair of porcelain willow pattern cups and saucers and a plain brown teapot.

'That's all the locked cabinets done,' said Hugh.

'So has the name "Brindle" been expunged from the records?'

'I hope so – we could offend three countries at once with him. I, eh . . . I wouldn't mention him again if I were you.'

'Don't be silly – I'm going to be the perfect ambassador's wife. Do you think we'll see him tomorrow?'

'More than likely – if he isn't busy trying to sell something to General Matsui, or hasn't chartered the whole bloody boat for himself and already gone.'

'Matsui?'

'The man who's coming our way.'

Sally gingerly hooked the kettle out of the fire and made some tea.

'Shall we go in?'

Hugh nodded towards the fire.

'I'd better stay a while,' he said. 'Make sure it all goes.'

They sat side by side on the steps, as seemingly content as two travellers by a campfire. Now and again Hugh raked the ashes, turning over still readable pages of print from where the paper lay densely packed. They would flare up quickly, delivering a brief rush of heat and light to their faces.

'We should try to get some sleep when this is done,' said Hugh. 'God knows what tomorrow will be like.'

'You realise how improper this is.'

'I don't think that's quite the word I would use.'

'All our chaperones have gone and here we still are. People will think the worst. Is war a mitigation or are we quite ruined?'

Hugh endured an almost physical struggle to find some suitable reply, but in the end said nothing. Sally put her hand over his wrist and squeezed till she could feel the slowing pulse beneath the skin. They both looked down on the dark pools of tea. From somewhere quite close, not more than a couple of streets away, there were two pistol shots and an outbreak of shouting. More distantly, a nervous burst of anti-aircraft fire rattled up into an empty sky. The slow, pulsed tremors on the surface of the tea did not change. They both smiled and knew that the exact same thought had entered their minds. They clinked the cups together.

'Sangfroid!'

A companion was essential.

'Oh, Geoffrey! Sally! What nonsense. How impossible!'

Thus had Mrs Marsden reacted to the first mention of her daughter going to China. But an impossibility divided, halved at a stroke in all its awful implications, might not be so impossible after all.

Sally spent a day on the telephone and sent a dozen letters. Celia's engagement had just been announced in *The Times* – she knew nothing but flowers, caterers' menus and bridesmaids' dresses.

'But it will be lovely, Sally. How clever of you. I wish I could come, I really do. You must tell Dick and me all about it when you're back. Next year we'll have a month on the Riviera all to ourselves – come then. Bring me back some tea!'

The conversation with her former friend had been a great horror to Sally. Celia had become a warning of just how quick the decline could be. The disease was virulent and insidious in its methods, always beginning by blinding the sufferer to the possibility that anything might be wrong with them. They had talked about it late into the night in their last year at Cambridge. They had determined all the symptoms, put themselves on watch for the slightest sign, declared themselves to be a private League of Nations, each member ready to come to the aid of the other whenever the dull or the insipid pressed too hard against their borders. Hands were clasped and held over a candle flame. An oath was taken. And now – poor Celia. It had all been for nothing. The disease was smarter than they knew and now, for Sally at least, China was fast becoming the only escape.

Others were briefer and more brittle in their excuses. Caroline was being 'finished' in Switzerland, her sense of irony already blunted. Phoebe also had marriage in mind, an alliance that would take her to Kenya, which would be more than enough adventure for her. Diana was writing for a magazine and plotting a crucial lunch with a youngish man from the *Daily Telegraph*. Agnes Van Otterloo, more a good acquaintance than a friend, had seemed by temperament to be the most promising prospect. Sally was right about that, but found herself baulked and her chest tight with envy as she listened to her talk excitedly on the telephone about an ambulance in Spain. Suddenly, it seemed hopeless and absurd and not such a good idea after all and Mrs Marsden was talking quite happily about a couple of weeks in Normandy instead when the telephone rang one long, silently screaming afternoon.

'Ambulance off! I'm furious, mad, quite enraged! A ghastly little man in Poplar had promised us a butcher's van – black-and-white promise – and we even went there to get it and he had just sold it to someone else for a guinea more. Can you believe that? We could get another, I suppose, but I don't know that I care to now. When people don't even try it's just too, too boring. Lunch?'

A department store in Knightsbridge provided a suitable setting for the plot (as Sally liked to think of it). The sinister rhetoric of contentment was all about them. Dead women in dead fashions gossiped eagerly about the young, about daughters and nieces and the respectable coffins they would like to hammer them into. The clash of cup on saucer cut through the noise. Sally glimpsed a bloody crescent of lipstick on its rim, the ashen, rilled face from which it had come. It seemed that it must be someone else's blood. Sally shuddered with revulsion and inwardly declared a new determination to escape. There were worrying signs of mould creeping around the edges of Agnes's bright, sternly phrased idealism. She was unhealthily encouraged when she heard that the itinerary would take them through Marseilles.

'Lovely! So close to Nice, to Antibes.'

'But just train to boat, I'm afraid,' said Sally, for whom France was immensely too near to offer anything of interest.

'Well, if it has to be. But we could make it a bit longer.'

'Perhaps.'

'And we'd be coming back the same way?'

'Of course, it's very close to Spain,' suggested Sally, suddenly taken with the idea of a double adventure.

'Spain and I are finished. Quite finished.'

The Suez Canal was another distraction for Agnes.

'Cairo, Pyramids and all that. What fun!'

The trip threatened to turn into a spinsterish Cook's tour. Sally could see it petering out in faintness and diarrhoea on some gruesome little Nile steamer, the two of them running back to London to smirking parents and friends who could only just forbear from saying, 'I told you so.' Still, if Agnes was unreliable, if her tether was likely to run out somewhere in the Middle East, that might work out rather well. All Sally

41

needed was someone to leave the country with – if she ended up having to go on alone, too bad.

Sally persuaded hard, smoothing away all objections and erring only very slightly on the far side of the truth. The project began to seem quite reasonable, and then an absolute requirement, a test of mettle and a cure-all to boot that no reasonable person could walk away from.

'Leave it to me.'

They were Agnes's parting words. Sally went home via a prodigiously expensive visit to Bartholomew's for maps and half a dozen volumes of universal timetables, advice, anecdote and guidance. By the time she got off her train a listless misery had settled on her. The whole thing was juvenile – not the idea, but the lunch, the excitement, the forced emotions, the deliberate erasure of the lines between imagination and reality. It always ended unhappily and Sally was angry with herself for still getting drawn into it at her age. The curtain always came down in the end, and there you were, shivering on a rainy street, bumping into a grumpy man in a mackintosh coming out the alley from the stage door – devil, king or angel hurrying back to a cold-water flat – and leaving you worse than before.

So it still seemed unreal two weeks later on Southampton Dock when her mother was fussing and giving her final orders for the tenth time and Agnes was already on board, leaning over the rail and waving down at them (Agnes's father, the sole surviving parent, had said his farewells in London and excused himself on the grounds of a summer cold). Sally at last managed to detach herself and a few minutes later stood beside Agnes, looking down on her parents and then waving too, quite guiltlessly, and with a thrilling leap of the heart as she felt the engines hum through the steel plates of the deck and the ship nudge out of its berth.

There was a night in Paris before taking the train south in the morning, then two in Marseilles while waiting to board their ship. Trips to Antibes or Nice were not possible. The two young women spent their time recuperating on the hotel café terrace, reading magazines, making up stories about themselves for the half-dozen men who, at various times, asked if the third chair at the table were free and tried their luck. Cables were sent reporting that all was well and then the *Orient Star* was boarded. Fellow passengers were examined, weighed in the balance, deck space was possessed, loungers claimed and the first of the five novels they had each brought with them begun as they steamed off into the hot, blue calm of the Mediterranean.

The Pyramids slipped by, invisible beneath the starboard horizon. The heat became fierce, driving passengers from the decks and enslaving the sweating stewards to a constant run between the galleys and the first-class cabins with pitchers of ice. Sally and Agnes rotated through all the tables in the dining room, greatly enjoying their status as attractive oddities among the missionaries, company agents, colonial administrators (British, French and Dutch) and the bishop of Calcutta. A neatly dressed German was said to be a colonel and a military adviser to the Chinese Nationalists. Sally was taken with the idea of espionage and engaged him in conversation one evening on the deck after dinner. But she quickly became bored as he frankly admitted his business and offered an unnecessarily detailed explanation of the excellent arrangements between the two governments. The telegrams schedule, to which both Sally and Agnes had been forced to swear an unwavering commitment by their respective parents, quickly fell by the wayside. Heat and the isolation of shipboard life made the two young women listless and they declined the chance of a brief examination of Djibouti during their ship's twenty-four-hour stay in its harbour. Incoming information was equally scant and no one seemed to mind very much. The English, French and German newspapers displayed in the lounges after every port call were already a week old and attracted little attention. The obligation to be informed slipped away. Magazines could be endlessly thumbed, novels exchanged, but newsprint was another matter. Most welcomed the chance to break the daily habit of absorbing information. What was a virtue on land had begun to seem a sort of tyranny which one could briefly escape on a liner. Sally readily agreed with an American that one of the great pleasures of the modern sea voyage was the first breakfast in the hotel on arrival, finding the world's stories refreshed by reading them as if waking from a sleep of several weeks. The only intrusion on this quiet was the ship's own newspaper – a single sheet distributed by a perpetually mobile fifteen-year-old boy in red trousers and white tunic. Tactfully edited for a shipboard readership, it concentrated largely on the high points of the deck-quoits tournament and reviews of the previous evening's most successful cocktail parties. The brief digest of news compiled by the RT officer was aimed at fuelling polite conversation and rigorously excluded anything that might cause anxiety or stimulate a debate.

So it was that in the King Edward Hotel in Bombay, where they sat together on the bed in Sally's room with the big windows open to the heat and the racket from outside and the mosquito net pluming down from the ceiling like an upturned cone of smoke and the letters that had been waiting for them strewn all around, Agnes opened a telegram and exclaimed in surprise.

'Good heavens! What on earth does that mean?' She looked grave and showed it to Sally. She read the words '*Return England immediately – international situation. Arrangements your behalf Mr Lethbridge, Cook's. Confirm receipt. More to follow. Father.'* The steady, civil chaos of Bombay roared on without any sign of an international situation.

'Perhaps it hasn't started yet?' suggested Agnes. 'It might still be a secret.'

Mr Lethbridge, a sad, stranded man, was not in the inner circle. Surely not yet past his early thirties, several years of Bombay heat and solitary nights had melted the hair from much of his head and polished it to a rosy gloss. The sympathy that went out from Sally on account of his aesthetic ill-luck quickly turned to contempt when she discovered his keenness to be back in England. She decided that he deserved his appearance, of which he seemed to be entirely unaware as he dabbed at his scarlet features with a handkerchief, sorted through a portfolio of tickets and declared: 'I'm quite quite green with envy. Back in England for autumn – the leaves falling in Green Park.'

He trailed off wistfully. Agnes and Sally remained silent throughout an indecently long pause. Mr Lethbridge hurried on, confirming the presence of all the necessary paperwork and handing it over to Agnes. He had received no instructions with respect to Sally.

'International situation? It's not then, if I may be so bold, a "personal return"? I do sometimes have customers who come a long way only to return immediately. The circumstances are usually distressing. In your case, Miss Van Otterloo, I may allay my fears?'

Two beads of perspiration swelled, merged into the fatness of a raindrop and ran down the side of his face. The handkerchief was applied, the broken fan deplored.

'Nothing like that,' said Agnes.

'As for international situations, all I can say is that bookings don't appear to be down. Of course, in Bombay, we are not always the first to know. You'll enjoy the *Antwerp* – an excellent ship. You have made your arrangements, Miss Marsden? I would be happy to help.'

The debate between the two young women, and various attempts at communication with London and the embassy in China continued for the next two days. Deeply buried in the *Times of India* were two column inches about misunderstandings and shots in the night. The next day's paper had nothing to add.

'Well, he does get nervous,' said Agnes, referring to her father. There was a half-heartedness in her remark that sounded a clear warning to Sally. She guessed, without much regret, that it was the beginning of an apology. Maps were consulted which reassured the two travellers that the supposed shots were some hundreds of miles from anywhere they were likely to be. Further indeed than Spain was from London, and who worried about that? Telegrams went to and fro. Mr Van Otterloo suggested his daughter and her friend might like to stay in Bombay for a month before coming back, which rather undermined the idea of a crisis. Hugh, from the embassy in Nanking, reported serenity and an ardent wish to see her.

Sally and Agnes sat on the veranda of the hotel on their second evening in the city. Two dripping Tom Collinses and a tattered issue of *The New Yorker* sat on the table. Sally fished the lime from her drink and bit out the half-moon of flesh.

'You know what this is all about really, don't you?'

Agnes said nothing. It had been an awkward day. The divide between them had widened with every hour until that moment, at six o'clock in the evening, when they both looked silently down on the hotel gardens and felt how painfully the mere pragmatism of their companionship had been exposed. Sally began to feel evangelical – here was a sister in danger of lapsing and she had a duty to save her.

'It's the call of England, that's what it is. The last roll of barbed wire before you get clean away. You don't have to go back.'

Agnes told her that she was a romantic, that Byron was passé, that the only people who really couldn't go back to England were criminals and undischarged bankrupts.

'Anyway, why can't it just be what it seems to be? My father should be in a position to know.'

A liveried waiter went down the steps beside them and made his way across the lawn with a tray of drinks for a party of four laughing loudly under the trees. Agnes pressed on, her decision already made.

'Sometimes one gets a mania for difference, but it's all a wild goose chase as far as I can see. You travel thousands of miles and all you get is this.' She gestured at the brash four-some, at the waiter bending by each shoulder in turn as he put down the drinks. 'Nothing's really different. Not that different. You've got to make your nest somewhere.'

It was their last day together and Agnes knew she could indulge in a small and to her mind entirely justified reckoning.

'In any case,' she said, 'it's not as if I have some man waiting for me back in England or, just between ourselves, any likelihood of such a thing for God knows how long. So, you see, the chasm doesn't yawn as widely for me as it does for you. One might almost say, Sally, that of the two of us you're the one who's going in the wrong direction.'

There was no way back from that. They were both happy to accept it and had a harmonious meal that evening talking of other things. The *Orient Star* was due to depart the next day at noon. Sally left the hotel at 5 a.m., determined to avoid any unfortunate encounters. She left a note for Agnes excusing her dawn departure and wishing her *bon voyage*. She gave her instructions to the taxi driver with a delightful lurch of excitement. Another knot had been slipped, another little victory won and it seemed as if only then something was starting at last.

Singapore and Canton punctuated the rest of the journey. The pages of books and magazines turned; Pearl Buck's earnest peasants laboured on the earth, men with moustaches at least her father's age were indulged and then frankly flirted with. Flowers appeared in her cabin when they were fresh after landfall, with invitation cards attached. And then there was the packing of suitcases, the crowding on to the foredecks and Shanghai itself, the grand, transplanted curve of the great buildings of the Bund looming out of a misty, humid morning – a Regent Street, a Kurfürstendamm, a Promenade des Anglais with a foreground of junks and somewhere, behind it all, China.

Sally stood still amid the bustle of the customs hall. She held her newly stamped passport in her pocket. People strode past her quickly towards the exits as if they had just stepped off a train. Others walked up and down the mounds of baggage with the torn-off halves of receipts in their hands and porters at their heels. Whenever a case was identified there was a sudden darting, like the attack of thrushes on a worm. The quickest would emerge struggling with the prize and bear it off across the concourse with the anxious owner behind, trying to make themselves heard through the porter's torrential stream of commissioned advice about taxis and hotels. She was excited and nervous at the same time – what if things had changed? She worried that perhaps for Hugh it was easier to love by correspondence than in the flesh, that a person mediated by telegram, or *par avion*, and without any of the irritations or untimeliness of an actual presence might have been more to his liking. It struck her as a dangerous moment, and all the more unnerving because she knew that everything would be clear in an instant when she first saw him. There would be a hesitation, something about a turn of the head, the painstaking contrivance of the smile. But all for nothing of course – if it was hopeless they would both know at once, or ought to. Such things weren't always accepted, however obvious. As she sifted the milling crowds for Hugh's face she recalled another scene her mother had told her of in a moment of particular sadness three years before. It had been a London railway station on that occasion and a hospital train coming up from the coast in 1916. Her father had been recuperating in France for two months. There was a band and streamers hanging from the iron pillars. He limped down the platform behind the stretcher-bearers. He wouldn't have to go back. It wasn't the same any more and everyone could see it. But how could she tell him? It had become a duty, a necessary sacrifice. They married three months later.

Sally watched her fellow passengers leaving on their own, in the clutches of Chinese porters or being greeted formally, with a smile or, here and there, with noise and embraces the way she would like it to be for herself. In her own mind, her solitude became glaring and she imagined it must be the reason why a neatly dressed, dark-haired young man some twenty yards away had twice caught her eye before looking away again. At last he approached her. She tried to look as discouraging as possible and prepared a stern reply. The man stopped in front of her and raised his panama hat.

'Excuse me, is it Miss Marsden? Sally Marsden?'

'Yes, it is.'

The man held out a letter and she recognised Hugh's writing on the envelope.

'Hugh's desperately sorry, he really is. Everything got into a bit of a mess and he couldn't get away. He'll be at the hotel this evening.'

As Sally looked down at the note some of its words began to blur. She kept her head down, pretending to read it over again.

'Do you have your baggage receipt?'

Sally handed over the printed cardboard stub and collected herself before the man came back with a trolley laden with several cases.

'Shall we take a cab to the hotel? It's only ten minutes.'

They were walking towards the exit when he stopped abruptly and Sally collided with his shoulder.

'I don't believe it. It's all been such a rush.'

The man apologised and then held out his hand.

'Peter Moss.'

For the rest of her time in Shanghai she did not see Hugh's journalist friend again.

'I can't remember exactly,' said Hugh when asked for the history of their connection. 'I don't know him that well. We probably got talking in the club – your typical friendly American.'

'Is that typical?'

'They'll talk to anyone. Of course, as a journalist one mustn't be naive about his motives. I'm not really supposed to know people like that.'

Hugh regretted the loss of Sally's travelling companion and worked hard to arrange entertainments for her during the day. Polo matches, greyhound races, museum visits and a succession of matronly 'at home' days followed. The Chinese opened doors, brought food and took away the empty plates. They would not look her in the eye. The mannerism was explained to her by the wife of a Jardine's director, but Sally thought it more likely that the Chinese simply preferred her and her sort not to be there. She readily agreed that no offence should be taken and was told that in only a few weeks she would be 'an old hand'.

By the beginning of the second week her reserves of tact were quite exhausted and she excused herself from all engagements on account of a 'minor indisposition'. For several days in a row she left the hotel immediately after breakfast with some money, a none too accurate map of the city and a desire to get lost. She wandered through the International Settlement and across its border with the French concession, a miniature Paris into which a gendarme waved her as queues of Chinese waited in front of sandbags and machine guns to show their work permits. She began to learn the species of Shanghai – the German Jews who were the great city's newest and least competent taxi drivers; the police officers of many nationalities and jurisdictions; their patient Chinese mirror images, the Kuomintang, who paced with their gleaming cavalry boots on the very border edges of the foreign concessions; the loitering agents of Japan, always with notebook and camera (Sally had been advised not to carry one herself), arrogantly obvious and too slow by half amid the frenetic human flow; the White Russian café owners in whose establishments old men nodded over chessboards under the eyes of murdered rulers looking down from ochre walls. High up, behind every bar, there were calendars for 1917 and stopped clocks. One other species was often talked about but not so easily seen – the communist could be tracked only through the murdered customs officer, the bomb in the presses of the government newspaper, the posters being scraped from the city's walls early in the morning.

Sally grew bolder and quickly understood that her skin, her features and her clothes were all the passport she needed. She crossed the borders of the International Settlement and walked for miles through the true Chinese city. Within the first few minutes of such expeditions the tramlines would peter out. The tang of ozone and vaporised steel that would crackle from their overhead cables went too, as did the sound and scent of cars and trucks. It was replaced by something more animal and by the smells of food from houses and the numerous sizzling roadside stalls and by the kerosene that fuelled the ubiquitous stoves and lamps. Another species of the city quickly disappeared – the New Chinese of the international areas, the nation's personified future – young Cagney dressalikes who sauntered about the cinemas and the French cafés, the print-dressed office girls with their silk stockings, waved hair and their Carol Lombard lips walking to the post office with armfuls of letters. Their eyes had met with Sally's on several occasions. No looking away by this new power, but rather the assertion of a bold claim. They were not to be found much outside the international areas, except in the mornings and the evenings, emerging from China to go to their work, or dissolving ineffectually back into it at the end of the day. Instead, there was the child's picture-book world Sally had been subconsciously trained to expect – silk tunics, pigtails, the broad pale circles of straw hats, old men with long, thin beards. One of them approached her with grandfatherly concern, declared 'Trafalgar Square!' as if that phrase might secretly reveal themselves to each other. He offered pidgin directions as to how she might find her way home again. Sally walked on, further into the city, not quite sure if she had been the subject of help or an attempted expulsion.

It was on the third of these days that Sally's mind was cast back to the scene in her parents' garden in England and her father reading from *The Times*. She saw a nanny in one of the narrow streets, uniformed in grey flannel precisely as one might see strolling in a London park. Here was one of those 'people out there' who might advertise in the 'situations sought' columns of English newspapers and a fellow adventuress, it seemed, deep inside Chinese Shanghai. It was enough for Sally to follow her and the little four-year-old girl in white tunic and blue silk pyjama trousers who held on tightly to one of the young woman's fingers. They went into a shop and Sally followed, getting a coin ready from her bag in case she should want to buy something. The place was dim, a single hissing gas mantle casting a weak limelight down from the central beam. Sally looked about at stacks of radio batteries and little red boxes of valves, at a rack of shirts and trousers, at two-gallon tins of kerosene, at bins of shapeless, dried things which she presumed must be edible, long-stemmed pipes, packets of needles, a barrel full of green tea with a tin scoop, a shelf of teapots and patterned bowls and a man standing motionless behind a wooden counter. The little girl dropped her nanny's hand and ran across the floor to a display of dolls. She examined several with great severity, a smile appearing on her face only when she was shown how to pull a cord at the back of each doll making its arms rise above its head. She made them all perform in this way before choosing the one dressed most like herself and placing it on the counter. Sally watched her solemnly lift up and open her left hand to show the large silver Chinese dollar she had been tightly holding all the way from home. It was while this offer was being made that three boys, perhaps fifteen years old at most, came in. They were dressed almost as recognisably as the nanny, in the khaki shirts, knee-length trousers and neckerchiefs of Boy Scouts. A stiff anxiety came with them. Sally sensed it immediately in the nanny who half turned round to watch them and to keep an eye on her charge at the same time. The shopkeeper followed them with his eyes, wrapping the doll in a sheet

of brown paper without looking at it. The three boys picked
things from the shelves without caring how they put them
back. One toyed with a radio valve while staring insolently
straight at Sally.

'American?' he demanded.

'I'm English.'

'English?'

'Yes.'

'OK.'

He showed her the box for the valve.

'You see?'

'What should I see?'

The boy thrust the box almost into her face and shouted
something in Chinese before adding, 'Made in Japan!'

He threw the valve down, smashing it on the floor. It was
the signal for his friends to start doing the same with everything they could lay their hands on. The shopkeeper did
nothing, not moving from behind his counter. The little girl,
now clutching the wrapped doll to her chest, began to cry.

Sally ran out of the shop and shouted to the policeman
she had seen on the way in. The noise of smashing and
shouting from the shop was all too obvious, but Sally understood at once how hopeless it was when she saw the policeman glance at her briefly then turn away and walk a few
paces before stopping again. Behind her the three Scouts
were making a pile of goods in the road. One came out
struggling under the weight of one of the large tins of
kerosene. A knife was produced, and a gash stabbed through
the thin metal. The other dolls were thrown on the pile and
the whole doused with kerosene. A box of matches was
suddenly to hand and the three boys stood around, ready to
enjoy the blaze. The little girl and her nanny were in the
doorway of the shop preparing to leave. They had only gone

two or three paces when the nearest Scout lunged forward and snatched the wrapped doll from the child's hands. The girl screamed with anguish and pulled forward with one arm outstretched to take back the doll. Her nanny pulled her away and she collapsed, roaring with infant grief, hanging from the adult hand, her knees in their beautiful blue silk dragging in the dirt of the street. The paper was torn from her doll, the tiny clothes soaked in kerosene and lit with a match. The child didn't see it. She was plucked up from the ground and her screaming face pressed against grey flannel as she was taken quickly up the street and out of sight. But even when the kerosene on the main pile caught and blazed up six or seven feet, Sally could still hear the child's cries.

She looked on in amazement as the shopkeeper stood by his shop, seemingly unmoved. Someone was leaning out of a window and shouting abuse at the policeman. He walked slowly with his hands clasped behind his back and turned the corner. The three boys stood in a row like soldiers on parade. They saluted the flames.

Sally walked quickly away and stopped in a quieter side street to look at her map. Everything was now alien and sinister, every direction equally mean and dingy. She had gone beyond the area in which street names appeared in the alphabet as well as in Chinese characters. She searched her map for some simpler symbol she could remember and compare with a sign, but as soon as she took her eyes from the paper she lost it as surely as one loses the digits of an unfamiliar telephone number. She decided that a particular direction was west and walked that way hoping to come across a police post somewhere on the borders of the international zone. She was sure the stares of the passing Chinese were now hostile rather then merely curious. The man photographing an anti-Japanese propaganda poster who looked up at her as she passed and followed her round three corners was now just another combustible particle in a city she had suddenly begun to understand and might burst into flames around her at any minute.

At last a police post and a striped red-and-white barrier across the narrow road appeared. She had strayed a little northwards to the French concession rather than the International Settlement. Two coolies by the barrier were being spoken to brusquely by a French officer. At every pause in the interrogation one of them pointed to a piece of paper the officer held in his hand. At the sight of Sally another officer touched his cap and gestured to where she should walk round the barrier. With a step she passed from China to France, or to a peculiar version of it at least. Within a few streets she found herself in the Avenue Joffre. She had a coffee and a trembling cognac at a table by the window in the Café de Montesquieu. The streets were full of cars again and a crowded tram rattled by. A Chinaman stopped abruptly in the street and stared at her through the glass. Calmed and quite safe now, Sally glared back through a painted screen of French, Chinese and Russian lettering. He was young and dressed as if poor. There was an intensity in his gaze that, half an hour before, would have terrified her. She decided that it was hatred, that he was a communist. Without the window there, without so many people to see he might throw a bomb under her chair and she would have a few inches in the papers back home. Sally considered writing a story about it. She was mentally describing her detached leg, still in its neat brown shoe, lying on its own in the middle of the road when the young man destroyed the vision with a tentative smile. The frigid, Western face looking back at him, too surprised and slow to respond, withered his hopes and he moved quickly on. Well, it didn't matter now – Sally walked south, into the international zone and the sanity of the Cathay Hotel.

Sally's evenings were altogether more reassuring. There were dinner parties in the old colonial villas in the hills and larger affairs in town in the course of which, if one wished, one could book oneself up for the next ten days. Sally found that her novelty (and Hugh's 'social age' was no more than a few months) was a valuable currency. They were the new couple in a jaded world, their union a firmly cemented *fait accompli* and in Shanghai no scandal at all. From time to time Sir Harold was down from the embassy in Nanking and the introductions would have a higher rank − middling scions of the Swire or Jardine stock, an American who added the term 'realtor' to her vocabulary and, most colourfully, the woman called Lady Berkshire. It was Lady Berkshire who conducted her conversation with a long, amber cigarette holder and instructed Sally in the impressionistic technique of deciphering Chinese characters. A vivacious forty-something and with a husband dead and long-forgotten, her private life was complex and much discussed. She took a liking to Sally, issued invitations which, Sally learned from others, were highly coveted. Lady Berkshire was the reason why she was approached one evening by a stylish, middle-aged man who let his hand rest on her back and signalled across the room with an empty glass.

'An admirer of yours, my dear. Been waiting for my opportunity. Tell me what you make of Shanghai.'

There was hardly time for a response.

'I see you have been taken up by our little duchess.'

'I'm sorry?'

'"Lady Berkshire" as she likes to call herself. But you must excuse me − that's been going for so long now that no one bothers any more, or ever did much for that matter. Very Shanghai, don't you think? Pots of money. Whole warehouses of the stuff, they say. And you know where she got it from . . .'

'I'm sure I have no idea.' Sally began to look uncomfortably about the room for a glimpse of Hugh.

'That's why she can't go home again,' said the man, switching his empty glass for a full one from a passing salver.

'Wherever home is, now. How is England, my dear? I don't know when I last talked to someone who had been there so recently. Has it changed much?'

'Since when?' Sally asked.

'Good God – you know, I'd rather you hadn't asked that. Since, well, since 1920. Yes, that was it – March 1920. I'd had a good war, money in the bank, young man, all that . . . you know.'

'I have no idea how it's changed. Anyway, it's a bore – and so are you. Would you take your hand away, please?'

'Awfully sorry. You're in this weekend, aren't you? With Lady B? Couldn't mention my name, I suppose? If the opportunity arose? Wouldn't do any harm.'

Perhaps he saw Hugh coming, but in any case he slipped away two seconds before he arrived.

'Who was that?'

'Horrid man, didn't say. I think I've had about enough of Shanghai.'

'Packing already?'

'I'll start this evening.'

Hugh pulled Sally in towards him and kissed her on the cheek. He kept his arm around her waist for everyone to see.

'Don't worry – you'll like Nanking. It's very different – new. It's all businessmen and missionaries and that sort of thing. Solid types.'

★ ★ ★

58

Margery Berkshire's latest affair was in the Cathay itself – she always retained one of the top-floor suites so she could do something bigger in town whenever the mood took her.

It was a memorable occasion. Sally and Hugh had walked along the harbour front that morning. They'd held hands and Hugh had talked of the future. He was attentive and seemed to have no doubts. Sally was happier than she had been since leaving Southampton. That afternoon, it was only beginning to get busy when the sirens started and two-thirds of the guests fled to the shelters in the basement. The last made for the stairs with Lady Berkshire's contempt ringing in their ears. She turned to Sally.

'Miss Marsden, I'm so glad. I had you down as someone with a little backbone and I'm never wrong about these things. There's really nothing at all to worry about. I was here in '32 and I can tell you there is no danger at all.'

She clapped her hands and assumed command of the remaining twelve or thirteen guests.

'We shall not let history pass us by! Up on to the roof, everyone! Life is memory, Miss Marsden. Some never miss the opportunity to stock up on new memories, others crouch in basements. This way.'

So a dozen or so disported themselves to their best advantage and talked and drank their cocktails in the early-evening air of Shanghai on the roof of the Cathay Hotel.

'A no-show?' someone suggested just as the distant drone could first be heard. Something like dust in the sky approached and resolved itself into individual specks.

'Here we go.'

Sally began to sweat. She could feel waves of creeping cold wash over the skin of her shoulders and neck. Her bare arm brushed the cloth of Hugh's jacket and she moved closer to him. Arms were held out straight, fingers pointing to the horizon.

'There!'

'Try this.'

Sally accepted a pair of opera glasses and aimed them along the line of the pointing fingers. Her body detected a succession of rapid pulses, like the beat of an inaudible drum. Through the trembling, magnified figure of eight, dark plumes of smoke and debris shot upwards. A weak thunder came to them, such as might threaten a light shower of rain. It carried with it a faint toylike bell, an antique fire engine ringing out a futile warning.

From high above in their fragile shells, navigators looked down on the city and compared it with the coloured shapes on their maps. They saw the denser, multi-storeyed texture of the International Settlement, how neatly it fitted the protective pencilled outlines they must not cross.

On the roof of the Cathay Hotel, Margery Berkshire bared her faultless teeth and picked an olive from a cocktail stick.

'I'll say one thing for living in China – it does teach you the most wonderful sangfroid.'

4

Hugh's secondment to Shanghai ended and he and Sally went inland to settle down to the routine of embassy life in Nanking. There were more museums for her to visit, before their contents were packed up in wooden cases and taken away. She climbed Purple Mountain, a modest hill in fact, and wandered about the vast mausoleum of Sun Yat-sen before the protective scaffolding was erected and army trucks concentrated in its grounds. She met the American preachers and the missionary doctors and the German engineers and the lecturers at the bright new university. She met Miss Vautrin and began regularly to visit her and her college girls for tea and English conversation.

Hugh was less busy and there was more time with him. There was embarrassment when she was referred to as Mrs Jerrold, but happiness later when strolling together around Hsuan Wu Lake it seemed to both of them no innocent mistake, rather a confirmation of what was right and must be, a piece of good advice from a wise world. There was the radio and the *North China Daily News* telling of the fighting in Shanghai and of its end and the efficient restoration of order. The forces of progress and Asian amity lapped up against the borders of the International Settlement and the French Concession and went no further. The stench from Shanghai Bay was worse for a few weeks, but that too soon returned to normal, Margery Berkshire wrote cheerfully from her suite in the Cathay Hotel. She had been right, of course – it was just as it had been in 1932, which was as much as to say that nothing had really happened at all. The Astor had caught a bad one. Among the dead were two valets in a lift. The bomb cut the cables and they fell nine floors, floating in a moment of weightlessness before being buried in the concrete of the sub-basement. But that was the Chinese, trying to bomb a Japanese gunboat and falling short. Typical, really – and it was all over now anyway.

There were telegrams and letters home explaining why no one must worry about anything they read in the papers. Her letters, particularly to her father, adopted an authoritative tone. In the language of leading articles, she explained the personal nature of modern warfare, how much it had changed since his day. Each conflict was its own bacillus, deadly to some, harmless to others. It was everywhere, like the meningococcus. Only the neurotic worried about it and its violence was nothing but a new style of normality, one of those chances of life like the robber with a knife or the car on the wrong side of the road that could strike you down at any time. She confessed, by the way, to a sudden enthusiasm for becoming a journalist. Did her father know anyone in that line? If she sent an article could he pass it on?

The season changed and inland, far from the mildness of the China Sea, the cold quickly became harsh and dry. She began to think more of England and of that March date on her ticket when she would set foot in it once again. Peter Moss came inland too, to cover the Kuomintang government after the fighting in Shanghai had died down. Peter, Hugh and Sally made a threesome from time to time in the International Club. Sally and Peter met by chance in one of the city's parks. They all went together to Qixia Temple with Sir Harold. They came back, or most of them. Hugh and Sally sat side by side at the back of the British Embassy, looking down into the dark, still circles of their cups by the light of burning documents.

'I don't suppose they would really have been interested in any of that,' said Hugh disconsolately. 'It just seemed the right thing to do.'

He teased apart large, fragile flakes of ash to find the last unburned paper at the heart of the fire. When it was gone, the intensity of the cold quickly made itself felt on hands and faces.

'We'd better go in − try to get some sleep.'

They moved slowly, uncertainly, taking up time with small unnecessary tasks. They spoke little to each other except occasionally to say what they were doing.

'I'll leave the lights on,' said Hugh.

And then upstairs as she was taking her shoes off, Sally told him: 'I'll just take my shoes off.'

The weak evening current that coaxed a brown light from the bulbs was no use for heating. No fires had been set and they could just see their breaths, even inside the embassy. Two old paraffin heaters were recomissioned and gave off a faint warmth and an oily scent. Sally held hers by its swinging wire handle and leaned against the doorway of the second guest bedroom that had been her home for the last few weeks.

'Early start,' said Hugh.

'Yes.'

Trucks rumbled by outside.

'Does it matter any more?' asked Sally.

She moved towards him and they stood facing each other in the corridor. Hugh looked awkward, resistant. It was one of those moments at which it always seemed to Sally that Hugh needed rescuing from something, that the best of him had been put under siege, perhaps many years ago, but could be led out again to fullness by her. It was this restored man, whose potential glimmered in her mind like the completion of a hobbyist's grand project, she would marry with perfect confidence. She grasped the handle of the Ambassador's bedroom and opened the door.

'What are you doing?'

'Doesn't it make sense?'

Within were the large windows looking out over the front grounds, the curtains not yet drawn; the heavy wardrobe, the two telephones on the bedside table and the double bed with the sharp laundry creases on the pillowcases and the satin-edged counterpane turned down at one corner. Sally went in and put her paraffin heater on the floor.

'We can't share a single bed, can we? I don't think I'll take anything off. I shan't sleep and I suppose we might have to move quickly.'

It was an inducement to a timid creature – something edible held by the tips of the fingers at the end of an outstretched arm. Sally had swung her feet up on the bed as she spoke the last words. She slipped under the cover and pulled its satin border up to her chin, a performance of modesty by a silent-film actress. She closed her eyes and concentrated on the sounds in the room – Hugh coming in and crossing to the other side of the bed, the side the Ambassador (and where was he? still on the back roads, bumping southwards to Shanghai? still alive?) did not sleep on. She heard him take his coat off, the soft sound of it slumping over a chair. He took his shoes off and let them clump heavily on the floor. This is the way it would always be, year after year. Sally concentrated hard, tried to imagine it as a reality, as an actual life. Hugh got into the bed. She wriggled closer to him and rested her head on his shoulder and there they lay, as chastely as two travellers on a train.

Sally was right about not sleeping. A half-dreamworld was as deep as she got, in which stories unfolded not under their own impulse or arbitrarily, but lazily directed by her semi-conscious mind, still smelling the kerosene, still feeling on cheek, or exposed hand the cold of a deserted embassy bedroom in Nanking. The tick of a typewriter entered one of these narratives and she swam up some time between four and five to find herself alone, the door ajar and a faint light coming in from the landing. From the office below she heard the last few letters striking home and the sheet being pulled from the cylinder. A shadow blocked the light and there was a moment of fear before Hugh came in. He slipped in beside her.

'Not yet,' he said. 'Just doing one last thing.'

Half an hour later she was making tea in the icy scullery, stamping her feet and keeping her hands tucked under her arms. Hugh had refused food and she wasn't hungry either, but she did go through cupboards and search the pantry to see what could be made of whatever the staff had left. She would put together something for later in the day, just in case they had to wait. This simple foresight pleased her greatly. She was providing. She would say nothing about it and then produce her ingenious lunch just when it was most needed in a memorable display of resourcefulness under fire. She had a foolishly pleasing vision of an ample woman in a parody of military uniform pinning a badge on her sleeve.

It was one of the details she would include in a letter to her mother once back in Shanghai.

She wrapped both hands round a cup of tea and carried it upstairs to Hugh. He was so absorbed in his task she was able to stand in the doorway and watch him. He smoothed, and then pinched the cloth of the pillowcases in an attempt to restore their appearance of having been newly ironed. He pulled back the quilt and carried out a close inspection, holding the lamp close. He pinched up a telltale long, black hair and sprinkled it fastidiously on the carpet where it would never be noticed. Sally didn't want to see any more.

'Here,' she said, holding out the cup.

There seemed to be a slight twitch as he first heard her voice. He took the tea with a flat 'thank you'.

They went downstairs and put on their coats. Hugh checked the doors and the window latches. He picked up the document he had completed an hour before.

'Ready?'

They went outside and stood on the spot from where their journey to the temple had started less than twenty-four hours earlier. Hugh locked the front door and pasted over the keyhole the signed and stamped sheet of paper – a threat from His Britannic Majesty against anyone who might dare to break the seal.

In the cold, early-morning darkness, they joined the already thickening stream of traffic towards Hsiakwan.

The great walls of Nanking, thrown up in the sixteenth century, were an unfulfilled ambition. They ran for miles around a vast enclave of land protected on one side by the river. Four hundred years later these defences still protected many barren acres on which no building had ever stood. There had been no failure of commerce, or of fertility –

tens of thousands lived beyond the walls in a pungent, noisy choleraic fringe of slum that ran round most of the perimeter. The opium was cheaper here, the whores more shameless, the tax collectors less efficient.

On that particular morning it was on fire. General Tang had ordered the incineration of all buildings beyond the walls. Chinese soldiers ran through the slums shouting warnings and banging cooking pots before setting fire to Chinese homes and workshops. There must be no concealment for the approaching enemy and no obstruction to the defenders' guns. The wind carried the smoke away, but the light of the fires was clear above the walls, a sinister dawn hours before the sun. The burned-out slum-dwellers were crowding into the city. Sally considered that what she had read in her guidebook about the walls and the homily on ambition might be all wrong. Perhaps their great size was merely forward planning for events such as this, which the town planners of the sixteenth century would have confidently expected once every generation or so. The city was purposely expandable and the new hordes would live by tilling the vacant acres, perhaps for years at a time until whatever had driven them in there changed its mind, wandered on after some new story of gold or honour, or simply dissolved away into the infinity of China, leaving a few half-breed children begging for bread at the gates.

Sally's policy was to have a modern mind – it was how she described herself to others and she was excited to be caught up in an essentially modern event. In London, or in the country for the weekend, this would be her Spain, her Abyssinia, a trumping identity card with which to ward off boring young men with their tales of Barcelona or learning to fire a rifle from the back of a camel. And yet, when there wasn't a truck rumbling by, or a street light glaring in her eye, her consciousness of everything about her would suddenly shift and veer backwards through countless centuries to when this happened for the first time (if there ever was a first time). The calm, the solemnity and the slow pace of the refugees' way towards the Y Chang Gate made it all seem ceremonial, not modern at all, an immemorial ritual, an old truth dramatically refreshed for a new generation. Perhaps that was the real meaning of the walls.

A car sounded its horn, faintly at first then more loudly. People parted and pressed themselves against the sides of the street. A Mercedes rolled by with a driver and two staff officers in the back.

'General Tang,' said Hugh, 'or I think it is.'

Faces turned as the car slid by. It was hard to see, but there were no obvious signs of hope.

Hsiakwan was the greatest part of Nanking's extramural growth, the port that had filled up all the land between the walls and the banks of the river and had become a town in its own right. At night it was a prowling ground for those who missed the pleasures of Shanghai, by day a busy jumble of trucks and carts and porters servicing the ships that supplied the city. Sally had visited it once, in its decent daylight hours, to see the river. The word had a new meaning in her mind when she came away – the Thames and the Seine would never be the same again, even the Rhine would not impress. More like a long sea than a river, there would have been nothing surprising about the ships that plied it if one were to come across them in the middle of the Atlantic. The sight made sense of stories about the Yangtze as China's sorrow, of it carrying off tens of thousands in its floods and some-times, once every brief century or two, countless hordes, millions it was said. Standing by the edge of its vast, turbid waters, it was all too easy to believe.

The river was their destination now, and in particular the

promised HMS *Bee*. Two days upstream to Hankow and back to Shanghai by train was all it would take, and then a deep hot bath in a room at the Cathay, a thick towel – just enough of an adventure.

A dense crowd was pressing itself against the high, arched gateway that led to Hsiakwan. There was a sudden crescendo of shouting and movement at the front. Hugh stretched up on his toes. He could see the caps of Chinese police and the threshing rise and fall of truncheons. A burst of machine-gun fire restored the peace.

'What is it?' asked Sally.

Hugh didn't answer, but grabbed her wrist tightly and pulled her round the outside of the crowd. At the barrier, he imperiously summoned a police officer and showed his diplomatic passport. The man waved them around the end of the barrier and spoke to two of his colleagues who immediately stood aside. They were through, and ran into the streets of the port suburb, unaware of the further outbreak of truncheon work behind them as a dozen Chinese tried to follow.

The darkness lifted, revealing a dispiriting grisaille of houses, workshops, shut-up tea shops, bordellos and creaking godowns, all spread out beneath the modern outline of the electricity works wherein Herr Rabe's turbines turned at a thrifty half speed. By the quays the clothes were different, and the languages too. The West was in the air – a little Italian could be heard, much German, some French and loud American English as the US chargé d'affaires separated his citizens off from the rest and began to marshal them into a line. The structure quickly broke down as a long day of waiting began.

Tea and noodle sellers quickly clustered round the tiny, shivering enclave of foreigners determined that, if they were going to leave, they should at least do so without any loose change in their pockets. Hugh ticked off his short list of nationals, including one very self-conscious Jamaican with a mandolin case under his arm and in a great hurry to get back to the cabaret clubs of Shanghai. Sally threw Hugh an inquisitive look.

'Member of the Blue Jay Boys, apparently.'

'What happened to the others?'

'Got out in a van, he says – while he was sleeping.'

Sally looked for Peter among the Americans, but he wasn't there. The day wore on through a rhythm of rumour and disappointment. The air-raid warnings sounded twice without consequence. There was, in any case, nowhere to take shelter and the sound quickly lost all meaning.

River junks and sampans tied up at the smaller landing stages, made deals with a steady stream of the more prosperous Chinese and left promptly. Around noon there was a negotiation between two Frenchmen and an Italian and one of these enterprising boat owners. It became noisy and ended in acrimony. The lives of Europeans were more important, argued the boatman – a more valuable cargo justified a higher fee. The three returned to the fold and waited to see what a government might do for them.

Before noon the *Kutwo* steamed in. The Germans and the Danish representative of the Texaco Oil Co. picked up their bags and struggled up the gangplank with a barely tactful show of relief. Without ever properly tying up, her sailors unhitched the cables and ran up after their dozen passengers as if there were some invisible pursuer on their heels. The water churned and the little ship moved out from the quayside. There were waves from the deck, best wishes, professions of optimism that all would be well. In a few minutes the *Kutwo*, three-quarters empty, was just a smouldering smokestack on the steely, sea-wide expanse of the Yangtze. Hugh looked at his watch and swore. Sally bought more tea.

As she sipped it a new crisis began to impinge on her. She looked around with increasing anxiety, but could see nothing hopeful. She stared hard at various Chinese characters, trying to use her imagination, as instructed, to make them mean what she needed them to mean. Nothing was remotely suggestive of what she was looking for, and in any case, it seemed unlikely that such things existed in that part of town. Modesty was not a practical possibility for most Chinese and was little understood, even as an idea. Her discomfort seemed to be communicating itself to Hugh who was taking a renewed interest in a document of some sort. Sally whispered in his ear.

'I have to go for a walk.'

'Right,' said Hugh tersely, unwilling to take a detailed interest in something with such a monumental potential for embarrassment.

Sally wandered about the dockside area without finding a solution to her problem. It did occur to her, in the last couple of minutes before it became impossible to think of anything else, how odd it was that it should be a problem only for her. Certainly, it was no problem for Chinese women, as she had seen so many times since arriving in the country, but for Sally, after a lifetime of genuflecting to the closeted decencies of white porcelain, it seemed an enormous barrier and at that particular moment quite the worst thing China had thrown in her way. Good fortune took her around the corner of some packing crates. The extremity of her condition must have been obvious to the elderly woman already squatting over the concrete gutter. She laughed and addressed Sally with a stream of those sharp, half-swallowed vowels that always seemed so emphatic. But it was impossible, outrageous. The woman gestured to the gutter and chattered on. And suddenly there was Sally too, breaking the stage fright in the last few seconds, hitching up her skirt, pulling her knickers down about her ankles as the woman talked on and men stepped over the steaming gutter, paying no attention at all.

'All right?' asked Hugh, when she returned to the quayside.

'Fine.'

For a while, elated by having coped with this test and with the sense of victory over a mildly contemptible weakness in her nature, she found it hard to worry too much about the non-appearance of the ship. Hugh paced, muttered, escalated through a series of encrypted demands that she share his anxieties and then, when she still did not, exploded loudly and crudely. Conversation stopped, faces turned in their direction as eagerly as to the sound of a slapped face at a cocktail party.

Several tea shops had opened to take advantage of this captive market while it lasted. Sally sat in one of them as the afternoon hours passed. Co-nationals came and went, sometimes sitting by themselves, sometimes making conversation. Two middle-aged businessmen competed for her attention. She never learned their names and was not even sure if they still had any – one had introduced himself as Asiatic Petroleum and the other wished only to be known as British American Tobacco. Sally smoked one of his products and listened to how tobacco consumption rose during wars. When Peter appeared in the doorway there was something so unmistakable in her reaction that Tobacco and Petrol, neither the most sensitive of men, both promptly touched their hats and left.

'Where have you been? I've been looking for you since this morning.'

'Observing, asking questions.'

'That's what soldiers call spying – you should be careful.'

'I've just spoken to Hugh. He told me you were in here.'

Sally nodded, but didn't speak. Peter put his precious camera carefully on the table.

'I was in the news agency when the last cables came in. The *Bee* has been stopped downriver by the Japanese.'

Sally looked alarmed.

'It's OK – you all get on the *Panay*. There won't be a problem. Hugh's fuming – already composing the diplomatic protests. It's a bit of a professional embarrassment, I suppose – getting out on an American ship.'

'Sign of the times.'

'You don't mind?'

'Why should I?'

'You'll go back to Shanghai?'

'Yes – and then London, sooner than planned. I think I'm going off adventures.'

Their eyes held each other for a moment. They waited. Peter looked away and took a notebook from inside his jacket.

'I have a lot of friends in London. I know someone who would like to meet you. Can I give you an address?'

A messenger, a go-between? So much was already understood.

'Of course. I'd like that.'

Peter tore the page from his notebook and handed it across the table.

'Anyway,' said Sally, 'we'll be together on the boat.'

There was a commotion outside.

'I'd better go and see.'

Sally and Peter stood together on the threshold of the tea shop and watched as a dozen Chinese soldiers appeared from a warehouse and started to clear an area of the quayside. At the same time, a relieved cheer went up from the huddled

Europeans as a gunboat came into view. The group compressed themselves, seized suitcases. The gunboat stopped in mid-channel. After a few minutes a fast launch appeared and surged towards the quay at the apex of a white V of foam. All polished wood and brass, a uniformed boatswain standing behind the wheel, the flag of the Chinese Republic fluttered at the stern. On a slight rise, Sally and Peter could see more clearly across the screen of soldiers that hid the landing stage from the crowd. They watched four men come out of the warehouse and walk briskly towards the launch.

'Good heavens!' said Sally.

Peter reached for his camera and quickly wound on to a new frame. There was a quiet click and then another as General Tang, his adjutant, an unknown officer and Mr Edward Brindle of the Lion Machine and Bearing Company climbed down to the launch and were borne away to safety. The Europeans and the Americans groaned, put down their suitcases, lit cigarettes and drifted apart.

The *Panay* did come. Captain Komatsu, who had established his light artillery on the north-western side of Purple Mountain half an hour before, examined her through his binoculars. He noted the American flag, recalled the standing orders relating to neutrals, speculated pleasingly on his great nation's future. He saw the torrential crowd pouring in from the Y Chang Gate where the police and soldiers had given up the fight against their own people. They had asked for instructions. A field telephone rang and rang in the outer office of General Tang's headquarters and they had understood. Captain Komatsu looked down on the dense, panicking swarm, on the last thin line of order that held up a fragile enclave of space around the foreigners queuing to board the ship. There could be no doubt about the meaning of this scene – Japan was being insulted.

On the quayside Hugh had twitched with irritation as the Americans embarked first. The French and the Italians roundly abused their rescuers in the safety of their native tongues. Peter was somewhere in the crowd of Chinese, trying to get a steady sixtieth of a second for a good picture of the *Panay*. At last it was the turn of the other nationalities. Sailors stood ready to cast off as Hugh took both the suitcases and went ahead.

'Be careful,' he said over his shoulder.

Sally straightened from picking up a comb that had fallen from her hair. It was then that she saw the first white plume spike up from the surface of the river. The noise from the gun that had caused it arrived and then another shell, smashing into one of the old warehouses. Sally picked herself up to see the tea house explode, filling the air with shattered timbers. Another shell exploded between her and the way back to the city, its detonation muffled by the flesh of the crowd.

The klaxons were sounding on the USS *Panay* and Sally could hear an amplified voice shouting a succession of brief phrases. Everyone was running. People were falling into the river, some jumping. Where was Peter? She crouched low as more buildings disintegrated. She watched a brick chimney topple on to a row of burning workshops. A man passed her, face black with blood, a bucket in his hand, a silhouette against yellow and orange as he walked unsteadily towards the fires.

Hugh's voice suddenly cut through and she remembered herself. She ran a dozen paces to the edge of the quay only to pull up at the ten-foot gap between land and ship. The water seethed as the *Panay*'s engines strained. Hugh was screaming at her, pointing to the stern as if something could still be done. Sally saw the last rope holding back the ship, and a sailor with an axe running towards it. Hugh was not coping well. She watched him run up and down in confusion. He headed for the bridge and got halfway up the iron steps before an officer stepped out of a doorway and blocked his way. Hugh remonstrated, waved towards Sally on the quay, tried to push by and was knocked tumbling down the steps and out of sight. The axe fell. The *Panay* lurched out of her berth, straddled by the fountain splashes of shells from Purple Mountain. Through the smoke and the spray that splattered down heavily on her coat Sally waved at someone standing in the stern and then turned away.

Fire took hold quickly. It made its own wind, sometimes gusting billows of flame right across the narrower streets so that people had to stop or throw themselves down flat into a puddle. Where the shells had fallen there were bodies too, parts of bodies, just as she had imagined, but not to be dwelt on now, just flashing through her consciousness for the duration of a frame or two, their reality still uncertain.

The heat was cut off abruptly when she regained the tunnel through the Y Chang Gate. She passed the abandoned barrier and stopped as soon as there were no fires near her and no one jostling her. The back of her hands, which she had held up to protect her face, tingled as with sunburn. Her eyebrows and the ends of her hair were gritty where they had been singed. She could smell herself burning. She took off her hat and sat down on a discarded crate of hand grenades.

Sally considered her situation with mounting astonishment. What to do? Which way to go? The paralysis crept on. How even should she make a decision, let alone act on it? How should the powerless say 'left' or 'right'? She fingered a coin in her coat pocket, but could not decide what heads or tails should signify.

An incomprehensible chaos swirled around her. It was Waterloo again, when a morning crowd prised her hand from her mother's and swirled her away into a dark current of giants. Solitary in the rushing strangeness, as an Englishwoman or a four-year-old child, she remembered the stares from all directions, and saw them now, so quickly disengaging from her isolation with an electric jolt of fear. Not their problem. She heard the piercing shriek of a steam whistle that had almost made her faint eighteen years before.

'Peter!'

She was sure it was him. The light was failing, but the man had his hands up to his face and the gesture made no sense to Sally unless there was a camera between them.

'Peter!'

She ran forward and called again, putting all her strength into it, convulsively, like a child's cry. There were a thousand people between them. The man lowered the camera and let it hang at his hip in a movement as distinctive as a signature.

'Peter!'

It was impossible that he could hear her. The man looked about himself and Sally was more certain than ever. As he turned towards a side street she ran forward and collided with a woman who grunted and pushed her away angrily. She caught a last glimpse of Peter, a fraction of a second, as he ran out of sight. The camera strap across his chest made him look like a soldier, the camera itself so like a pistol or a wallet of ammunition.

There were few civilians left. Orderless policemen and soldiers milled about until a little violence by a cart heaped high with clothes gave them a new direction. The owners were quickly overpowered by three soldiers. Policemen immediately got involved, forming a line to facilitate the theft. As soon as the idea became clear, there was a violent assault on every shop in the area. Police smashed windows with their truncheons, soldiers kicked in doors. They staggered out under armfuls of clothes, fought each other. Seams ripped, blood streamed from heads clubbed with rifles. Sally watched from her packing crate as caps were thrown on the ground, tunics torn off, boots kicked away as if their very touch was poison. Stripped to their underwear, steaming with exertion and fear, they struggled into whatever they had been able to steal and disappeared.

Sally was almost alone, an indistinct irrelevance in the binoculars of Captain Komatsu as he looked down from Purple Mountain. A cloth army lay scattered about the street and the pavements. Trousers with boots to march in, jackets with identity papers to hand, army issue watches with which to time their attacks.

Glass cracked under the pressure of a new Dunlop. Sally looked up. She saw a swastika painted on the car door. The door was pushed open and there was Herr Rabe, one hand on the steering wheel, the other holding his hat two inches above his head.

'Miss Marsden – you stayed. I'm so glad.'

He indicated the passenger seat of his car.

'May I?'

5

A few days passed. The fires outside the walls burned out. The ashes of Hsiakwan went cold. The precious electricity plant remained unharmed – a testament to the virtuous precision of modern artillery.

Gunfire was continuous. Sally learned the dialects of rifle, machine gun, field gun and mortar. It was never more than desultory and never gave hope. The argument became one-sided – the endless explosive repetition of an orator's climax, but never a response. There was a night and then a morning of silence. On Chung Yang Street they waited for the rumble of armoured cars.

For the score or so of Westerners still in the city it was the most exhausting and the most energised few days of their lives. Ordinary people about to be made special by circumstance, they seemed to be lit up by the drama of their choice, half-strangers to themselves and capable of anything. They had come together in a group and elected the little German with the moustache to be their leader.

Schooled to the invoice, the contract and the order, an engineer's agent in China of some twenty years' standing, he was a man of the industrial age. Organisation was a sensual pleasure to Herr John Rabe, be it in the matter of delivering a set of searchlights or a sack of rice. Tenacious in the retention of customers, supple in the appeasement of superiors, he was an acknowledged artist of the common purpose. Things came together around John Rabe. He was the man for the job and had accepted it with humility two hours before collecting Sally in his little car by the Y Chang Gate amid the litter of discarded uniforms.

The six hundred women and children who had crammed themselves into the grounds of his house since the earliest hours of that morning knew nothing of these dry considerations. Their instinct was to put themselves as close as possible to anything foreign, to anything that was wholly alien to them and to their cousin-enemies. Anyone, to be more precise – it was a witness they needed. A telltale who might prevent whatever would be done to them if there were no one to tell tales. They did not take refuge in the gardens of the Japanese Embassy. Neither did they arrange their straw mats and string up their blanket tents around the American Embassy, or the British with Hugh's pompous seal on the door. There was no one left to look out of those windows, or to take a photograph or compile an aide-mémoire. They went to John Rabe's house. The earliest arrivals made their home under the red roof of a vast Nazi flag staked out in the garden as a charm against bombs.

They called themselves the International Committee of the Nanking Safety Zone and wrote to General Matsui through the good offices of the Japanese Embassy, hoping that he would accept their neutrality and humanity and that they could rely on the best traditions of the Japanese Imperial Army being maintained. The General was feverish and much put upon of late. The old problem made him sweat and turn the night through on his camp bed.

At Ninhai Lu, in the spacious house of a departed government minister, typewriters were being carried up the steps. Two preachers, a lecturer, the administrator of the local YMCA and a handful of businessmen were making their headquarters. The Chinese had begun to refer to John Rabe as the Mayor of Nanking, and without in the least intending it, this little group discovered that they had become a government. To what remained of Chinese officialdom their requests had the power of an instruction from on high. They had a treasury in the form of the safe in the corner of the main office, well stocked with Kuomintang funds. When one of the last policemen caught a thief, he hauled the cowering boy before John Rabe for punishment.

The first night, when Rabe brought her back, Sally slept on a sofa on the ground floor under a pile of coats. The activity never quite stopped and she drifted in and out of a vague awareness of conversations, the ticking of typewriters, the rattling and then the cursing of telephones some time towards dawn when they finally stopped working.

From under an astrakhan collar she watched Rabe add columns of figures by the light of an oil lamp, mumbling the results as he made notes with a pencil. She jumped as he shouted loudly through the open doorway.

'Three hundred and seventy tons!'

'Good,' replied an American voice.

'Good? It's a disaster. It's seven days, maybe eight. They're not birds.'

'Sorry!'

The reply was cheerful.

Sally got up and went to the window. There were low voices from outside, a new baby gasping, working up to a full roar of hunger. A dark fall of humanity had covered all the lawns. Only the path was clear, a light concrete stripe from steps to gate. Breath and smoke from small fires thickened the morning mist. Rabe came to join her at the window and they both looked up at the sound of a single aircraft. Black puffs of flak from Japanese positions began to track it across the sky until it pulled up into the clouds.

'Chinese,' said Rabe. 'He'll fly back to Hankow and say all is quiet, apart from the ack-ack. I hope it doesn't snow.'

The American came in and offered his hand.

'Lewis Smythe, I'm at the university. Well . . . was.'

He smiled broadly, excited by his enforced change of role.

Sally gave her name in return and was about to explain how she had come to miss the last boat when Rabe interrupted her.

'This is the young woman I told you of. The planes and the British Ambassador?'

Smythe reacted.

'She's been through more than any of us.'

The professor could think of nothing other than to seize her hand again and give it another more vigorous shake.

'Well done!' he exclaimed. 'We need everyone we can get. Thank you for staying.'

He spoke quickly to Rabe about another warehouse in the East City which was said to be full of rice. Liu would show him where it was. They would go in the car and should not be more than an hour. With any luck there would be some left.

The fiction of Sally's voluntary presence bothered her at first, all the more so because she was sure Rabe must have known the truth and had quite deliberately awarded her this moral promotion. She felt herself inexplicably in possession of someone else's property and that every failure to confess was another failure to give it back.

It was on that first morning she suddenly said to Rabe, 'I have a hundred pounds sterling and my watch is gold.'

She was taking it off. But he just poured more coffee for her and said, 'I'll remember that.'

Rabe showed her a map of the city and explained what they were trying to do.

'Do you know Nanking well?' he asked.

'I've spent enough time walking around it.'

'I wonder if you would like to help?'

The morning was spent slowly piloting Rabe's car around the city marking out the borders of their defenceless enclave. At every stop a flag would be taken – any piece of white cloth attached with upholsterers' tacks to a length of broom handle commandeered from a hardware store – and set up in a prominent place. The task took longer than it might have done because of the many interruptions that Rabe had to deal with. Sally lost count of the number of times he exchanged a few words of pidgin with passing Chinese, each encounter beginning with the simultaneous observation 'Still here!' He seemed to know a third of the city. Sally stood by, silent and unnecessary. She was at least visible and her mood lifted towards the end of the morning when she received a nod from a whiskered, silk-hatted old gentleman Rabe must have spoken to earlier. She had never been greeted by a Chinaman before.

Rabe drew on his map with a coloured pencil, thickening the line they had just marked out in reality.

'There.'

He showed Sally the blue-edged oblong that contained the university, most of the embassies, the International Club and Rabe's own house.

'Tell me, Miss Marsden, have you ever been entertained by a lion-tamer?'

83

'I wouldn't say entertained.'

'But you've seen them?'

'Yes.'

'I saw one as a child. He held the animal off with a chair, or pretended to anyway. And what I couldn't understand was what the lion thought about the chair. Did you ever wonder about that?'

'I don't think so – I can't remember really.'

'I thought – I was perhaps ten or eleven – the lion must have some idea about the chair, a misunderstanding. And perhaps the whole thing depended on the tamer's ability to make the lion believe this lie about the chair.'

Rabe stopped the car in front of the Committee Headquarters and they got out. He tapped the map and said he would get it printed as a poster and distributed across the city.

The grounds of 5 Ninhai Road were even more densely populated than before. People were settling on the narrow grass verges beyond the walls. The road would soon be impassable. The German businessman and the young English tourist attracted universal attention as they walked along the path and up the steps.

'There must have been some trick he had,' said Rabe. 'I only wish I had paid more attention.'

Peevish and still with two degrees of fever, General Matsui was in no mood to listen to his inferiors. Operations outside the walls were complete but how sure could he be of what lay within? The reports were all positive. The comical Mr Fukuda of the Japanese Embassy told of apathy and disorder. He solicited instructions for the victory parade. Captain Komatsu reported what he had seen through his binoculars and explained, with some generosity to himself, the beneficial effects of his work on Hsiakwan. The General pressed his seal on to the formal dispatches that mentioned the good Captain's name.

'No.'

The General was a student of history. For him there was no modernity in warfare. The sword he wore was no ornament. The machine gun was a sword, the bomber was a sword. Always the bayonet rather than the bullet — that is what he told his men. He brooded on the ignominy of trinitrotoluene and the piston engine, on the pursuit of a great vocation in a vulgar age. The walls of Nanking troubled him. They were centuries old and not to be despised. He could sense the spirits of the men who built them and felt again that bite of regret he could not possibly share with his juniors. Like the walls, the errors of generalship were ancient and always the same. General Matsui's mess anecdotes were all of failed optimists.

'No, wait. Make them wait.'

He got up heavily and padded into the inner room of his billet, pulling the screen behind him.

'Send out forage parties.'

The Sun Emperor's soldiers fanned out across the countryside emptying the storehouses and the granaries, tainting with old engine oil whatever they did not need or was not to their taste. They burned the villas on Purple Mountain, sending smoke signals down to the city below. It was unrewarding work and the city's great walls and everything that lay within them began to prey on their minds. Shanghai had been hard work and there had been no time to rest after the surrender. They had been much offended by China's cold welcome.

In the city the delay was not wasted. Half or more of the remaining population huddled into the Safety Zone.

Government buildings, the university, the post office and anything else with much floor space was organised into a series of huge dormitories. Gardens and verges were obliterated by humanity. The roads silted up with families bivouacking under blankets pinned to the telegraph poles. Almost at once, Shanghai Road became the thoroughfare of this new city, a seething barter market where every meagre surplus found its value – only what could not feed, clothe, shelter, warm or salve was worthless. Countless thousands remained outside – optimists perhaps, or without faith in the power of white flags.

The members of the International Committee audited the resources left to them – rice, flour, oil, coal – and mobilised the fragmentary police force into guarding them. Soup kitchens were set up, rations calculated. A doctor toured the pharmacies with a crowbar and delivered their contents to the hospital. Phials of insulin were handed in at 5 Ninhai Road where they were gratefully received by John Rabe and tucked away at the back of the safe. He handed another sheet of figures to Sally. She worked hard to justify her place, but the halting rhythm of her typing still made Dr Rabe smile as he put on his coat and hat and went out to pay another visit to the Japanese Embassy.

A hundred miles away on the lacquered, sea-broad expanse of the Yangtze, Hugh stood on his own at the rail of the USS *Panay*. Everyone knew his story. He had colluded just a little with the drama by claiming that he and Sally were actually engaged and had then lost his temper with one of the journalists, telling him in return for his kindness that he just wanted a piece for his paper. He had composed in his mind a whole sheaf of telegrams to be fired off as soon as he set foot in Hankow. He was going to mobilise the resources of HMG. Metaphors of aggression swarmed in his mind as relentlessly as the latest tunes. They rose to a pitch with the phrase 'strongest possible terms', a switch that threw a voltage across his dead limbs, startling them into a confused movement. Consequences would be threatened. The words would sting in Tokyo.

What if she were dead? The thought slipped into him from behind. Hugh clung to the rail and put his head down, expecting to find something literally draining out of him. For a moment he couldn't see or count the impossible rate of his heartbeats. He bent lower over the rail, putting all his weight on it. His heart punched the inside of his ribs with a convulsive blow that made his whole body jump. The last, surely. No. He opened his eyes and watched as shapes swam back to the true and colours became themselves again.

'Sir?'

A young sailor was at his elbow, asking for the second or perhaps third time if he could get by. Hugh apologised and straightened. He watched the man attend to a piece of machinery he couldn't name near the bow. All day it had been sunny, dry and bitterly cold. The shadow of the *Panay*'s main gun fell over the sailor as he worked. Hugh's heart rate slid back down to normal. No, Sally wasn't dead. That just wasn't possible. But even so . . . A leaden futility settled over him as he watched the distant banks peel by. He reviewed the few years of his adult life with dejection. Was it merely by chance that he had made all the wrong choices? That could change, especially at such an early stage. But for how long could one be blamelessly unlucky? For a year now the other, unacknowledged theory had been gaining ground – the guilty self, the reliably faulty compass in the deepest innards of the machine that would always misdirect it. Well, at least he could save Sally. He could call the whole stupid nonsense off before it did any more harm. He went below in search of a drink and to make peace with the journalist.

The *Panay* ploughed on. Her bow pleated the river into spreading furrows of light and dark. The pattern was clearest from above. Through ten thousand feet of glacial air it was unmistakable.

In Nanking the water was off. Peter walked back from Hsuan Wu Lake with a brimming tin pail and set to improvising some coffee in an abandoned house on Chungyang Road. He tucked a dollar into an empty ginger jar and settled down, picking his spot with his camera held to his eye. He had made his guess as to where they would come through first and drifted into happy contemplations of what the shot might bring him. The word 'Life' glimmered richly in his mind. 'Cover photo by . . .' Yes. There was luck for some, even in the midst of all this.

His worst hours had been two days before and he felt good now, the momentum of relief pushing on into a thoughtless happiness. He had kept his head down when the shells had started to fall. An avalanche of hessian sacks tied up into bales had knocked him off his feet and pressed him to the ground. He might tell it differently one day, but he did nothing to scramble out until the explosions had stopped. He got a shot of the departing USS *Panay* and then started to shake as his mind flicked back to the last clear frame before the attack – Hugh struggling to get on board with two cases, Sally standing on the quay. Where was she? There was a lot of blood. He took in several dead at once and the injured were calling out. His mind skimmed over the scene, panicking for what it might find – a recognised pattern of cloth, one of those costly light tan shoes, a green hat. He looked for her among the living – easy to find, surely.

The chaos was complete. Someone thrust a bucket into his hand and he spent several minutes in a chain trying to douse a warehouse. It was clearly futile and the heat was hard to bear. Gaps began to appear in the line and after a while Peter also slipped away. He searched for over an hour, for a while being pinned to an area close to the water when the fire was at its height. When the embers were collapsing in on themselves he went back up the road into the city. He went through the dark coolness of the tunnel and scuffed through the discarded weapons and uniforms. An entrepreneurial boy ran here and there picking up watches, identity papers, a pistol. Then he was quite alone.

He heard almost immediately about the Safety Zone and had gone to their headquarters as a last hope after failing to find any trace of Sally at the Red Swastika Society, the YMCA or the abandoned British Embassy. He had walked through the crowded grounds in mid-morning, had run up the steps straight towards the possibilities he most feared. The place exuded a calming air of organisation. Suddenly deprived of what he wanted to say, he positioned himself in front of the noticeboard and there read Sally's name on one of her own inexpertly typed sheets, a businesslike 'SM' at the bottom right-hand corner, just as Rabe had instructed.

'She's out flagging,' someone told him. 'Have you registered? Any special skills in that box please.'

'I'm a journalist.'

'Just name and nationality, then.'

Peter folded a note to Sally and pinned it to the board on top of the list of names.

'You'll make sure she gets it?'

He encountered half a dozen of the flags but always missed Sally and Rabe.

His note became a bookmark. In a back room at 5 Ninhai

Road, behind a sheet tacked up to preserve her privacy and that of the young Reverend Weston snoring on the other side of it, Sally slipped it out from between 'Carburettors' and 'Centrifugal-type Superchargers' and read it for the twentieth time.

On their last day of grace Sally found her niche. While on a liaison visit from her Ginling Girls' College, the redoubtable Miss Vautrin had noticed her name on the typed sheet pinned to the noticeboard. She had not, perhaps, been much use as a tutor in English conversation. At the end of their afternoon together a dozen of Miss Vautrin's girls were able to give the birth and death dates of Shelley and recite 'Look on my works, ye Mighty, and despair!' but were not much further on in the business of telephoning a hotel or instructing a tailor to make alterations. Minnie Vautrin had taken to the young Englishwoman nevertheless. She had not missed the signs of isolation, nor failed to understand the eagerness with which Sally accepted her invitation to come again to what could hardly be a very stimulating engagement.

The appearance of Sally's name on the noticeboard of the International Safety Zone Committee had come as a surprise to Minnie Vautrin. She reproached herself with this uncharitable habit of mind, but could still not hold back from sorting everyone she could think of into the only two categories of humanity that mattered any more – stayers and goers. Sally hadn't been down on her stayers list. She came up at the end of a long exchange with John Rabe about food reserves, medical supplies, the whereabouts of more sandbags and the capacity of the basements under Ginling's main dormitories and science building during air raids. Whether anything was given in exchange Sally never dared to ask, but somehow she found herself transferred from Dr

Rabe to Miss Vautrin. She found her new mistress waiting for her on the bench in the hallway and noted the transformation from when they had last met – the muscular, portly calves exposed, the stout hiking shoes with white ribbed socks rolled down in a thick ring of wool around the top, the sturdy skirt and matching jacket of a colour so close to khaki that the whole effect was such that Sally looked for the rifle she ought to be carrying with her.

Minnie Vautrin sprang up and delivered a firm, cheerful handshake.

'Hello again. I hope you don't mind but I think you're mine now. Is that all right?'

'Well, yes – of course,' said Sally, too taken aback to think of anything else.

Miss Vautrin claimed that John Rabe had been most reluctant to let her go but she had been persistent and had finally persuaded him.

'They don't really need women here and we do. You'll see what I mean in a few minutes. I think I can promise the accommodation will be better too. Is there anything you want to bring with you?'

Sally ran upstairs and gathered together her few things, not forgetting to slip Caldwell's slender *Fundamentals of Aero Engines* into her coat pocket.

It was partly the pace and partly the density of the crowds filling the Safety Zone that forced Sally to walk behind Minnie Vautrin as she shouted her explanations back over her shoulder. Often they had to turn side-on to ease a passage. Minnie's English was constantly broken by Chinese apologies and forceful demands to make way.

'It wasn't really planned, or not at first, but we've become a women's refugee camp – there are so many without men because of the war and now they're our problem.

'We stopped the girls coming back for the new term by writing to as many as we could and then putting notices in the papers. We only have three with us – we haven't been able to contact their families. So with all the dormitories and the kitchens and so on we were well set up. We couldn't say no.'

It was the last phrase that pulled Sally's attention back to what Minnie was saying. It seemed odd in her mouth, as if borrowed awkwardly from a more ordinary person who could even contemplate saying no. Sally had been looking down a side street as they made their way over a swarming junction. She saw one of the flags she had helped set up two days before. Beyond it was the broad Sikang Street, by no means deserted, but with a Sunday traffic of the occasional bicycle rickshaw and a handful of curious strollers. What did they think the flags meant? And those crowding inside the Safety Zone – what did they think?

'I hope you'll call me Minnie – it's for Wilhelmina, before you ask. Everyone does. I've outlived my name – who could possibly call themselves Wilhelmina these days? I got called Kaiser Wilhelmina at school.'

'Sally,' said Sally.

'We can go in this way.'

Minnie took out a key and the two women went through an unobtrusive door in a brick wall and into the secluded grounds of Ginling Girls' College.

On her first and only previous visit Sally had walked up the broad front steps and into the central courtyard and gardens of something very like a temple. Pantiles and rooflines with upward curving vertices were everywhere. It was an American architect's concept of what would be acceptable and had resulted in one of Nanking's most traditional buildings. These gestures sat atop modern buildings no more than twenty years old. The institution as a whole was the product of the Protestant religion and American money and justified optimism. The alumni of Ginling were proving themselves all over China and beyond. Their photographs advanced inexorably across the walls.

Minnie enumerated the changes since Sally's first visit – the four tons of sand at the end of the assembly hall for smothering phosphorous incendiaries, the patchy grey paint on the roofs which was believed to confuse artillery spotters, the bright scarlet exclamations of new fire extinguishers bracketed to the uprights of the covered walkways, the vast Stars and Stripes flag stitched together by her own pupils and staked out on the grass to do for her charges what John Rabe's swastika did for his. Men were digging trenches across an expanse of lawn.

'For air-raid protection,' said Minnie, 'but I don't suppose they'll bomb now it's theirs. It'll be the Chinese we have to worry about now and they don't have much, I'm pleased to say. One of war's little ironies. We'll turn them into latrines. We'll be needing them soon.'

The fragments of a female and childish society were busy making the best. Washing hung, drying slowly in the cold air. Vegetables were being peeled near a row of large aluminium pans while others were being planted in former flower beds. They encountered the three remaining pupils coming from the science building with trays of fragile glassware and skull-and-crossboned bottles. They snapped to attention as best they could on seeing Minnie and were presented solemnly to Sally. They bowed, looking very serious with their badges and 'Service Corps' armbands. Sally bowed back as the last in the line rhythmically announced 'Look on my works, ye Mighty, and despair!' and everyone laughed. Minnie said a few words to them in Chinese and they went on their way. Sally tried hard to retain the alien syllables of their names. She recited them silently for a few seconds until they became jumbled and she had to give up.

'I'll show you your room.'

They went on to the Principal's house, a substantial mansion which stood to one side and on a rise that gave an overview of the whole site. The stained glass in the front door presaged it, and then the scent of the place on opening the door and the wainscoting inside and the half-moon table by the wall with its vase of dried flowers all powerfully added to the pang of homesickness.

'My goodness,' said Sally, meaning nothing in particular. She felt a little dizzy for a moment and stopped with her hand over her mouth.

Minnie was already climbing the stairs.

'I know,' she was saying. 'They could have found something better to spend their money on. I look at it now and all I can think is firewood – we're very short of coal, you know. It's up here.'

Two floors up Minnie opened a door and stood aside. Sally stepped into a large room with windows on two sides. A brownish rug covered the central square of polished bare boards. The walls were white. A single unadorned cross hung from a picture hook. A simple iron bed frame protruded at either end of a colourful bedspread that Sally suspected was not the standard issue. There was a chest of drawers and a bedside table of the same pattern. There was a pitcher of water capped with an upturned glass, a Bible and a useless electric lamp. A narrow wardrobe stood in the corner like an upturned coffin.

Sally put her book on the table and leaned forward to get a better view from the window. She could see a corner of the college grounds, the front perimeter and the quiet roadway beyond. Thirty hours later, exhausted and happy, she stood on the same spot with the window open a few inches. Across the city Peter had taken his photographs and had stood by the roadside, holding up his American passport as the first units warily went by. A runner had come from John Rabe to say the occupation had begun. The Safety Zone Committee's letter had been delivered to the Embassy of Japan and to the High Command. They were hopeful of good behaviour. Sally looked down on the improvised Japanese flags that had appeared outside many houses just that morning. She watched the first foot patrol trot up the front steps and rattle the college gates. They turned away, unconcerned. The bicycle rickshaw, piled high with winter greens, tipped over carrying the rider with it. For several seconds the shot seemed separate, even as Sally watched the rider trying to rise, falling back again and again as half his body no longer responded. The three soldiers approached, obscuring the man. They made signs over him and Sally heard the short, deep sigh of petrol as it explodes into flames. The soldiers stepped back from a high bright heat and then moved on without looking back. The flames died back quickly. Sally looked down on the black outline of a man – still moving, still trying to get up.

6

'*What crimes have not been committed these last few days . . . ?*'
How to go on? Minnie raised her head. Her own
hand cast too large a shadow over the page and she moved
the oil lamp a little closer. The darkness crept onwards by
half a degree, the black lee side of roof timbers and the
outlines of iron-framed beds edging round, the dozen black
heads stark on new-laundered whiteness unchanged, a shifting glint in the one pair of open eyes.

'Go to sleep, Siao-sung.'

A blink, and darker still.

Minnie looked over at the young Englishwoman slumped
awkwardly in a straight-backed chair. Her long legs were
stretched out and crossed one ankle over the other. Her dark
hair hung down, her neck bent sharply over the top rung
of the chair, the mouth slightly open. Her clothes were
crumpled, she smelled strongly of labour and exhaustion. It
would be painful when she woke. She had learned a lot
about her – her brotherless and sisterless life in England, the
mother and father whose full weight she had to bear, the
strange and, to Minnie, rather pointless history of her presence

in China. It was nothing but a self-indulgent game between the three of them from what she could see, though that was more than had actually been said. She had heard the rumours about the Ambassador and the cars confirmed, she listened to the whole stony recitation of the horror and sudden violence with which the bubble about this young life had burst. When Sally talked, the effect was as precise and passionless as a photograph developing in Minnie's mind, the holes in the car coldly equivalent to the holes in the man. It had the air of a painstaking, forensic testimony pared down to the bare bones of noun and verb as if anything more would risk dishonouring the truth.

She had heard about Hugh too – an economical account, and the conclusion that he was safe somewhere. She had asked no questions, sensing perhaps that this was the way to soften the steel she had come so much to rely on through the first nightmarish week of the occupation. She had learned about the American photographer when he had come three days in, following up what he had been told by a member of the Safety Zone Committee. She had been there when he and Sally met. Nothing was certain, but a life of selflessness had by no means deafened Minnie Vautrin's ear for such things and she did wonder how different that encounter might have been without her spinsterish presence. She looked over again at the lightly snoring body – not at its best, an unguarded, husband's view. The little blue book was on the floorboards beside her, the notes protruding from the top edge – two from the journalist and the one from Herr Rabe delivered that morning with his own little drawing of a Christmas tree and angel. Minnie had asked her about the book.

'Not Shelley now, Sally?'
'No, not now.'

And she would say no more about it. Minnie listened, her heart and senses preparing for another crisis. But no, it was quiet for now. She turned back to her diary.

'*Dr Wilson of the University Hospital reports countless cases of . . .*'

Sally tried to swallow, straightened her head then woke herself with the pain in her neck and shoulders. She winced as she turned to see Minnie writing in her diary. The oil lamp gave the only light in the whole vast cavern. Beneath them was the gymnasium and assembly hall. Sally's view down the ribbed expanse of roof space was cut off halfway by the weakness of the light. A triangular blackness obscured everything beyond. In the day, a feeble glimmer from two mired skylights and the odd bright needle shaft where a tile had slipped revealed the discarded, broken or outmoded hardware of twenty years of education. Minnie had been a part of it almost from the start and had taken the lamp round late one night – 'just to see if there is anything useful,' she said. She came back, tiptoeing between the beds, to sit at her invigilator's desk and hold her pen immobile over the surface of her diary, knowing only that expansive, slightly awed estrangement from one's own life that suddenly stops the unsuspecting rummager after shoe or comb when they discover instead the forgotten parcel of letters, the electrifying photograph.

'Just another middle-aged virgin,' had been Sally's first thought on meeting Miss Wilhelmina Vautrin three weeks before, 'pouring her heart into second-best.'

She would do whatever Minnie asked now. There was no time for questions, nor even the slightest defect in trust by which they might arise in the first place. The process had begun at once – even as Sally followed her out of the headquarters of the Safety Zone Committee, only too happy to find her life being taken over and made use of by others.

An unused freedom was being given up. At least now there would be something to do.

Sally sat up straight on her chair, narrowed her shoulders, arched her spine to get the sluggishness out of her body. The twelve white beds just visible by the light of the oil lamp were arranged in two straight rows of six. The pattern suggested a cylinder block to Sally – the absurd incongruity of the image making her smile and pleasing her, oddly, as confirmation of the new creature she had decided to become. The thought threatened to go too far, into something ghastly and involuntary, transforming twelve sleeping children into harsh metal, heat and power. The last ten days had got inside her. Could things ever be put back? Maybe. After the price had been paid. Long after. For now there was just the hatred – the joyous, energising, nurtured hatred that said 'yes' to everything, to whatever was required. It had been one of the first lessons of Sally's war – that never in her life before had she known what hatred really was. Now she did.

She watched Minnie put aside her exercise book diary and take up instead the slender New Testament. The smell of smoke from outside made itself noticeable again. Sally looked up at the high round window in the gable end to check that its blackout cloth had not slipped. There was a shot from outside, two shouted syllables then another shot. Just a dog-bark of war to which neither woman reacted. It was past midnight and they were already grateful for a quiet night. Neither was it strange for Sally that she was watching over hidden children in an attic, that the stairs lay flat on the floor and must be lowered down to the storeroom below on freshly oiled rollers, or that she was alerted to the murmured syllables of her companion because they were in English rather than the more familiar rhythms of the Lord's Prayer in Chinese. It was the two coloured paper lanterns between the rows of beds that struck her as odd, and the flimsy decorations tacked to the rafters and the invitation from Herr Rabe with its charming little drawing. It was Christmas Eve, the first that Sally had lived through without even a vestige of childishness.

The outer walls of Ginling College offered no great encouragement to an occupying army. They were not obviously flammable. They did not appear to enclose a military establishment. Neither was there anything particular about them that promised rewards, material or sensual, for the hard-working soldier. There was nothing immediately offensive about their politics – to be sure, there were no abject, patchwork rising suns above the gates and the prostrate American flag within was just a dot of colour in a pilot's eye and quite invisible to the unsuspecting foot patrols that passed outside, walking by the burned remains of the rickshaw and the blackened struts and shafts of its owner.

Three days' grace was the result of this unobtrusiveness. Sally continued to make the lists Minnie had asked for, touring the dormitories and halls and then the open areas too in the company of Mr Wang, the college's Chinese secretary. He would ask the questions and then haltingly interpret the answers from which Sally would weave columns and rows, learning quickly how to transliterate the Chinese names, how to excuse herself, apologise and say 'please' and 'My name is Sally'.

'Sao-li?'

'Sally.'

'Sao-li!'

Sao-li it was, the deep opening vowels curling the tongue into the back of the throat, the end as sharp as glass. It was another step away, another thread cut. She wrote an unsendable letter to her parents and callously signed it Sao-li, knowing full well that the words 'no longer your daughter' were written invisibly beneath.

What is your name, what is your age, what relatives have you in the college, where is your husband, brother, father, son? The answers were various, hesitant and coded. Who could be trusted, to what purposes might such a list be put? Men were usually 'away' or had altogether slipped out of existence. No one was in the army, no one was with the communists.

'Don't know.'

'Don't know.'

'I'm hungry.'

'Don't know.'

'Why you ask that?'

'Don't know.'

'That's all right,' Mr Wang would say. 'It doesn't matter. It's all right.'

Sally could see how the syllables reassured. She learned them quickly and began to repeat them over and again in the gaps of anxious, one-sided conversations, none of which she could understand.

Have you brought food? Do you have any money? The answers here were still surprisingly honest – a gesture to a sack of rice, an opened palm with a row of small coins, or an empty one perhaps, a shaking of silent purse and pockets as if to say to Mr Wang, 'You see? Whatever you think, I'm not a liar yet.' In the latter case another mark was made in another column and a red tag given which could be offered instead of money at either of the campus rice kitchens that steamed all day from morning to night. The bowl was taken back after the rice had been eaten and exchanged for another numbered tag. The low numbers were replaced with high ones and vice versa. Under Minnie Vautrin the first would indeed be last and the last first, a longer hunger one day, a shorter the next. This very rational essay in fairness had been threatened from an early stage by a vigorously competitive mêlée nearly upsetting five gallons of rice porridge. Sally found herself absurdly equipped with a walking stick and ordered, with the help of a young interpreter from the Service Corps, to take charge of queuing lessons. For the girl who, only five years before, had denied the difference between a prefect and a collaborator the experience was distinctly uncomfortable. She would make courteous suggestions to the interpreter who would then fill her lungs and bellow at the crowd and raise her hand to threaten the reluctant or the merely slow. It was only when this fragilely theatrical authority seemed about to fail that Sally, on a single occasion, lunged forward, makeshift shillelagh held high and shouting in a voice she hardly recognised. Everyone within twenty feet cringed away and did not raise their heads again until re-formed in an unmistakable queue. For Sally it was a disconcerting pleasure and she was glad not to have to do it again.

'Do you have anywhere else to go?'

'No.'

'Are you pregnant?'

'Don't know.'

'More than six months?'

The figure in that column went down the second night as the first of several new 'Minnies' was born in a science classroom.

'How old are you?'

'Don't know.'

'Where were you living?'

'Don't send me back.'

'Where is your mother?'

'Gone.'

'Dead.'

'Taken.'

'Away.'

'Don't know.'

'Taken?'

The lists were handed to Minnie at the end of the day, at eleven perhaps, or past midnight, after hours of compiling by candlelight and when it simply wasn't possible to do any more. She pored over them in the grand reception room of the Principal's mansion. For the moment it did not impose. All the intentions behind the panelling, the heavy, brass-hinged shutters and the plasterwork were lost in darkness, far beyond the dim cave of light in which Minnie worked, habitually close to the cold hearth on which she would allow no coal to be wasted. The smell of smoke and even, at times, the visible haze of it came from outside. Light came too, dimly adding to the glow of the oil lamp. There was a permanent dawn over the walls of the college. It confused the birds and made them sing at midnight. Outside, street by street, the city ceased to exist.

Intuitively perhaps, in the early hours long after the rational powers had revolted, certain patterns emerged from these sheets of information as Minnie shuffled and reshuffled them, no longer with any clear idea of what she was doing. Certain blanknesses in the columns became articulate, sharp pitches of deprivation that stood above the already immeasurable need that flowed into her college every day. Her heart chose them for its own reasons – it is not easy to love a crowd or to receive back from it the least grain of authentic affection. Her head prepared excuses – they were quite on their own (column after column empty), they were too old for her to be sure of the soldiers leaving them alone, too young to understand, to turn the face away, resist with resignation before getting up and walking on. They were souls, as much as all the others to be sure, and here, as she had always been taught, there could be no more or less, no tipping of mercy's balance – but more vulnerable, less roughened by life, with more still to save. Minnie admitted to herself that the reasons were not very good, but she gathered them up early next morning nevertheless, a dozen ten-, eleven- and twelve-year-old girls, plucked out from the flood with a mercy as arbitrary as any god's.

That day was the last that Sally spent trying to count and describe the lives streaming into Ginling College. A week before Minnie had calculated the floor space of the cleared buildings and divided it by the area occupied by a sleeping human. The answer – 2,750 – had been exceeded within two days. The refugees squeezed together more tightly and then camped out in the freezing cold. There was a permanent crowd of supplicants at the gate. Minnie told them to go to the Nanking University, to the hospital. She didn't mention Herr Rabe whose compound, she knew, must be at least as crowded as hers. All efforts at control were given up. Through the short daylight hours the gates were left open. By the end of that day Sally and Minnie looked down from the steps of the Principal's house on a roofless town, a small city even, that had obliterated the beloved Ginling College – ten thousand, eleven, more? Eleven thousand and twelve.

They brought their stories with them, and their injuries. Certainly, something was driving them in. On the street corners outside, in three- or four-man huddles of khaki the joke was good. The soldiers had hardly lifted a finger, and yet the greatest brothel in China was being made just for them.

★   ★   ★

Smoke was the smell of those first few days, the firing squad was their sound. It was always distant, unthreatening. Echoed and lost in the city, the source was never clear – you could think it was your neighbourhood or tell yourself, if you preferred, that it must be somewhere else. It was all down by the river some said, having thought out the practicalities for themselves, or in the Mufu hills or to the south sometimes in the woods beyond the flower terraces of Yuhua. Then again, in the opinion of others, that was just a change in the wind. The sound was not recognised at first for what it was – faint shouted orders (a vaguely sporting sound in Sally's ear) followed by the brief, snare-drum beat of rifle fire. Just a celebration perhaps? A ceremony? Competing explanations were gradually given up and the matter discussed no more as the sound was heard again and again and again.

One morning, when the muddy roads were still hard with frost, a motorcycle dispatch rider had been happy to ride out of the city in search of his general. Iwane Matsui was awake. Tired from sleeplessness he wandered the rooms of the antiquated country house, browsing the books and the pictures and thinking of what pleasant conversations he might have had with its owner in other times. He regarded the dispatch rider with contempt. The mere sight of the documents sent by his inferiors filled him with irritation. The General had heard of improprieties – was that true? The dispatch rider bowed low and regretted he did not understand. The General slapped his face for lying. He was not interested in the colour of the horse or the preparations of the embassy staff. How could he enter the city when there were still improprieties? The dispatch rider bent lower and sweated with shame. As for these papers – were all his officers fools? Did they not know that men must sometimes do what could not be written down? General Matsui sat, he blew on the ashes of the hearth. Did prisoners of war not eat, did they not drink? Those were his orders. The dispatch rider returned to Nanking and the noise of the firing squads redoubled.

It was to feed this machine that the soldiers came battering at the gates of Ginling College. Old Du, the gatekeeper since the place had been built, was thrown to the ground and swept out of the way as soon as he withdrew the last bolt. An officer positioned himself to one side and shouted continually at the stream of soldiers running past him into the campus. In two minutes six machine guns were positioned throughout the college and Minnie was running across the main square with the jangling ring of master keys and Mr Wang breathlessly on her heels. The officer shouted at Minnie and then at Mr Wang who kept his eyes firmly on the ground. He slapped Mr Wang hard across the face and then turned to summon a small man in civilian clothes. Mr Kikuchi bowed, gave his name and position at the Japanese Embassy. The officer shouted at Mr Kikuchi.

'Many Chinese soldiers hiding,' said Mr Kikuchi. 'Must find to correctly process.'

'To process correctly,' said Minnie. 'In any case you are mistaken, there are no Chinese soldiers in this college.'

The officer shouted again at Mr Kikuchi who looked miserably nervous and kept his eyes away from everyone else's. They accidentally connected with Sally's as she arrived on the scene. She experienced an instant loathing for this creature, even more than for the vacantly expressionless soldiers who had all focused on this unexpected young Westerner. Mr Kikuchi was forced to shift his gaze again as he mumbled, 'It must be.'

A soldier had found a plan of the college in the gatehouse. He smashed the glass, kicked the frame to pieces and tore out the card. The officer took it from him and with a red pencil at the ready ordered the inspection to begin. Every room was gone through and marked off on the card. Stored furniture and supplies were pushed about to find all the hiding spaces in between, the sheets and blankets in the linen cupboards were bayoneted, the access hatches in the floors were all opened and the voids inspected with torches. Soldiers stalked through the crowded classrooms, the assembly hall and the gymnasium, looking into every face for a concealed enemy. While crossing from one building to another Minnie spoke a few quick words to Sally. She was worried about the other groups of soldiers independently searching the grounds and understood that no Chinese member of the college's staff could stand in their way without the likelihood of being killed. Sally slowed her pace and when almost at the back of the group turned to go along another path. A soldier ran a few steps to get ahead of her and blocked her way with his long rifle and bayonet held across his chest. The officer was shouting again. Mr Kikuchi had more questions for Minnie.

'Other foreigners here?'

'What do you mean?'

'Americans, English, French, Germans – foreigners.'

'None.'

'Americans?'

'Apart from myself, none.'

'No?'

'No.'

Kikuchi reported to the officer and they moved on as a group, the interpreter and a single rearguard soldier on Sally's heels to make sure she did not stray again. Sally watched Minnie closely, observing her breathing, her closed expression, her manner with the keys as she struggled to control her fear. As every lock was turned and every door opened there seemed to be more to hide as the search made its way with relentless thoroughness towards the hidden orphans. Other attics were occupied. The soldiers had seen them, searched through the children and the older women, roughly of course, abusively, but without taking any prisoners or lives. This time it would be different – the concealment, the obvious, enraging intention to deceive would condemn them. Who ever hides a treasure not worth taking?

Minnie turned another key and stood aside. A disused classroom was revealed, just a huddle of desks cleared up to one end, pale winter light on the last lesson chalked on the board. The officer gestured upwards. They were close now, on the third floor with only the roof above them. Sally remained in the corridor as the small senior dormitories were searched. On the right, doors were kicked open and incomprehensible orders shouted to the refugees within. On the left, a row of windows looked down on the miserable expanse of the college grounds. A movement caught Sally's eye. It made no sense at first – something human about it, certainly, but not right. The outline was wrong, baffling the eye, at the same time demanding and troubling to the attention like a jumble of disassembled mannequins in a shop window glimpsed in the middle of an otherwise safe and civilised city. There was khaki camouflaged against mud, the boundaries far from clear. The more noticeable darkness of civilian cloth was visible too and the paler tones of human skin exposed to the chilly air. There was resistance in Sally's mind, but when it broke through at last to every nerve of her consciousness she started violently and almost cried out. There was the inverted V of the legs kicked apart and the rumpled black trousers hanging off one ankle. Between them the confusing, hunched khaki shape became a soldier whose thighs and naked buttocks, half exposed beneath his shirt-tails, convulsed in a casual, brutish rutting. Sally could briefly see the side of his face as he turned to say two or three words to his companions standing nearby. There was laughter and then he was getting up and moving aside. It was then that Sally could see the woman clearly. The skin was dark below the knees where it had been tanned by the sun in last summer's fields. Otherwise it was almost as white as Sally's own, the black tuft of hair between the legs stark in contrast – provocative, would they say? The woman's abdomen and breasts were also exposed, the tunic and two or three layers of winter vests pulled up to cover the shoulders and face. For a moment Sally wondered if she was still alive. An arm moved and then a leg as if she was about to get up. Another soldier came over and kicked her in the thigh. He threw away his cigarette and stood between her legs. Sally looked down on his foreshortened form – head, shoulders and the heels of his boots as on a single plane. His arms, slightly apart, were cut off from her view just above his hips, the angle suggesting a meeting of the hands in some intricate task. The pose brought a precise childhood memory of a man in the Abbey Park standing with his face to a wall and her mother hurrying her on, urgently shushing the unacceptable question. Here it was again, but now ramifying into a revelatory explanation of everything she had not understood between these two moments. Calmer now that she knew what to expect, she watched this second soldier drop his trousers and kneel on the muddy grass. He shuffled forward on his knees and leaned over his motionless partner. His friends lit new cigarettes from the embers of the old.

Twenty-five feet up, observing it all through the bare branches of a tree, Sally became aware of Mr Kikuchi's breath on her neck. He stood at her shoulder with his left arm curved around her waist, pushing anxiously into the three inches of charged, magnetic space that always separated them.

'Please.'

He indicated the required direction, leaned into it to make a more persuasive argument. His expression was one of wary, crafted solicitude as if all that mattered was that Sally should be spared any further unpleasantness.

'Please – this way.'

The search party had moved on. In the washroom the doors of shower and lavatory cubicles were being kicked open. They echoed loudly in the tiled space. A clear warning, hoped Minnie, for the girls who were now just the other side of the thin plaster ceiling. The officer, his soldiers and Mr Kikuchi stared at their ghostly images – the white cotton shifts hung up across the window to dry and just below them, pegged to another string, a row of white, child-sized underwear. Minnie prepared an explanation, but the question never came.

There was only the storeroom left, the storeroom with the large rectangular hatch in its ceiling and the two feet of rope hanging down and the oiled and cleverly telescoped stairs ready to unfurl and show the way. Minnie remembered the rope, slipped past a key on her ring and made a show of attempting to unlock the storeroom door while all the time talking unnecessarily. When the fourth key failed a soldier pushed her aside and tried the handle. The door flew open into a cluttered darkness. Cones of yellowish electric torchlight swept the contents – sheets, towels, bottles of disinfectant, stacked bricks of soap in their wax paper packets, one of them unwrapped and cautiously sniffed. One soldier absurdly looked behind the door, the other threw some towels on the floor, kicked over a stand of mops. The officer shouted. Mr Kikuchi explained that it was time to go back to the front gate. Minnie closed the door behind them, concentrating hard on keeping her head level as she turned up her eyes as far as she could to see the candlewick stump of rope where someone had cut it off.

Just inside the gate soldiers idled on the path waiting for orders. They ignored the two rows of people they had selected from the thousands in the college and its grounds. One was of a dozen men, kneeling on the mud, heads bowed, necks teasingly bared. The other row was of shorter, standing figures – examples of the new species that had been created over the previous few days, pulled out for ridicule and ceremonial exposure. The men consisted of ten members of the college staff and two elderly hot-water sellers whom Minnie had agreed to admit with their coal-fired mobile boilers, exchanging a measure of safety for a measure of comfort and cleanliness. She was asked to identify each of them. Hesitating over the names of the two most recently engaged, Mr Wang, also crouching in the line, volunteered the information and was kicked forward to lie flat on the ground. The hands and feet of the two men were examined – had they marched, had they arrogantly worked the bolt of a rifle? Their shirts were pulled off their shoulders to see where the straps of knapsacks might have rubbed the skin raw. The city's porters and its needle-calloused tailors had already died on the strength of such evidence.

The officer seemed uninterested. He directed two soldiers to gather up the enormous Stars and Stripes pinned to the grass and then turned his attention to the other row. From the second day of the occupation young women had started to come into the college with their hair cut off, their faces smeared with dirt and ashes greying their heads, bent over with improvised walking sticks or in the clothes of men or boys. Now Sally and Minnie had to watch as the joke began by which the officer and his men pretended to be convinced by these disguises. Mr Kikuchi aided their understanding, his features flickering mechanically between avid complicity and a grim-faced concern depending on the direction he was facing at the time.

'They are soldiers,' he dared to say.

'Aren't you ashamed?' asked Minnie.

But the show had started. The mock men imitated the corporal in front of them, putting their hands on top of their heads. More soldiers collected to watch. Laughter started as one of their number went down the line roughly clutching between the young women's legs to see what sort of soldiers they might be. The soldier saluted and reported his findings to the officer. Mr Kikuchi, absorbed by the game, excitedly explained in English that the officer was not satisfied and that a further inspection was necessary. His last few words tailed away before the two Westerners' frozen expressions as he realised how disastrously he had confused his roles.

'Sorry,' said Mr Kikuchi, 'very sorry,' before turning back to watch.

To mounting laughter, hoots and excited calls the same soldier went back along the line of women pulling all clothing below the waist down around their ankles. The last in the line took her hands from her head to defend herself. There was a burst of cheering from the soldiers as a brief fight started over the waistband of her trousers. The soldier slapped the woman twice. Someone called out in Chinese and she put her hands back on her head. Sally examined the row of faces – the fighter's now lined with grief and weeping loudly, silent tears elsewhere, some stolid and fixed, one at least proudly unmoved, refusing all possibility of humiliation. The officer inspected his parody parade front and back and then decided he had done enough to placate his troops for one day. He spoke to Kikuchi who in turn conveyed to Minnie and Sally that the inspection of the college was over.

The troops began to leave. The machine-gun crews laboured out under their heavy weapons. An infantryman went by with a wall clock under his arm, another with a wheezing piano accordion, a third with a gallon jar of preserving alcohol from the kitchens. Soon only two soldiers were left, struggling with the monstrous American flag. They had thought to fold the thing up and carry it off like a bedsheet, but they had not undertsood its size and with every redoubling of the heavy cloth it had grown into an ever more unmanageable mound. Sally, Minnie, the dozen staff regaining their feet and several hundred refugees looked on in silence as the two youths – mere boys in Minnie's mind – struggled to lift the dewy, candy-striped lump on to a bicycle. One attempted to ride the bicycle while the other walked alongside balancing the folded flag on the rear mudguard. The arrangement soon collapsed and they abandoned the bicycle, walking sideways down the front steps with the flag between them. They stopped in the middle of the street, just past the blackened tangle of the rickshaw and its unburied owner, the bent wheel rims crusted with the remains of the tyres, the white blaze of teeth clear where the flesh of the face had tightened and pulled back. The two young soldiers became aware of their audience on the college steps and of the embarrassing inadequacy of their orders. What were they to do with this vast, cumbersome heap of cloth? The road was straight and long in both directions – were they simply to walk along with it indefinitely and so obviously without any purpose? Confused as to where their duty lay, they first failed to set fire to it with a cigarette lighter, then urinated on it and kicked it into a ditch.

To the constant smoke from the fires and the frequent sound of the firing squads there was added the nightly trial of defending the perimeter of the college. By the end of that day of the first inspection some sixteen rapes had come to Minnie's attention, all committed within two hours that morning. The news was not slow in getting back to the hive and the college at once became the first stop on the nightly sexual itinerary of the Safety Zone. Minnie had hardly completed her report that evening when one of the young members of the Service Corps burst in shouting and crying. Minnie followed and found the quiet aftermath of another attack – a few older women sitting around looking away and in the middle, at the focus of their aversion, a younger one who wouldn't answer Minnie's questions or even look up at her and who shrugged off her hand angrily when it burned her shoulder.

The rules were quickly established. For the woman to resist or for another Chinese to intervene brought violence, often fatal. But under the eyes of a Westerner everything changed. For the corporal or the private soldier, that powerful, repelling strangeness that had kept Mr Kikuchi's arm from ever touching Sally's waist exerted an even greater force. No Westerner had yet been killed and their vulnerability remained hypothetical. The consequences of one more casual shot, of another stroke of a sub lieutenant's sword retained that slight taint of uncertainty that made it wise to hold back. Over the sake in the field headquarters worries took the form of the neutral gunboat just around the bend in the river, of the naval demonstration and the telegram from Tokyo reminding of the latest legal advice. For the young soldier who had gone to the trouble of climbing over the walls of Ginling College or into John Rabe's crowded garden or the grounds of the University Hospital, the last look round as he unbuttoned his flies was a simpler matter. Would the lion-tamer come? The incomprehensible figure with his strange clothes and meaningless words and his absurd, flimsy chair and his stage-prop bullwhip, so evidently useless that it must surely conceal some devilish power.

Minnie forbade the college's Chinese staff to throw away their lives in pointless gestures. A procedure was laid down by which they were positioned throughout the college at night but would only run to summon her to an intrusion. If she could arrive in time the rape could be prevented, or at least curtailed. Her initial intention to study the Japanese phrase book from the college library and perfect the lines 'What would your mother say?' and 'How would you feel if your sister were treated this way?' came to nothing. Her presence was enough, not because Minnie Vautrin was in any way especially formidable, but merely because she was present, she was human and, apart from the rapist, the first human on the scene. It was the casualness of these assaults that confirmed the unhumanity of the Chinese. The soldiery would engage in rape in the midst of a crowd or by the side of the road in the afternoon as people walked by. They were always alone when they did so, in the way that a man is alone when he settles down in his own home of an evening to masturbate in the company of his dog or his pet canary. Only when Minnie arrived, or Dr Rabe in his little car with its proud swastikas or the Reverend Magee or Professor Smythe or others from the Safety Zone Committee was the door thrown open, the light switched on and the moral solitude destroyed.

The frequency of the attacks increased so that it was soon impossible for Minnie to be present at even half of them. She forbade Sally to help her – too young, was her unspoken thought, too attractive. But it was the old way of thinking. Sally knew it and felt as safe as any of the thirty or so foreigners still in the city. As safe as Dr Rabe, even, or as safe as Peter, wherever he might be with his newsman's trench coat straight from the movies and nothing more offensive in his hands than a camera. She accepted Minnie's authority nevertheless, not straying from service with the rice kitchens or night vigils in the attic with the dozen young orphans whom Minnie gradually began to teach, dress and drill into a miniature of the school she had lost. She would be relieved towards the end of the night, with two or three hours of darkness left, and would stumble back to her room in the Principal's house. She had to pick her way carefully with a storm lantern through the snoring, coughing, gently steaming field of human forms. She paused on the threshold to listen and then lit her way up the stairs to the plain maid's bedroom Minnie had shown her into a week before. She extinguished the lamp before entering so that nothing could be seen from the roadway. She kicked off her shoes and stood at the window to perform the rite of her private religion, looking down on the burned rickshaw and its owner or on the darkness that concealed him. She reached back to her childhood and brought from it a fresh belief in magic, immeasurable powers, the repair of the irreparable. She sent an imagined limb of her mind out into the night, searching all over the school atlas contours of China, calling out to Hugh, being heard, receiving her answer. Fully clothed, she crawled into her bed, taking care not to leave an ear or finger out in the cold, falling into safety through the rich nest-scent of herself as her body warmed the sheets.

Minnie left the college early next morning and walked the half-mile to the headquarters of the Safety Zone Committee. She carried her passport in her pocket and kept tight hold of it all the way. Patrols of Japanese soldiers were everywhere – ambling groups of three or four young men with their long rifles and bayonets menacingly fixed as they walked through a city of old men and grandmothers not daring to look them in the eye. Many wooden buildings had already been destroyed. Façades of brick and stone now fronted nothing but empty spaces floored with tangles of collapsed roof beams. Only the concrete remained largely untouched, all part of the fatherly plan – the new command headquarters, the new officers' mess, the new Army Press Liaison Office where Peter bowed back to a uniformed clerk behind the counter, accepted his baffling credentials and tested the English of his fellow correspondents from the *Asahi Shimbun*, the *Mainichi*, the *Tokyo Nichi Nichi* and the Domei Agency.

Three soldiers came out of a shop, one walking backwards, throwing something through the broken doorway and colliding heavily with Minnie as she walked by. The boy turned angrily, his open hand already raised as his colleagues advanced and the two dozen nearest Chinese froze. They saw what they expected to see – a sudden check as he was forced to look up into Minnie's eyes, a surprise, an embarrassment, a drawing back. Smoke was already beginning to stream from the shop. One of the older soldiers spoke. There was a hand on an arm and the three went off together, the arsonist casting a sulky, oddly juvenile backward glare. Minnie was left at the centre of a circle of resentful Chinese curiosity. She recognised one of the faces – a man once employed by the college as a gardener. He did not respond to her greeting and she moved on.

Minnie returned to Ginling just before noon, reluctant to be drawn on what she had seen in the city. She would say only that others had it no better and no worse than themselves. She reported that Dr Rabe was well – 'indomitable' she said – and his colleagues on the committee alive and working hard. One of their cars had been stolen by a Japanese sergeant who had been most polite and had given them a handwritten receipt saying, 'Very thankyou one car soon back ~ Japan.' Rabe cheerfully admitted he did not expect to see it again. The markings on his own car had spared it for the time being.

Minnie had gone to the committee to make a specific arrangement and it began at once. Every evening from then on one member of the committee would arrive at the college late in the afternoon and stay until first light the next day. With this help, it was supposed, twice as many rapes could be prevented.

Sally would often sit with these guardians, drowsing, talking of other things – polite enquiries as to occupation, home, exchanges of likes and dislikes; the talk of strangers on a train, growing cautiously but never quite without reserve. There was the dry Mr Sperling of the Shanghai Insurance Company, who knew it was wrong but could never entirely prevent himself from fretting about replacement costs, or attempting some worldly observation on policy exemptions for acts of war and God. He mumbled to himself while half asleep, blending the two words into a single term through half a dozen languages so that the insurers of the future could express themselves more efficiently – acts of *dieurre*, acts of *krott*, acts of *sperl*. The alarm would be called and there would be sudden running through the darkness, shouting, waving of arms, an underwriter's hand on a soldier's collar, the other heroic, dreamed-of life momentarily real and afterwards the sweating, the tremor in the voice, the nausea, the hollow joke and the plain amazement at still being alive.

There were others more personable and no less courageous. Professor Smythe from the university came one evening.

'Call me Lewis,' he insisted, renewing their acquaintance by shaking her hand as firmly as if she were a man.

In the quiet periods he would work over the notes for his sociological treatise on the new warfare. He had felt the want of educated company recently and could become enthusiastic when discussing his ideas. Sally kept the green tea hot and picked listlessly through her new book – a pristine work from the college library on the winding of transformer coils. Their conversations tended nevertheless to poets or novels they both enjoyed. When the Professor asked her about her reading matter she was embarrassed by the explanation.

'I've taken a vow never to read another useless book again.'

It hardly seemed possible to say something more jejune, but the expected laugh didn't come, nor even a smile. Lewis Smythe just looked away and said vaguely, 'Yes, I suppose so.'

The Reverend Magee would come, another from the hopeful American mould. He would bring his Bible and his cine-camera, staying on the next morning to add to the shaky images of what he called his 'testament'.

Twice John Rabe came himself, parking close by the rickshaw and its owner and walking up the steps of the college in an impressive display of confidence that his car would still be there when he got back. Sally liked these nights best and looked forward to when he would come again. Dr Rabe was her father's age, perhaps a bit more, but little like him in any other respect. He would take both her hands

in his and hold them there firmly as he greeted her, demanding to know how she was, how she really was and making
her blush by telling how he had heard from Minnie of all
her indispensable services. He brought a pocketful of whis-
tles. Coloured ribbon was found to tie through the rings
and they were distributed as badges of high office. Their
sound would summon witnesses across the college at night.

Disturbances were frequent. By running with Rabe to the
latest incursion Sally was able to get round Minnie's desire
to keep her away from the worst. She was unwilling to be
censored or protected and increasingly failed to see the need
for it as she watched time and again as a middle-aged
engineer's agent waded in against armed soldiers, often not
contenting himself with mere words. What kept them alive
was a mystery, but it was real. It was easy for Sally to get
there first and she did on one occasion, proving her own
immunity before a startled, fumbling corporal. There was her
curious, starved animal self too, refusing to look away and
horribly alive for the second or two between the soldier
struggling to his feet and him cringing, turning away, pulling
up his khaki trousers in a stage convention of shame.

A breathless John Rabe came up behind and delivered
some furious instructions in German to the retreating soldier.
He was angry with Sally and kept repeating on the way
back that she should be careful. Sally was still excited by the
incident and for several minutes afterwards her confidence
could not be breached. That was when he stopped her.

'Don't you understand?'

Rabe could just see the pale face framed in its short,
curved bob of hair blacker than the night. A thought of his
own daughter caught him off balance and there was a tremor
when he spoke again.

'We must all be careful − if they kill one of us there'll be no reason why they shouldn't kill us all. Once they see how easy it is, that it doesn't really make any difference . . .'

They settled back in their guard post − a cleared classroom shimmering dimly in the light of a single kerosene lamp. Rabe took out a sheet of paper and excused himself as he added another paragraph to the letter he was writing to his wife. Sally read her book. Her head nodded over its sterile phrases, its very vocabulary made her suffer and she wondered if she must despair of ever being useful. She angled the cover so that it caught the light of the lamp and sent out a shy signal to Rabe that conversation should restart as soon as he was willing.

'Transformers!' he said at last. 'A fascinating subject, Miss Marsden.'

Sally deplored the difficulty of the slender little primer.

'The author must be incompetent,' declared Rabe. 'No one but a blockhead could make them dull.'

Rabe rekindled her enthusiasm and she enjoyed for a while the happy delusion that all the obduracies of engineering and science might fall away as she eased effortlessly into her new self-made mind. It was the tone of Rabe's own mind that did her such good − beautiful because foreign, formed beyond the pale of letters, history and the arts of administration that had been the stamp of every articulate person she had yet known. Understanding these other things, these strangenesses, fitted perfectly with the compulsive aesthetic of escape that had brought her to China in the first place. Her project of being useful dreamily confused itself with the old desire simply to be different. As she contemplated herself Rabe talked.

'I can take you to see the searchlights and to Hsiakwan too to see the power station − Siemens turbines. The Japanese want to restart them so they must be nice to me. I must be nice to them too, you understand? It is my plan to make customers of them. I never like to lose a customer. The telephone exchange would interest you, I think. I know how to make that work too – and they don't.'

Sally was no longer able to stifle a yawn. Rabe apologised and moved on. She heard about his wife and children safe in Shanghai, about his thirty years in China, the German elementary school he had set up in his garden years ago, now a crowded, trampled laager every bit as much as the grounds of Ginling College. He told her some of what was happening beyond the college and even beyond the safety zone. He had to patrol his own garden in just the same way and delighted in recounting how he had stood in wait for booted feet to appear over the wall, seizing them and pushing upwards with a vigorous shove. The reward was a cry of alarm, the soft thump and grunt of pain from the other side of the wall.

'You too must be careful.'

He shrugged and happily contradicted himself.

'I'm German.'

Sally made more tea and the talk turned to home. John Rabe was a great enthusiast for the Führer. She heard all about the new roads and factories, the great public buildings, everywhere the turbines whining, the lights burning bright, new pride for a beaten people.

'I get letters from friends. John, they say, when are you coming home? Such changes everywhere. Such opportunities for a good man like you. If you don't come soon you won't recognise the place. When was I last there? Was it . . . yes, my God, 1930. Can you imagine?'

'I was fifteen in 1930,' said Sally. 'I remember being fifteen, but nothing about 1930.'

'I sent a telegram to the Reich Chancellery, you know. Addressed to Herr Hitler himself – I am sure he got it. I told him all about the Safety Zone. That is why the Japanese never bombed it – a note from the Führer to Tokyo was all it took.'

Sally nodded but said nothing.

'There is never much about Germany in the *North China Daily News*. I get the *Ostasiatischer Lloyd* by post, but even that is mostly about China. It comes and goes, you know – Germany for me now. Something very strong and clear comes into my mind and it's a surprise because I realise only then that I haven't thought about the place for three months. You have been in Germany, Miss Marsden?'

'Sally, please. Yes, years ago. Two weeks with my parents – Schwarzwald, Zugspitze and a funny castle somewhere.'

'Charming spots.'

'It was lovely.'

'You were going to stay in China long?'

'Three months.'

'Ah.'

Rabe paused. He pulled a handkerchief from his pocket, a long white stripe in the gloom, tugged out by one corner as if by a conjuror. He polished the round lenses of his glasses.

'Is it strange? Sometimes, just recently, I have found myself thinking how much easier it would be if I were Chinese. I close my eyes before the mirror in the morning, wonder what those few little changes would look like and then I open them, like a child standing before a present. It's still me – it's just that I don't have to go home any more, or rather that I am home and with the people around me, really with them – you understand?'

'Now might not be the best time for such a transformation.'

It sounded smart and cold – the hated undergraduate

coming back to the surface. Sally started to apologise but Rabe interrupted her, holding his hand up, laughing.

'No, no, you are right of course. Someone would come along and cut off my head and then what use would I be?'

Was it a joke? Was that really happening? Sally momentarily thought of asking but missed her chance.

'What do they think when they look at us? The young want to seem old, the women to seem like men, you've seen them. But none of that for us. We are excused suffering. How can we still seem human?'

Rabe replaced his glasses, tucked his handkerchief into his pocket.

'I suppose I'll have to go back now. My firm wanted me to leave weeks ago – "valuable staff member" was how they put it. I tried to explain, but they really didn't understand. I just made an excuse and then sent a last telegram saying it was too late.'

Something clarified in Rabe's mind and he turned to Sally with a new brightness.

'Everything is decided too soon, don't you think? What home is, what's strange. You can ignore it for thirty years, forget all about it, but in the end it's still there. Like . . . I don't know . . .'

He spread his arms out wide, sketched sharp square edges.

'Like a huge block of stone. It was your tenth birthday present and you were told never to lose it. A month ago I was fifty-five and it's still there – my God, there's not even a chip off one corner!'

Sally declined a cigarette.

'You don't mind?'

Rabe gingerly lifted the hot glass cover of the lantern and bent close to the flame. He stretched against the stiffness in his muscles, laid his head back. The thick whiteness in his mouth vanished as he breathed in.

'Think of our beloved Miss Vautrin, here even longer than me and yet what could be more American? Think of me, of...'

'Go on,' said Sally. 'I don't mind. I know it's true.'

'Of you, my dear. Maybe it's being out here, but when I look at you, when I hear your voice – it's England.'

'I know. It's why I came.'

Sally went to the window and opened it an inch to the cold early-morning air.

'It's dawn,' she said.

Rabe spoke from behind her.

'If only I can do something and then go back. Well, it's been a quiet night.'

Sally looked through her reflection in the window. Translucent glimmers passed over the glass and there was the ghost of John Rabe close by her side. She felt his hand on her hair, a gentle pressure on a thick black lock as it ran through his fingers. She remembered it hadn't been washed in a week and edged a little closer to the window.

'Forgive me, my dear.'

Sally turned and Rabe recoiled a little, covering his embarrassment by turning all his attention to his jacket pocket.

'Miss Vautrin is not wrong to worry about you, I think. I remember when I first saw you – perhaps you did not notice me – I was standing on the hotel steps talking to Mr Moss and I could see someone through the window of the car. It was early, misty, that was part of it no doubt, but I was not sure until later whether you were Chinese or not. I have been very frightened that I might not be the only one to make such a mistake.'

An inch of folded, neatly ironed scarlet protruded from either end of his hand. Sally rejected Rabe's idea – it was just silly, who could think of such a thing?

'At night?' he persisted. 'A momentary mistake? Miss Marsden, you would not think it an impertinence if I ask you to accept something from me and to keep it with you?'

The red cloth passed from hand to hand and what harm could it do – a token, a fatherly, sentimental indulgence.

'Thank you.'

Sally unfolded it to see the white circle and within it the black, broken cross.

Thus the ten days before Christmas 1937 – for Sally, for John Rabe, for Wilhelmina Vautrin, for China and for the fatherly forces of progress. For General Matsui too, hesitating in his country billet, spending the days close to the fire with a borrowed book of Chinese poems, well-turned laments from a thousand years ago, yearnings of an unregarded servant of the state for his hut in the hills, graceful syntheses of solitude and decency. The General's inferiors wore him down – they might make less noise if he chose to believe their lies. And so the chestnut horse was called up from the rear, the harness and the boots polished, the white gloves pulled on. Matsui stepped from the river launch, turned his mount to face the Imperial Palace in Tokyo, turned it again to walk himself, his reputation and the name of his forefathers between the leafless trees and the ranks of troops. The animal skittered nervously, smoke and blood stinging its nostrils. Peter pushed forward to get a better shot, rubbing shoulders with the urbane, anglophone Moriyama of the *Osaka Asahi Shimbun*.

The victory banquet at the Metropolitan Hotel became a sombre affair and broke up early. The General could not get an answer to his questions. He lost his appetite and assumed a distant look. Loitering journalists hustled for his press release in the early hours of the morning. Peter and Moriyama read by the light of the same car headlamps – deep emotion, a million innocents, and yet – until China showed respect, until she repented . . . Peter heard about the incident upriver, vaguenesses about an attack on neutral shipping, the barrage of telegrams between Washington and Tokyo, the arid regrets, the casualties.

'Names?'

'No names.'

'An Englishman?'

A shrug, an exchange of hip-flask whiskies and a parting of the ways.

It was a good ten days for Major Komatsu. Promoted in the field then quickly forgotten, he found himself the unconstitutional monarch of Hsiakwan. Supplies came in smoothly, unloaded by teams of coolies whose pay was a daily rice ration and their own continued right to exist. He had the honour also of supervising the departure of General Matsui on a river destroyer. The General was eager to get back to Shanghai as soon as possible and his fellow officers were entirely in agreement.

Major Komatsu did not know of John Rabe or his bargaining with his country's embassy and with other more senior officers in the city. He could not conceive of being, as he was in the view of this most strange Mr Rabe, a customer to be retained, a pampered commercial cultivar to be worked over with cigars and cognac in hope of a most precious return. Accordingly, he took no great interest in the origins of the forty-three Chinese electricity plant workers who reported to his office one morning. There was nothing to indicate they might be part of a bargain. No one had told him. Though to be fair to the Major, the knowledge would have made no difference to his actions which were, as ever, in conformity with his nation's high purpose.

The machines had a hold on him. He would go into the plant now and again and stare at the vast German turbines and at the two score Chinese preparing them for operation. How did they work? What, even, were their basic principles? The Major, a soldier since his sixteenth year and son of a permanent peasantry, scowled down unhappily from an inspection gantry. The Chinese engineers, dirty and clothed in little more than rags, performed obscure and complex rites, consulted each other on the finer points, sang until the Major shouted at them to stop, cooperated with a troubling precision. He began to doubt whether they would ever truly love Japan.

It was early the next morning, in one of the less damaged rooms in Herr Hempel's little Port Hotel, that Major Komatsu had a strange awakening. The tuning panel of the radiogram glimmered dimly in the darkness. English words blended alarmingly with an unpleasant dream and then snapped him into abrupt wakefulness. A report of the weather (he guessed) in Tientsin, Shanghai and Canton came to an end. The racing results from Hong Kong and Singapore were more cryptic. A terrible thought came to him – telephones, cables, were they the same? would they work now? could someone be speaking to Shanghai at that moment? With furious, panicked understanding he ran out of the ruined hotel, shouting to rouse his most reliable platoon.

Across Nanking, on the eleventh day of its occupation, lights went on, a handful of forgotten records began to turn and sound, electric fires glowed and shattered wiring sparked, starting a dozen new fires.

In Hsiakwan, in the shadow of the electricity plant, twenty-two of the workers were already standing with their heels over the edge of the quay. Fire from a machine gun knocked them back into the freezing water. The other twenty-one, with hands tied behind their backs, were led to the same position and treated the same way. Soldiers came forward with poles and staved the bodies off into the river's flow.

The unstoked fires in the electricity plant cooled and died away. The turbines slowed. In the city, wirelesses began to mumble and then fell silent. Light bulbs had an hour of brownish half-life before going quite dark.

'Too good to be true,' Minnie had said halfway through the morning.

7

Chang, who bore with great pride the title of Number One Houseboy for John Rabe, had been engaged in secret activities for some days. A branch of a fir tree had appeared fortuitously in the street, stripped by a tank round perhaps, plucked off by a mortar blast from a tree that he could no longer see. He took it back to Rabe's house, carrying it past the Japanese patrols, unsure at each moment whether the possession of an evergreen might prove to be one of the capital offences of this strange new society. He accepted other, greater dangers − asking questions, looking up old friends (mostly fled, one dead in his own home) − to bring back a haul of coloured candles and a length of ribbon. Beyond the Safety Zone he located the little glasshouse in his uncle's garden and collected from its miraculous completeness a dozen pink and yellow roses, their opening buds a cold brand borne past innumerable corpses as he made his way back in the last half-hour before curfew.

These things, and others gathered from their hiding places within the household, had all been carefully concealed from Chang's employer. Rabe, for his part, had taken equal care not to see anything he shouldn't. Now the Westerners' special day had come and Chang had been busy since long before dawn, dressing the stage for the rituals he had watched and learned through happier years. Ribbons hung from the mantelpiece and were tied in bows around the bases of candles. Half a dozen kerosene lamps had sprigs of fir attached. Three were hazardously wrapped in coloured cellophane saved from old packages. Chang's most meticulous task was the setting out of the Nativity Scene. A square of green cloth had already been scattered with straw and the stable with its open double doors placed on top. What next? Chang searched his memory and stirred through his box of props. He knew that animals were at the centre of this religion and decided that a horse and a donkey would be rational choices. He tried half a dozen arrangements but the scene failed to move him. He delved more deeply and added a magnificent pig the size of a bus, a seven-inch Tyrannosaurus rex and a kangaroo, mistaking the latter for a deplorably inaccurate rat. It was beginning to work. He recalled that the animals should all be looking in one direction, as if they were about to be fed. Chang agonised over the missing centrepiece, the dramatic element that would drive the whole story and explain its strange significance to the foreigners. It was perhaps the hungry look on the tyrannosaurus's face that reminded him it was in essence a tale of cruelty to children. Sure enough, there was the tiny wooden manger that must so contemptuously double as a crib, the impoverished, grasping mother with her stony heart and the three swarthy no-good fellows about to buy and bear off this helpless girl to some- where much like Canton. Chang arranged these final figures, carefully balancing coins on the hands of the three kings so that they seemed to be holding out golden dinner plates. Yes, that must be it — there was a satisfying, confirmatory

131

catch at his heart as he felt the power of the story. He knew it would all end well – something about coming back as a chicken. But that was Easter and not today's problem.

Chang's thoughts were interrupted by a pain in his belly. His Nativity took on a new and more practical significance – divinity now shone from the pig and it was with true reverence that he picked up that Zeppelin porker and placed its huge body on the manger. Mentally, Chang lit the straw beneath the pig. He closed his eyes as pork fat began to sizzle and tormenting smells filled his nostrils. What a prince a man would be with a pig like that! Especially now when there was not one in the whole city or even, it was said, for a hundred miles about.

It was in such a state of dreamy feeding that Chang was discovered by Rabe. Flustered by his employer's silent appearance, Chang knocked over several of the figures into a less blasphemous arrangement. Rabe made a few adjustments, as if tutoring a novice chess player, and all was quickly as it should be. Chang studied the tableau, already thinking of next year.

'Merry Christmas!' said Rabe.

The Chinaman repeated the meaningless greeting.

Through the chilly, early-morning gloom Rabe slowly took in the ribbons, the candles, the coloured lamps and the 'tree'. He had been woken by a dream of his wife and these domesticities went straight to his heart. In a moment of thoughtlessness he advanced on his servant, arms widening. Appalled by the prospect of an embrace, Chang drew back and bowed his best and most formal bow. Rabe bowed back and both men quickly looked away from each other.

With the guttering candle stub he had brought down from his bedroom, Rabe made his way to his office. He shivered and his breath misted densely in the air. He inhaled and held like a swimmer and then cupped his hands against the weak glare of the candle to get a clear view through the glass of the French windows. Ever the clerk, he knew precisely what he was looking at – 602 souls penned in the 5,500 square feet of his garden. His Christmas guests, those who were free to travel, those indeed who were still alive to see the morning, were expected at eleven. John Rabe peered out at the six hundred and felt his own life tremble on the needle bearing of their fate. How they had annihilated the last fifty years – what would matter now from that old life if only he could save them? What of any importance could possibly come after? Even his family seemed threatened by this huge burden – he could have been with them now. Why did he insist on doing the impossible? The whole thing was making him ill.

Chang entered with a tray and offered an ingenious cup of coffee, nine-tenths ersatz but with a trace of reality from the last washed-out grounds in the house. Rabe could just smell it as he spooned in his sugary breakfast and stirred.

'Good night, yes?' asked Chang.

It had been – no rapes, no murders, the new system of guards working well and still too cold for the diseases to have started. All in all a remarkable absence of evil.

'Eleven o'clock all ready,' Chang asserted vigorously. 'You see. Wait!'

Rabe swallowed, winced at his own reflection in the black glass. Although the idea had not greatly troubled him in the past he received at that moment, as if handed down from on high, the certainty that he would never go mad – not now, not after this. He contemplated the five hours that lay ahead – organising teams for the scrabble for firewood (perhaps today the release of a little more of his precious coal), the rice dole, negotiating the entry of the sickest into the University Hospital, never turning one's back on the walls or the gate, walking by the dead as uncaringly as if they had never lived. Another day of cat and mouse in the kingdom of the cats. He prayed for it to be over. He relished it too – the modest greatness that could never be defeated, the good conscience it would buy, sweet as sleep, when he sat down at eleven to whatever surprises Chang was still hiding from him.

Sally had left the attic at two thirty that morning, pushing the stairs up behind her with a broom handle. She had made her way out of the building by the failing light of an electric torch and then, with the help of a half-moon, through the hunched masses of women and children, a miserable six-thousand-soul town of tottering, improvised tents, bivouacs, lean-tos of old floorboards and shelterless bodies under nothing but a few blankets or a pile of old coats. New fires had been started nearby, close enough for Sally to feel the heat on one cheek and for sparks to soar over the roofs of the college. A dozen of the young armbanded Service Corps were awake and standing by red buckets of sand and water. Sally was greeted with her Chinese name and answered in the same stage whisper. She felt a sudden, absurd leap of happiness, of lightness. That nameless, sluggish weight within her, the old undiagnosed problem was gone and she did not believe she would feel it again. She climbed the stairs in the Principal's house and pressed the torch to the face of her travelling clock before turning it off. She embraced herself tightly beneath the frigid sheets and held fast to the luminous pattern of the clock face – her father's practical gift presented in the last days before her departure. In England it was still Christmas Eve. It was seven o'clock and a variety concert was starting on the wireless. The comfortless newspaper had been read and the telegrams from Hugh lay open on the table. It was too much and the tears came – a hot, selfish, convulsive flood, and then sleep.

Sally had granted herself four hours. The alarm ran down, causing nothing more than a dream of telephones. Three hours later she woke just before ten with a rich ache in every muscle. She burrowed out, exposing her face to the cold air to be confronted first by the unbelievable time on the clock and then by a Christmas card from Minnie and a small package wrapped in the pages of a magazine. She read the earnest message and tore off the paper to find a packet of dates, a hard brown brick, on half of which she break-fasted immediately, working it into a soft stickiness in her hands. The gift filled her with energy. She ran down with her bucket to wait in line by the hot-water seller's steaming cart and rushed back to stand in shivering nakedness in a dry bath and do the best she could with those few pints of warmth. Not entirely confident of the results, she liberally treated herself with the rather masculine cologne someone had left in her room. In her second-most decent set of clothes (the best she still held back for some unspecified occasion), and in shoes dully polished on a corner of the bedspread, Sally considered herself in the mirror. Something like a jaded London typist looked back. It didn't matter. It was only a costume now, the outer appearance of a person she would never become, even if she didn't marry after all. She played up to the role with a frumpy look, something fierce enough to scare away soldiers. She checked for her passport and Rabe's soft, folded swastika. She was still laugh-ing as she grabbed her coat and ran down the stairs.

Ginling College was in defiantly cheerful activity. Carols were being sung. Games organised for the children had taken root and were becoming boisterous. The rice was red and yellow and smelled sweetly of cinnamon. Sally edged through the crowded grounds towards the front gate, diverting her way to catch up with Minnie, happily in command as she gestured with a large, gilt-edged Bible in an attempt to get some order into the procession that would soon move off to the hall for the Christmas service. The two women kissed.

'You're alive!' said Minnie.

Everyone had policed their speech in the first few days but had long since given up the effort to avoid indelicate ironies.

'I'm so sorry. I got your present – wonderful, thank you. I'm afraid I've eaten half of it already. I have nothing. It's awful. Last night?'

Minnie made the sign for so-so and reported three incursions, one rape, no fatalities. Sally apologised again.

'Not another word like that – you deserved it, the sleep I mean. And the dates. I don't want to have to worry about you too.'

Someone called out in Chinese and Minnie answered sharply in the same impenetrable code.

'They're getting impatient. You're going to Rabe's?'

'Yes.'

'Good. You should be safe. Get someone to come back with you, before dark of course.'

A silent glance of meaning passed between them as they both heard the strange ordinariness of these maternal instructions.

'Tell him "Merry Christmas" from me and bring back all his news. You've got your passport?'

Minnie turned back to her organising and Sally went to the gate where she fretted about the time while Old Du muttered incomprehensible warnings and fumbled with an elaborate entanglement of chains, padlocks and bolts. Sally threaded a reluctant eighteen-inch gap and heard the gate clang noisily behind her.

Outside, she walked down the steps into an ambiguously forbidden territory. Screened off through ten transforming days, there had been only the occasional guarded testimony from outside, the smell of war, the glint of its firelight and its refugees to work on the mind. Most of all there had been its sound, endlessly suggestive, a tireless remote voice crackling through a cavernous, dream-dark horn – an eerie performance of gunshots, screams and the dry, crumbling implosions of exhausted buildings. What scenes, what feelings must fill out these traces when she stepped out into the middle of it? She was disappointed by a memory of school – the self-dramatised frisson of stepping out of bounds. Would the ancient threats be made good, was it – such a revelation – not really wrong at all? The inadequacy of the analogy embarrassed her and she tried to push it away. She tested herself by standing close to the burned flesh of the rickshaw coolie and the rusting frame of his living. She watched a fly, woken by arson's summery heat, creep sluggishly across the surface of this immeasurable feast. It would soon be dead of the cold.

The high-revving whine of a truck engine sent the half-dozen Chinese she could see running off the road. The vehicle appeared, patches of fresh paint over its Kuomintang markings and soldiers in the back, clinging to its sides as the driver seemed jauntily determined to shake them off. He stamped on the brakes, freezing the wheels and sending long clouds of road dust scudding up into the air. His passengers were rammed up against the back of the cab and complained loudly. The driver stared fixedly at Sally and it became clear that she was the cause of this abrupt halt. The soldiers in the back got to their feet and looked down from the nearside of the truck. There were exchanges in Japanese – in Sally too, the mere sound of the language now triggered a skip of the heart, a feral moistening of the skin. A second face appeared at the front window, leaning over from the other seat to get a view of this oddity. From the back of the truck there was laughter and a sudden guttural emphasis. One of them was willing to entertain and had almost completed the unbuttoning of his flies when the truck violently jerked forwards forcing all hands to reach for the nearest anchorage. The driver swerved to crush a chicken and was gone. For a few seconds Sally held the attention of the remaining audience before a race started towards the settling cloud of feathers.

The city's new concrete buildings had, by and large, resisted the erosions of war. The polished architectural predictions Sally had made in her letter to her father had come true of an instant and it was by these prominences and by her recollection of the basic street plan that she now plotted her way to Rabe's compound. Much of the rest of Nanking was ashes. Smoke and small flames still rose from the timbers of the most recently attacked buildings. Groups of townspeople gathered close to the warmth or raked through the cooling fly ash with sticks for something useful or saleable or precious to the memory. A shift in the wind startled her with the strong smell of burned sugar as she passed the remains of the Kiessling and Bader German Bakery – forum and taste of home for the city's Europeans for twenty years. Yes – Sally admitted it – she did care about that particular wreck so much more than the others to the left and the right of it, the ones she had not even noticed until now.

The bodies came every fifty yards. On many the sword had been used and there were surrounding black crusts where the arteries had emptied themselves in the last seconds. Sally's ten-day meditation on the rickshaw coolie outside the college had devalued these individual corpses. Attempts at regret now resulted in nothing more than a performance or, colder and more necessary still, a brief mental address to the effect that 'your body does not frighten, appal, shock or grieve me'. These were the new city manners – only Country Mouse would stare, recoil, widen the eyes or hold hand over mouth. Something more was needed to move her now and Sally found it several times on her short walk – the heap of a dozen together, the headless ones for ever shut out of heaven, the mother and child side by side, the boy three perhaps or a little more, only the two dark lines as wide as bayonet blades marring his perfection. If Madonna was caricatured, so was the Resurrection – two feet protruding from an alleyway, dead surely, but then twitching, jerkily inching backwards. Why did no one help? Sally drew level to find a dog in the role of puppet master, rhythmically tugging an arm. Image after image simultaneously cut and cauterised the heart. Was there a single poem to the poignancy of second love? Second horror was no less insipid. Sally arrived before the gates of Rabe's house. She passed the drainage ditches mounded with dead, gloomily contemplating the public health.

Sally approached the door with Christmas card in hand – the brandishing of documents had become a general habit. The door opened, coincidentally perhaps, from the unprepared expression of the man standing there. Lewis Smythe, Professor of Sociology, snatched a yellow paper crown from his head and bounded down the stairs.

'Merry Christmas! Miss . . . Miss . . . Oh, dear.'

The Professor laughed and reddened a little. Sally was conscious of doing the same as the miracle cure of this sudden, unquestionable warmth flushed through her. Her hand was between both of his. The next words failed them, but the touch carried through, verging on intimacy.

'Sally,' said Sally. 'No Miss anything, please.'

Smythe pulled one hand away to theatrically strike his forehead.

'Of course, of course. I'm so sorry – what with everything.' And then, with sudden solemnity – 'And you're all right?'

'Fine, yes. Absolutely fine.'

Smythe asked again, the real question this time, the one that gave permission to talk about oneself.

'Fine, really. Well – you know what I mean.'

'I didn't worry. As soon as I met you I thought, if I may say so, "There's one I don't have to worry about."'

It was an inch too far. Sally's eyes filled and her smile weakened.

The sounds of a childish commotion could be heard coming through the house. They were suddenly louder and Smythe, keen to leave his mistake behind, took Sally by the arm and guided her into the house.

'Come and see,' he said. 'Our leader is fighting for his life.'

The two figures stepped across the threshold, through as complete and confusing a membrane as that between wings and stage. The colourful ingenuity of Chang and his two inferiors was everywhere – paper ornaments on the walls, the fragmented brands of biscuits or scouring powders just detectable in the new patterns, candles in coloured jars, a light haze of temple incense.

Smythe hurried her through hallway and lounge. In the dining room at the back of the house she exchanged greetings with Reverend Magee, heraldic cine-camera still attached to his hand. She gave a plain 'hello' to a third man she did not recognise. Attention was firmly fixed on events beyond the French windows. The stranger spoke – evidently another German.

'My God! I don't think he's going to make it. The Safety Committee's first casualty – it's so tragic.'

The French windows were opened.

'Run for it, Johnny!' shouted Professor Smythe.

He ushered Sally forward to where she could see. There was a boiling, heaving ground of black-haired heads (at the height of the average seven-year-old) and above it a tentacular chaos of skinny, tan arms confusedly dividing their efforts between attack and beating each other off. The outsized prey of this pack stood in the middle, his glasses hanging from one ear and a scratch already on his cheek when Sally first caught sight of him. He pulled his hands from his pockets and held them out in an Old Masterish gesture of appeal. From one, sweets were plucked with a fury that Sally had only seen before in the pigeons of Trafalgar Square. From the other a decoy of coins was sown on the ground. Rabe took his chance, dashing for the French windows with only four or five on his heels. They caught him on the edge of safety, hooked him by every accessible pocket. Adult hands seized him from the other side. To the sounds of laughter, screams shrill as gulls and tearing cloth, he was pulled in and the window slammed firmly shut. Rabe stood on the mat, his features red and glinting with sweat. A torn pocket dangled from its two remaining seams. Mud streaked trousers that had been laboriously pressed for the occasion. He polished and replaced his glasses, dabbed at his face and seemed, from his eyes and smile, acutely delighted as if straight from some unparalleled success.

'I think I got about half of them. I'll have to go out again later.'

'You must be mad!' declared the unknown German.

'They will all have to get something, Krischan — there will only be more fighting if they don't. Anyway,' Rabe fanned himself with the flat of his hand and tucked away his handkerchief, 'perhaps I am mad, but I rather enjoyed it.'

He noticed Sally.

'I am so pleased. Tell me, Miss Marsden, who don't you know?'

Christian Kröger was introduced.

'Carlowitz of Nanking,' he explained to the accompaniment of some practically Prussian gestures and a formal conveyance of best Christmas wishes.

Someone was pulling on the bell at the front. Chang appeared leading two men. The first displayed a meticulous, downward sweeping, middling fair moustache and a matching windswept mane of cinematic drama. He unbuttoned a heavy greatcoat, its frankly military cut and hue making him seem very much like a soldier and proclaiming his contempt for his own safety. He threw the coat over the nearest houseboy without looking at him and stood with his hands on his hips, an unexpectedly small, but energetic and distinctly Cagneyesque figure.

'My God! All still alive? Hell is too good for us, they've turned us back from the gates.'

A small gilt and enamel decoration glittered on his chest, at its centre the miniature image of a bearded, uniformed figure crossed by a sky-blue sash. Sally had to discipline herself not to stare at the man's boots — outsized and black with an obsidian gleam, they reached up almost to the knee and suggested that a detachment of cavalry must be waiting outside, poised for his word.

'Oi, oi, oi, oi.'

The man lunged at the departing houseboy and pulled him

back by the hem of his own coat. He delved into a cavernous pocket and produced a full-sized bottle with a flourish. It was half empty. He clowned a dejected expression and measured his way down the bottle with his finger.

'The cost of humanitarianism, I'm sorry to say. At this point the sergeant was going to kill them all, when we got down here he thought they might just be coolies after all, here we were blood brothers and the rest is for you. Merry Christmas!'

The introductions began again, Rabe thriving as host. He presented the newcomer to Sally.

'Cola Podshivaloff – Red Cross Committee.'

Sally smiled and made to shake hands. The Russian turned her hand downwards and bent stylishly to deliver a lingering kiss. Sally laughed pointlessly and shifted her feet. The sensation of her colour rising made her hotter still.

'There,' said Podshivaloff, showing a playful lack of remorse for her embarrassment. 'I have my present already and it's more than I deserve.'

Sally began to pray for another female guest, though without much hope.

'And . . .'

Rabe turned to the other man who had stood by throughout with the indulgent, head-shaking smile of an old friend who had seen this performance too many times before.

'André Delage of the Agence Havas.'

Sally and this self-deprecating, immeasurably worldly Parisian exchanged a few lines in French. He complimented her implausibly on her skill and extracted the outlines of her story with a professional economy while offering cigarettes to left and right from a blue carton on which camels processed past a scene of pyramids. He interspersed his interrogation with comments to the room as a whole.

'I have more – quite a supply. You must let me know if you take to them. I am ashamed to come without any wine. Oh, yes? Of course! But I am holding back a few for bribes.'

'Aren't we all,' said someone.

'So,' Delage concluded to Sally, 'you came first with . . . the Red Cross? You are not a doctor just yet? Not, I think, a missionary? Ah, I see – for love.'

He looked about the room to see which of these men might be the young English diplomat.

Sally explained Hugh's absence. There was a steady tightness in her voice as she tried to make sense of the moment of separation. The name of the ship may have been mentioned. The Frenchman, perhaps from having seen too much, or perhaps merely from tact, declined to sympathise.

'You are like me, more or less – a victim of unpunctuality. I missed the last French gunboat and was somehow too incompetent to get myself on the Jardine's steamer or that shiny American boat. So here I am stranded among heroes making up unsendable dispatches – I'll have to spend a month in the telegraph office as soon as I get out of here.'

Finally, he extended the carton to Sally and raised an eyebrow.

'You smoke?'

She took the oval cigarette with its pale blue, curved lettering at one end – Cairo. She wanted to be there.

'For Madame.'

Delage produced an amber holder from his pocket and connected it neatly with the cigarette. Sally happily played up, deriving as much release from its golden four inches as from an entire theatrical costume. She leaned forward to the flame of Delage's match, straightened and sent up an exotic blue plume. Toughness and elegance was what she aimed at – some ideal and hopefully not too laughable hybrid of Bette

144

Davis and Ingrid Bergman. Delage was charmed, and perhaps it really was for him – an acquaintance of all of three minutes. Sally understood how much she had needed this and she could see it too on all the other faces. Everything human in the room was heightened, acutely needy. Words, smiles, laughter, how the men touched each other all had a magnified boldness as if intended to be read from a billboard or to convey right to the very back row and without the slightest loss the exceptional meaning of a Christmas party. Much clinking of glassware started up. Cheers greeted the opening of a bottle.

'The Shanghai Sherry Test!' announced Rabe. 'No one is excused.'

Into assorted glasses he began to pour the notorious fraud – water, alcohol, a little caramel for the colour, a hint of concentrated grape juice in the better brands. Yet another common adversity.

The glasses were being handed out and apocryphal stories exchanged about the preparation of the so-called sherry when another guest arrived. Sally turned at once to the newcomer. An American accent came from the dimness of the corridor as he struggled to free his arms from his coat.

'I can't stay,' he began before even entering the room. 'I really shouldn't be here at all.'

There was a general cheer as Dr Wilson appeared with a bottle of claret in each hand. He handed them over rather sheepishly and continued to complain against himself for deserting his post at the University Hospital.

'I told them where I would be.'

'Well, there you are,' said Rabe taking receipt of the bottles. 'You can be here until they come and get you. You don't have to be a saint.'

Kröger snorted with laughter.

'Listen to that – and it's a saint who's telling you, so you had better do what he says.'

Sally remembered only later that she had heard the door open and close one more time. But in the moment itself it seemed a perfect, unheralded surprise with the sherry being handed round, and the glasses clinking and the smell of food from the kitchen and the room at last warming up and the air getting softly thick with incense and Egyptian tobacco and the polyphony of Christmas best wishes all quite properly and innocently propelling her into Peter's arms as he came in from the corridor apologising for his lateness. She could just hear Rabe – 'Now everyone's here' – as she squeezed Peter tightly and pressed her cheek to his, receiving a tingling shock of fresh cold.

'Peter. Thank God.'

Peter filled his lungs with the heavy scent she had put on that morning. About what, he could not have said, but he experienced a surge of certainty and a happiness sharp as a needle. A sudden quiet in the room indicated that they had become the centre of attention. They stepped back and turned to find five wryly curious expressions, the two junior house-boys staring straight ahead as stiff as guardsmen and Chang, poised with a drumstick over a miniature gong awaiting the beat from an unseen social conductor.

'I've been holding everyone up,' said Peter.

Rabe denied it warmly and described his arrival as perfect timing as he came forward with two more doses of Shanghai Sherry. Sally and Delage connected for half a second. She received in facial shorthand the indulgent scepticism of a man who was often forced to disbelieve what he had been told. 'I will not look around for Hugh any more,' he seemed to say. For a few minutes she wanted to hate him and then thought no more about it. Chang struck. To a short, unresounding clang the party took their seats around the table.

Chang had avoided the winter vegetables of the area as being too Chinese for such an exceptional meal. His raw materials, therefore, consisted of a slender selection of whatever was capable of being tinned, dried or powdered. He considered it to be a meal of the future – one day, when this was all over and the rewards had been reaped, the Chinese too would eat like this.

Reverend Magee stood up again and went to get something from the corridor. He came back with his stills camera. He held it up.

'No one minds?'

There was a murmur of acquiescence.

'History demands no less,' declared Podshivaloff, emptying another glass of his own vodka. He swept the table with an uninterpretable half-smile which ended lingeringly on Sally.

'Everyone ready?'

Eight faces turned to the lens and composed themselves. The shutter clicked, releasing the houseboys who had been standing in the doorway with plates of brown soup. They were delivered to each place and loyally declared by Chang to be soup Berlin. As with the following courses he undermined its very acceptable appearance by explaining how it had been made – 'lunching meat' thinned with a brew of beef extract and garlic powder and garnished with basil. The toothed leaves of a dandelion sat stiffly on the varnished surface. The imperturbable Rabe beamed at his guests.

'Think of it as another adventure,' he advised.

Several hands were on spoons before it was realised that Reverend Magee was still standing. They guiltily slunk back beneath the table. He gave a missionary's swift grace and then forestalled the hands a second time by moving on in a more solemn tone.

'He shall cover thee with his feathers, and under his wings shalt thou trust: his truth shall be thy shield and buckler. Thou shalt not be afraid for the terror by night; nor for the arrow that flieth by day; nor for the pestilence that walketh in darkness; nor for the destruction that wasteth at noonday. A thousand shall fall at thy side, and ten thousand at thy right hand; but it shall not come nigh thee.'

Magee stood motionless for five or six seconds. Regretful at the depth of this silence, or satisfied? Sally took a sly upward glance from her prayerful position over the soup but couldn't decide. Magee sat down. His jacket button clinked the wide lip of his plate and small sounds broke out across the table. Magee himself signalled the 'stand easy' by taking up his spoon and addressing the soup.

'Terrors, arrows, pestilence, destruction – but nothing about soup. I hope I haven't spoken too soon.'

Christmas lunch 1937 passed as a rushing express of relief, hilarity, forgetting and occasional moments of heat through four largely unnoticed hours. Conceptual worries about the soup proved unfounded. However oddly constructed the effect was all and everyone agreed it was an entire success. Under Chang's sentry gaze even the dandelion leaves were consumed. Their peppery sourness was complimented and everyone felt very brave. Professor Smythe insisted he would not leave without the recipe. Chang bowed in ecstasy. A traditional roast followed, moulded from the clay of half a dozen tins of corned beef and tied about with string according to one of Chang's memories from an earlier, English employer. There was a mock competition for this string. Podshivaloff started it, gathering several lengths to his plate and turning them around his fork. It was perhaps '*ficelle parisienne*', suggested Delage, so hard to get right. When it was clear that Chang misunderstood, the game got out of hand. 'Now which bit do we eat again?' Chang was on his third explanation and showing signs of distress when Rabe intervened with a headmasterly word. The soup reappeared in a gravy boat.

'The second coming, Reverend,' said Smythe jovially.

'The faithful shall have their reward.' Magee leaned over to help his countryman to his dubious deserts.

The wine was served.

'*Vraiment?*' Delage grabbed a bottle and studied the label.

Dr Wilson couldn't hold back an expression of guilty satisfaction.

'I hoped no one would embarrass me by asking about that.'

'Was this not on the wine list at the Metropolitan?' asked Delage in an investigative tone.

Dr Wilson confessed he thought the man had been a waiter. Delage winked at Peter and tried to rope him into a joint journalistic pursuit of the guilty doctor.

'I didn't believe they ever really had this. I thought it was only there for prestige.'

'I treated his wife after she gave birth. The man pressed them on me and then practically ran off. I've been wondering what to do with them ever since.'

Kröger nonchalantly raised his glass.

'Let us share your burden.'

Rabe followed suit and nodded at the exquisite patterned jars at either end of his mantelpiece.

'Ming – we're all looters now. And as for your cigarettes, Monsieur Delage, it would be a discourtesy even to be aware of them.'

History had not made a chronicler of Sally, as it had of so many others. It was a pleasure for her to drift uncaringly through the normality of such table-talk without any thought of making a record. She was content to remember only her own synopsis, the words, glances and sensations that carried the burrs to hold fast to her particular mind. The protocol at first was to say nothing of the realities beyond the room. China itself, in any year of its history, had become a prickly untouchable, mere mention of which threatened a collective relapse into gloom and anxiety. Home was the most acceptable theme. A new concession was made, a godown of home comforts, as memories of Germany, America, France, Russia and England were imported and stacked to the ceiling. With Magee, Smythe, Wilson and Peter as compatriots it was America that dominated as the roast corned beef went down and the wine disappeared even more quickly. There were sudden loud spikes of enthusiasm as they discovered common experiences in recondite corners of New York or Chicago and even a mutual attendance at a particular baseball game – a day never to be forgotten for Peter and Professor Smythe, though for reasons that mystified everyone else around the table. Outsiders attempted a few well-meaning contributions but quickly gave up and went their own way. Sally recalled later the fragments of this broken talk, the sudden brief clarities of an aimlessly tuned radio, the menagerie of accents, the essential uncommunicativeness of the exchanges. Under ascending American volume Paris was praised – the little pied-à-terre that would soon be returned to, Sunday-morning walks in the Palais Royal. The superiority of Berlin was loyally asserted. No, no – St Petersburg was the place, an impossible city, Venice's only true twin. If only it wasn't for those bastards who had it now, those swine who had made such a filthy sty of Holy

Russia. There was an exaggerated hawking sound, a chorus of laughter and pacification, a clink of bottle on glass.

Thoughts of home bred desire. The guests compared their interrupted travel plans and calculated when they could each expect to be on native soil again. The talk was all of 'leave' or 'furlough'. Even Professor Smythe could think of little more than a sabbatical in his home country. Sally chipped in with the date of her steamer ticket – an unchanged 16 March. She could see Peter absorbing the information, giving and receiving back from her, as two strokes in a harmless social game, the idea that it was meant especially for him.

'I'll go home too, shall I?'

Podshivaloff's tone was angry. The company was being accused of insensitivity, but only eyed the level in his vodka bottle to see how much more they might have to put up with.

'Home again, just one last time. And for that –'

He made a choking noise and held his fist above his head to pull tight the imaginary Bolshevik noose. Delage put a hand on his friend's arm and told him it wouldn't always be like that, but the Russian just shook his head and looked tearful.

Return for Sally, if no bomb or bullet found her, would not be temporary or problematic. There could never be anything contingent about England. For Peter and Delage it would be the next story, for Podshivaloff a rented room in Shanghai – memories, hatreds, endless chess and idleness, the exile's futile tenacity; either that or unclean dealings in pursuit of someone else's stolen passport. She drifted from the conversation and instead watched Chang and his juniors coming to and from the kitchen. When there was nothing to do they stood in a rigid parade line in front of the side table. How much more of this would they tolerate? Never mind the Japanese – here was history's true farewell parade whatever these Western angels thought. She noticed one of the refugee children peering through the French windows, eyes wide, hands pressed white against museum glass.

One boy shook more coal on to the fire, Chang and the other collected plates. Magee led the praises for his efforts and there was unspoken relief as the conversation broke from its threatening direction and turned to harmless trivia. What was the first thing they were going to do when this was all over? what was their greatest unfulfilled ambition? what would they do with a million pounds?

'No, no,' said Wilson as Reverend Magee began some piously selfless programme of expenditure. 'That doesn't tell us anything. You're only allowed to spend it on yourself.'

Others cheerfully agreed, but the new rule quite stymied Magee and he could only say he would think about it. Sally bought Brighton Pavilion and lived the rest of her life in nightly champagne parties with the least boring people in the world.

'Do I get an invite?' asked Peter, audible only to her. She nudged back against the pressure of his foot under the table.

Dr Wilson elected a motor yacht endlessly circling around the jewels of the Mediterranean. It would have its own ship's doctor so that he would never more be troubled by anyone's ailments. For Smythe it was a private library and a machine to calculate all the sociological statistics one could wish at the touch of a button. Podshivaloff bought the gun with which he himself assassinated Stalin before orchestrating the display of the body through the streets of Moscow under the greatest fireworks display the world would ever see. Peter built his own cinema, locked the doors, sat down in the middle of row G and bade the outside world goodbye.

Films were discussed. Sally admitted that she had gone to

see *The Good Earth* in preparation for her journey but that it had been of little use so far. Another hare was set running – what should their Christmas film be, what should they go and see right now if Nanking's cinemas were not all vandalised wrecks? Podshivaloff regained some gallantry, of a sort at least – he raised his glass to Sally and insisted that it must be *Snow White and the Seven Dwarfs*. Professor Smythe counted round the table – no, that wouldn't quite do.

'*One Hundred Men and a Girl* – what about that?'

Smythe detected the unsavoury implications of his suggestion a moment too late. He sensed Delage's louche amusement and said nothing more for a while.

'Well, I am a Frenchman – we invented chauvinism and I feel I should not disappoint you.'

'Hear, hear.'

'So it has to be – let me think now. Something to introduce you poor people to the greatness of French culture. Ah yes, I saw it only a few months ago – *The Life of Emile Zola*.'

There was a general groan of boredom but Delage, who seemed to have spoken particularly to the two Germans, was happy with his private joke.

'Or perhaps you would prefer *La Grande Illusion*?'

'What about *The Awful Truth*?' said Peter. 'No, no – it's a comedy.' He explained the theme to Sally – 'People don't know what's good for them, but they get it in the end anyway.'

Rabe and Kröger had been in a Germanic huddle of their own for some time. Sally, sitting on Kröger's left, had kept an ear out for whatever fitted within her school German and her occasional later attempts at linguistic self-improvement. She caught a few isolated phrases and began to concentrate hard on them as if it was her job to crack this code. The affair of the wildcat swastikas and the German Shanghai taxi drivers was, she thought, one topic of interest. She half guessed, more from tone than anything else, that Berlin's new policy towards Japan was not approved of – bad for business. After some fruitless searching of her memory she realised that the word 'Rosen' must be a name, one of the German Embassy staff she deduced, the only one to have stayed in the city. Had they noticed her listening? The two men were suddenly quieter and Sally pretended to take an interest in the latest arch film titles being batted about the rest of the table. One of them said something about life on the reserve list, there was head-shaking, regret, surprise at the revelation – *eine jüdische Großmutter.* Rabe abruptly brightened and she lost all track of what he was saying as his words bounded off in the swift rhythm of an anecdote. It ended with a blast of laughter, table-banging and the wiping of tears from eyes. An explanation was demanded.

'Two mutual friends of ours.'

'Acquaintances, I think.'

'Very well, acquaintances. These two very proper and rather old-fashioned gentlemen misunderstood each other on a certain business matter. Trenches were dug, accusations thrown, the good advice of friends rejected. And then they found themselves in each other's company in the German Club in Hong Kong. A wrong word was spoken at the end of a reconciliation drink and within two minutes a challenge to a duel was made and accepted before a score of witnesses. The police visited them that evening and reminded them that when in Hong Kong they must do as the British do and they would have no nonsense about any duels. Raging about honour, they both ran to the nearest steamship office and booked passages back to Germany where such things are not yet dead. The last I heard was that they had inadvertently booked themselves on the same ship. One spends his days fuming on his recliner at the bow, the other at the stern. They eat in the diagonal corners of the dining room and look the other way whenever they are forced to pass. All they can think of is getting home to Hamburg where they will immediately set about killing each other.'

Not everyone found the story so funny, but Rabe was reassuring.

'Oh, don't worry, I know them well – one of them anyway. It will all come to nothing.'

Chang had been loitering for some time with increasingly urgent intent. A nod from Rabe allowed him to begin a stately procession from the kitchen with the high point of his Christmas lunch. For some time he had been baffled by two slightly soft, foil-wrapped bricks that had been left on a high pantry shelf for as long as he could remember. He had meant to ask Frau Rabe, but she left for the coast with her daughters before an opportunity arose. The essential issue, that of its edibility or otherwise, was answered by the mouse that gnawed away one corner and penetrated almost far enough to make a snug, delicious cave for itself. The firm, plastic consistency of the material reminded Chang of a childhood talent long unexercised. Happy memories came with the thought and were powerfully intensified as he rolled a ball of the sticky, off-white paste and cautiously tasted it himself. No one would ever know what it cost him not to eat another ounce but to hold, with something close to fanaticism, to his sudden vision of a moment of high table-drama at the meal that was already beginning to prey on his mind. That was three months before, when it still seemed possible that war might pass them by. Everything else had changed, but this one ephemeral treasure Chang had carried through fire and slaughter like a basket of eggs.

The roses came first, held back for just this moment.

'Are they paper?' asked someone.

'Too good,' thought Smythe. 'They must be silk.'

The wonder and appreciation of their reality prepared the way.

'Good heavens!' said Rabe. He adjusted his glasses on the bridge of his nose as if it might correct an optical illusion hovering above his plate.

Peter repeated Chang's original question, though this time very much as a compliment.

'Is it edible? It seems a shame.'

Chang discreetly indicated the dessert forks.

'Look,' said Sally, 'they're all different.'

Chang commended her with a bow.

'And the colours, the little roof tiles, everything. They're extraordinary – where do they come from?'

'Chang make. Chang make all.'

With three entrances from the kitchen Chang and the junior houseboys delivered nine tiny pagodas, intricately modelled in marzipan. They were coloured for the hours of the day and the seasons. One was rosy with dawn, another midnight black. One had greenery about its base, another sat under a thick snow of sugar. Past a terracotta roof, on a hair-thin wire, a white marzipan crane crooked its wings to land. It was Podshivaloff who exclaimed in his own language and, finding even that unsatisfactory, began the energetic round of applause. The Americans were loud in praise, Delage silenced by aesthetic shock, John Rabe forced to wipe a mist of emotion from his spectacle lenses. Sally and Peter enthused together over their own pagodas, pointing out the peculiar details, as delighted as if they had given them to each other. Green tea was served with apologies.

Chang stood by the side table in the deepening gloom. He looked on with satisfaction at the purely oriental end he had contrived to the Westerners' strange meal. It was good that neither his employer nor any of his guests had intruded on the privacy of his plan. There was no thought in their minds that they were eating models of actual, recognisable buildings. Still less did they read the language of the roses, their peach edges darkening through red almost to black near the base – an allusion to the sky outside as precise, one would have thought, as Reverend Magee's chapter and verse. It was Chang's alone to enjoy.

'I wonder what Germany will make of me now.'

The second tranche of Delage's cigarettes was being handed round and a few volunteers were being served with the last of the sherry. Three exhausted radio batteries had been wired together and weakly powered the wireless. Something pretty and French could just be heard from one of the Shanghai stations. The diners were tired and content to leave the floor open for Rabe.

'I don't know if I've changed, but I'm sure she has – she might look on me now as something rather old-fashioned. I've had the odd postcard from friends over the last few years. The words on the back are the same as ever but the pictures are all of motorways and parade grounds – not at all the sort of thing you would look at twice. If I get out of here I'll have a chance to find out what it means. I shall have three months there, I think, and then back in harness. It will be a busy time, all the same. I have a plan, you see.'

Rabe sat up very straight and leaned forward on the table. There was an excitement in his voice that began to wake the others. Delage prepared a sceptical expression while Professor Smythe shifted uneasily as if in the face of an oncoming embarrassment.

'Herr Hitler is very concerned about what is happening here. I am sure one or two of my last telegrams got through.

They must have been forwarded to the Chancellery and that is why the bombing stopped – a note must have been sent to Tokyo.'

'They just didn't want to bomb their own troops, perhaps?' asked Delage.

'No. It stopped earlier than that, I'm sure. And it was different in Shanghai.'

Around the table Rabe's guests felt the awkwardness of their own rather different memories.

'The Führer is a compassionate man. He shares the suffering of the Chinese people even though he doesn't know a tenth of what is happening here. Once he knows the truth he will not rest – I am certain of that, absolutely certain. If only people know the truth they will act. I will take a copy of Reverend Magee's film with me and tell them everything I have seen.'

The light of a great and proven discovery was in Rabe's face. The others around the table began to understand that they had not been invited merely for a Christmas lunch in bizarre circumstances. Rabe indicated Magee with his right hand and went on excitedly.

'John will show his film in America, all being well. Professor Smythe here is a distinguished man – if you write to your Mr Roosevelt he will read it, surely?'

Smythe made to deny his significance, but the little German could not be stopped and his tone quickly brought the Professor onside.

'But a letter, just a letter or two. Others to your colleagues in the universities. And the students, won't they care?'

Smythe seemed to bridle at having such a campaign planned for him, but conceded that he might write a few letters and again mentioned his sociological analysis of urban destruction – someone would publish it, perhaps?

'That's it, excellent. And Mr Moss here will be helping.'

Only at this point did Peter fully wake up. He straightened in his chair. Sally felt the gentle pressure of his leg leaving hers beneath the table.

'Journalists are a great power these days, especially those who take photographs. All that is needed is for people to see the truth and you'll show it to them.'

'I'll try to earn my living, that's for sure.'

'And you can write to Roosevelt too.'

Peter smiled. 'He's not an easy man to interest in foreign affairs.'

'Make the newspaper readers interested. Then he'll have to be interested too, won't he?'

'It's certainly logical.'

It all seemed to Rabe to be an avalanche of assent. Momentum was building. It could really happen. Here, as he knew so well, was the great secret of sealing at last that difficult contract – the self-fulfilling belief in the inevitability of the inevitable. He moved on.

'Dr Wilson will tell all his colleagues what swords and bayonets and rifles do.'

'You're damn right I will!' said the good doctor, entering into the spirit of humane world government.

'I'll write to Mr Chamberlain as soon as I get home,' volunteered Sally. 'And I'll keep it up too – every week if I have to.'

'And you, Cola, what about you? Russia watches every move Japan makes. You'll get a hearing in –'

Podshivaloff twitched with irritation. 'Don't say it. Don't even mention his name! I'll cut his Georgian throat for him and then I'll write a letter to his successor.'

'Oh, well,' said Rabe equably. 'That'll have to do.'

'Unless Japan attacks Russia that is. One of their dirty feet over our border and I'll join the Red Army myself.'

Delage for once seemed even gloomier than his Russian friend. Rabe waded on and when he talked again of his faith in the power of the press Delage tonelessly agreed that, like Peter, he too would have his bills to pay and if he could find readers to read and newspapers to publish he would happily work for them.

'And to your government too,' insisted Rabe. 'You can write to . . . to Monsieur . . .'

Delage refused the prompt but offered instead the national gesture – a shrug of extreme diffidence.

'There you have it, my friend. There, exactly, is the question – who speaks for France now?'

Rabe did not doubt that someone must speak for France and that Delage could, after all, be relied upon to write them an excellent letter. The job seemed done.

'There,' said the President of the International Safety Committee.

The pale lustre on his broad, bald head suggested to Sally something spiritual, immovable. Golden lamplight glittered obscuringly on the lenses of his glasses. Jazz fluttered weakly on the radio – a high-soaring rhapsody on the trumpet over a scuffling snare drum and the heartbeat base. The signal began to fail. Chang tried some adjustments but nothing seemed to work and Rabe quickly told him not to bother. A wire was pulled and there was silence.

'Better to save it for the news.'

'Lies,' drawled Podshivaloff.

The Europeans sat in silence. The three Chinese stood in a line and looked on from the side – mystified, if they had not been so wholly indifferent to the meaning of everything that had just been said.

'Ah, well . . .'

It was Dr Wilson, insisting that at last he really must get

back to his powerless University Hospital and face whatever the day had brought. There was a general preparation for departure. In the narrow hallway shoulders and elbows bumped as coats were struggled into and the chorus of thanks was loud. Peter held Sally's coat and helped her into it, pulling the lapels together as he leaned over her from behind and spoke so that only she could hear.

'I have to speak to you.'

'Yes,' said Sally, just as quietly.

Delage had got to the door first. He seemed to be holding it closed until all the noise and movement was over. He turned to look back on the crowded hallway and unnerved them with a vulpine smile.

'Ready?'

8

Everyone was frightened of New Year. The god of the intervening days was Registration and by throwing themselves into its numbing repetitiveness it was possible for Minnie and Sally briefly to forget the approach of this new threat.

Registration was now the most important thing in the world – so said the men with the guns. Two hundred thousand people must be recorded in ten days. Nothing mattered more and every refugee centre in the city scrambled to turn itself into a bureaucracy. For those with a capacity for hope it seemed a good thing. At least the instruments were different – perhaps paper, pen and ink would now be in the ascendant, one facet of modern man had exhausted itself and another would now come to the fore. There were other straws to clutch at. Certain units had been seen in Hsiakwan embarking for leave in Shanghai – surely their replacements could not behave as badly. The firing squad was heard less frequently and the rumour that this was due only to the greater use of the sword and the bayonet could not always be confirmed. The beginnings of a Chinese administration appeared. Names were mentioned and on rare occasions nervous former officials and a few businessmen were seen being taxied about the ruins, always at the centre of a knot of Japanese bodyguards. It was said that, even more than the corpses in the streets, they had the look of those who were already dead. A fictional Japanese police force was instituted – the ghostly, almost humorous arms and legs of a civilisation, but with a very real head. It was this Police Chief Takadama who narrowly missed Rabe's Christmas guests late in the afternoon of the twenty-fifth. An ascetic figure in pristine, ballooning jodhpurs and treacle-black cavalry boots, his shell-rimmed spectacles rested on two high cheekbones beneath which were such deeply shadowed concavities that it seemed he must contain a powerful inner vacuum that threatened to suck him into nothingness at any moment. The fear in Chang's face was very real as he led this visitor through the corridor and into the dining room where Rabe sat alone at the half-cleared table and received him without surprise. Takadama spoke a mannered, only occasionally peculiar English. He deplored his poor timekeeping, regretted that he could not yet meet Rabe's excellent colleagues. He offered a box of cigars, accepted in return a Siemens calendar diary and, because he had admired them so, Chang's roses, Rabe himself shaking the water from their stems and wrapping them in paper.

'What do you want?' he said to Chang after the Police Chief had gone. 'That I should be proud and let someone else die? I'll get my pride back when this is over. For now, I do what I can – with this.'

Rabe tapped the side of his head with his finger. The Chinaman returned to the kitchen without giving any sign of having understood.

It was the same Takadama who offered a detachment of gendarmes to guard Ginling College at night and was thus mistaken for one of the possible signs of improvement. He was concerned too about what he referred to as 'offences against women'. The Police Chief was one of the last men in Nanking to put much faith in euphemisms. There was a risk to the reputation of the Japanese Army, especially with foreign elements still in the city, and it was felt that the men should be catered for in a more organised way. So it was that a detachment of officers and a member of the nascent Chinese Self-Government Committee arrived at the college just after Christmas asserting that it contained a hundred prostitutes who must now return to their former profession in the new licensed army brothel. Minnie insisted there were no such women in the college but could not prevent a search which seemed likely to be as arbitrary as the earlier searches for escaped soldiers. As a single organism Ginling's huddled city of women fluently reorganised itself, keeping the younger ones as far as possible from the searchers, placing the matronly and uncommercial to the fore. The soldiers made little progress. Twice, dragging prizes by the arm, they lost them to kicking, screaming attacks of seven or eight defenders at a time. They began to look uncertain, as if the weaponless multitude might suddenly prove too much for them. Their officer twitched with irritation and shouted orders in a rising pitch, sending his men chaotically one way and then the other. Humiliation threatened when the Chinese collaborator had a quiet word in his ear and was left to thread his own way through the grounds calling out the Masonic word of Nanking's night town. Minnie was appalled when this invocation produced twenty-one volunteers who filed through the gates without looking at her on their way to the promised food, heat and regular work.

'Seventy-nine,' insisted the Major. 'Seventy-nine more — we come back.'

The gendarmes came at dusk. At night they climbed the walls.

For registering one received a piece of paper. It was a good offer – show yourself to your enemy and you may live; come out and we won't kill you. Only the enemies of Japan would refuse such an offer. To have no permit, to have lost it, left it, to have had it burned to ashes with everything you owned, to have had it stolen from you by someone cleverer, stronger, more damned, more determined to live than you entailed a summary death by bayonet. In every camp in the city, the citizens of Nanking queued for permits to live.

In the University of Nanking, a mile to the east and practically overlooking the Japanese Embassy itself, there was the jostling, reeking male mirror to Ginling College. Its inhabitants listened carefully to a short speech from a member of the Chinese Self-Government Committee. He would repeat himself every twenty yards as exactly as a machine as he made his methodical way through the crowd, a Japanese sergeant always at his shoulder. The men strained at his meaning, weighed the odds, weighed and weighed again through endless, tormenting inconclusions. The speaker was one of them, in likeness at least, but his eyes gave nothing away. Was he frightened, was this the price for his own survival, for the life of his child? There was no way through. The rules were too simple – to play is to lose; you must play. The little speech was repeated again – former soldiers could declare themselves, be joined to work parties and be assured of two bowls of rice a day and one meat meal a week. Men denying their military status and subsequently found to be soldiers must be shot. Five minutes to decide, one and only chance. The Japanese soldiers and their nervous, unhappy Chinese instrument assembled in front of the crowd and stood motionless as the minutes went by in silence. At length the sergeant shouted out a phrase and held up a single finger – one minute left. One man shifted his position, settled again, looked about himself. Another stood up. The sergeant beckoned and he limped forward to stand behind the khaki line. Another stood up, then two or three and the flow began. It was some thirty-six hours later that a single man scrambled through the night towards Dr Wilson's hospital. Six wounds drained his strength and when at last he was found fainting in a corridor he told the nurses of bayonet practice and of lying for hours under the dead bodies of his comrades. He had seen or heard no other sign of life and believed that of more than two hundred he alone had survived. Before long, not even that was true.

When Captain Hayashi, his sergeant and half a dozen boyish privates turned up at the gates of Ginling College to begin registration there the story was already well known and no one was expecting volunteers. Setting up three tables in the main quadrangle and marshalling the refugees into long lines, Hayashi and his men drew out their presence in the college for three full days and were a troubling presence. An assistant manager in an Osaka insurance company until four years previously, Hayashi had never thrown away the shameful poems and watercolour landscapes of his youth. Another route had been blocked the year before by his unsatisfactory reaction to his country's attack on Shanghai in '32. A tainted man, commerce was his punishment, an internal exile which seemed to promise nothing but a lifetime of eating lunch on his own. One strange day he could still not quite explain, deep in a blend of despair, moral fatigue and a tormenting restlessness, he joined the army. He started by questioning once again the college's male staff, even Old Du the gatekeeper, so evidently long past soldiering. He did not object to Minnie intervening with her own explanations and at the end of several hours of translated questions and answers issued certificates to them all, stamping them like parcels in a post office and smiling as he handed them out. He set his men a leisurely pace. Much tea was drunk and two hours spent over lunch on the last day. The great surplus of rations he ordered for his men was passed on to Minnie for distribution. Two bottles of mercurochrome and a jar of aspirin tablets appeared unaccountably on a table in the gatehouse.

When it came to registering Ginling's general populace Minnie brought the girls down from the attic early one morning and distributed them among a number of fictional mothers and grandmothers who each made a convincing show before Hayashi's increasingly lackadaisical tribunal. With their new legitimacy in Nippon's empire the orphan girls were left to roam the college during the day before being shepherded back to the attic at night. Their paper mothers were keen to keep them with them and Minnie watched with satisfaction as these bureaucratic relationships quickly became real. Sally and Minnie were standing together close to the soldiers as they watched one of the orphans, teased beyond endurance, burst into tears and know already who she should run to.

'The Hundred Families,' said Minnie.

'What?'

'That's what they call themselves, all the Chinese together – the Hundred Old Families.'

One of the soldier-clerks handed out another identity and beckoned to the next in line.

'What a waste of time all this is. Just another Yangtze flood. Millions die, the waters recede and nothing has changed. Don't you think they must know that?'

Sally said nothing.

'I'm sure they do, especially the big ones back in Japan. That's at the heart of it – a madness for throwing yourself against the infinite. Either that or I don't know what.'

Captain Hayashi walked by. He bowed a few degrees and smiled ingratiatingly, an expression so unique on a uniformed Japanese that Sally had to stifle an urge to laugh.

'I don't trust that man.'

When the score or so of young men who were indeed hiding among the women of Ginling College were exposed and dragged forward for questioning every one, without exception, found a grandmother on hand to weep and plead and grovel for the life of her only support and comfort, a good simple boy who had never been anything more than a coolie. Hayashi's soldiers presented their catches with enthusiasm at first, tying their wrists behind their backs even before the questioning began. The Captain took half an hour over the first, keeping the quaking, shaven-headed adolescent in thorough fear of his life before brusquely ordering the cords to be cut and sending him back into the crowd. The inquisitions became shorter and more casual, the results always the same. Hayashi's men became listless, occasionally good-humoured like the players of a friendly, unscored game. Only one, the thinnest, most feral of the lot, seemed unhappy. He did not talk to his fellows after the second day and sat apart whenever they were idle. On the last morning, just before the detachment departed, he got involved in a loud confrontation with Hayashi on the grounds that the woman pleading for the life of her only son had done exactly the same two days before on behalf of some other probable soldier. Hayashi shouted him down, seemed to issue threats, pointed at his insignia and in the end slapped him hard across the face. Sally stared in amazement and saw that it was the Captain who was trembling more violently as he walked away from his inferior and struggled to light a cigarette.

Over the three days of their acquaintance Hayashi intruded more disturbingly on Sally than any other Easterner. Idly supervising his men, he spent most of his time walking up and down behind them or sitting on a camp stool smoking an endless succession of Camels with a screen-world intricacy that suggested a man in need of gestures. He never gave up trying to engage passing children with a smile and a word, or with something edible. He offered his cigarettes to Sally and tried the gambit again three or four times, always pretending he had forgotten how she had told him she didn't smoke. He was proud of his English and persistent in letting her know what books he had read, his admiration for *The Old Curiosity Shop*, his great desire to know her own opinions on such matters. Sally did her best to maintain a silent coldness but was drawn in once or twice, cutting him off guiltily only when she found herself the subject of Chinese scrutiny. It was at the end, when the sheaves of forms and the stamps and the inkpads were being packed away, that he spoke to her for the last time. He came to stand close to her, but looked straight ahead over the mass of the camp from which not a single soul had been removed.

'Don't you know how lucky you have been?'

Sally pressed her teeth together hard. She neither spoke nor moved to acknowledge the question.

'It's wrong of you to hate me.'

The line sounded petulant, grotesquely inadequate as if quoted from a merely childish falling-out.

'How do I know what you've done?' asked Sally.

Hayashi indicated the refugees.

'How do I know what else you've done?'

The Captain shrugged. He looked to his side and stood

back a little so that Sally too could see the starved dog-soldier glaring at them, poised. Hayashi turned to face her, hiding their last exchange. He nodded over his shoulder, pointed a finger at his own chest.

'You know I'll have to pay for this?'

'What do I care? You'll get nothing from me.'

Hayashi and his men left and were not seen again. Exhausted, half drowsing that night in the attic with Minnie, Sally knew he had indeed been the college's first stroke of luck. She knew she should have regretted her last words to him, but could not. She went over the moment in her mind, tried to perform more generous emotions, but found instead only emptiness, a hard steely coldness that was now a great treasure and which she would not give up at any price.

The young orphan girls had been gathered up, lectured sternly on the importance of the permits they had just been given and were then shepherded back to their hidden night quarters. Pails of hot water were hauled up to the top floor and poured through improvised shower heads down on to a parade of shrieking, laughing bodies, childish or just leaving that state, a dense steamy chaos of black hair and tan flesh, briefly finding form to compose itself into tableaux of *baigneuses* or of Spartan athletes even, made small by distance. Back in the chilly air, the girls shivered, became little priest-esses, robed in thin white towelling. They processed out of the washroom, down the corridor, into the cleaners' cupboard and up the frail stairway which itself climbs up after them leaving only a rectangular shape in the ceiling and the barely visible stump of cut-off rope.

The girls' quiet chatter slowed and finally gave way to nothing but the steady breath of sleep. Minnie pressed the heels of her hands into her eyes. She closed and put aside the little New Testament and smiled across at Sally.

'You're wonderful, Sally,' she said. 'How you've coped with all this, I don't know. I'm very grateful, you know? I haven't always had time to say it.'

Sally demurred, returned the compliment. Minnie would have none of it – what were great virtues in others she would not allow in herself to be anything other than common duty.

'Besides,' she added, 'this must all be so strange and new to you, but for me – you see, I've been through it all before. This isn't the first attic I've slept in.'

She began to talk quietly, steadily, wistful sometimes, slow and cautious at others, defusing the memories before holding them out in the lamplight. In an hour Sally had the whole story and learned how wrong she had been. She heard of the little school in Hofei, all her own, made from nothing but hope and will-power a quarter of a century ago, of changing slowly from Vautrin to Hua Chuan. She heard of the man she would marry (though never his name), of Ginling College when it was an idea, a drawing on a table and forty acres of land, of the buildings rising course by course, of the chrysanthemums Minnie cultivated in the first college garden and their escape and colourful rampage down the banks of the Yangtze. It was while on furlough in America that the letter came offering her the acting presidency of the college. She took her time, prayed and in the end was granted the courage. She would have the flimsy rattle of the rickshaw rather than the roar of the subway or the El. She would have her pupils – behind her an abandoned fiancé and an oath to have no other, a burned bridge of love to hold her to something greater.

Sally learned too about the anti-Christianity federations of the 1920s, the riots and the seizure of mission schools and, cutting through the whole life of the nation, Chiang Kai-shek's Great Northern Expedition to root out the warlords and make China one. Its troops came through Nanking. It was the Chinese officers in those days, almost exactly ten years before, who cut the leash and set their men burning and looting, and raping too. The new Chinese nationalism was their master, so then the Chinese were safe and the foreigners were hunted. Mission schools, embassies and consulates burned, half a dozen Westerners were killed, more injured. Minnie and her colleagues were hustled up to the very same attic in which she was now speaking a decade later. At night they made it across to the university and thence, under covering fire from American and British gunboats, through another flaming Hsiakwan and downriver to the safety of Shanghai.

Minnie gazed up at the wooden rafter-ribs of their hiding place as if looking for a mark, a remembered sign from this other crisis.

'You can't go through that twice. It sears, toughens whether you like it or not. That's what I've learned – there are things no one can feel twice in one life. And then, I always remember that I chose it. And I never regretted that choice, not in '27, not even now, not when youngsters look at me with their icy compassion and think "poor old maid, poor crusty dried-up old thing, how sad that it never happened for her". But it did. It's happening now. You could even say I was selfish. I knew I could never love a man like this.'

Minnie turned to Sally, reached out to place a hand on her arm.

'You know about the *Panay*?'

Sally looked down. Caring, or merely intrusive? She couldn't decide and found herself regretting and feeling relieved by the question at the same time. She nodded, made a false start on a word, cleared her throat.

'Yes, I know about it.'

It was Peter who had told her, whispering that he must speak with her, easing the sleeves of her coat over her arms, wrapping it close about her as they stood together in Rabe's busy hallway. Outside, the Christmas diners picked their way through the fringe of refugees and past the flesh-clogged ditch. They took their leave of one another – the missionary, the doctor, the journalist, the exile, the professor; the invulnerable ones, history's new opium traders, each going their way to pour a little cooling water on someone else's hell. Sally and Peter walked away together, the discrete movements of the others seeming to confirm their connection. Podshivaloff, unsteady on his feet, shouted a hearty valediction in Russian. Delage gave the pair a casual salute and a suggestive farewell smile.

The American journalist and the young Englishwoman walked back through the thickening darkness. They passed the bloodied, sometimes the headless shadows on the ground with nonchalance. At a crossroads they could look eastwards to where a tattered, lopsided white flag could still be seen marking the edge of the Safety Zone.

'You've been out?' asked Sally conversationally. 'Beyond the zone?' She began to shiver in the plunging cold.

Peter answered with a monosyllable, returning at once to the inner debate of what he had to tell Sally, of what it might mean to her, of the dangerous possibilities of misunderstanding. He should have spoken to someone else, perhaps? Used the safety of an intermediary? He admitted to himself awkwardly that he saw the moment as an opportunity, that he wanted very much to be there, to find those traces in her voice and face when she heard the news and weighed its uncertainties. A glimpse of his motives churned his stomach. They were not crude or uncompassionate in his heart, but he closed his mouth again and looked away as he saw how easily they could be misread and the dizzying scale of disaster – all the way from mere tactlessness to a gross hovering by the graveside of the departed rival. They went on in silence passing small defiances – a stall with a handful of pale turnips, a hot-water seller pushing home, the fire bright under his dented boiler, the flames inching along a collection of sawn-off table legs. The humour of the day was there too. Five men peered over a wall as Sally and Peter passed. They caught Sally's eye and confused it too – they were too close together and there was some trick being played with the wall so that they seemed to be coming through it rather than standing behind. Peter understood more quickly and she felt his arm around her waist hurrying her away from the heads, from their wide eyes and the unlit cigarettes between their lips.

Without another word being spoken they arrived before the steps and main gate of Ginling College. A patrol of four Japanese soldiers ambled by on the other side of the wide road. They paused at the sight of Sally and Peter and advanced a few paces just for the pleasure of threatening them before moving on. Sally felt for her passport, pressing its hard corners harshly into her hand. She spoke quickly to Peter.

'Say nothing.'

The soldiers went on their way, the last turning to clown a childish wave as they disappeared round the corner. Peter reached a pitch of anxiety and then suddenly found stillness. Sally waited, caught his eye to solicit whatever this announcement might be and then looked away again almost at once. The dim form of the burned rickshaw puller was no more than ten feet from them. Sally had already seen with a tiny startle of the heart the wire-stemmed, silk carnation on the scorched chest where some fierce little Antigone had defied the law. A doubt held her back from mentioning it. Sally experienced the peculiar realisation that this was her corpse – a relation was there, and a strong one too, impinging on her for the first time. Hers and not Peter's – there were after all so many to choose from. Had he even seen this one before? The thought slid her forward into her own future, talking with the old friend who never asked about her children – better to be silent than to try and fail again to understand.

Eager to break the mood, Sally swung her arms and hips to and fro, parodying the screen cliché of winsome girlish awkwardness. She put on a bad American accent.

'Well, Mr Moss – you've walked me home.'

'You mustn't worry,' said Peter. 'I think it's all right. It almost certainly is but . . .'

Sally stood still, alive with a new, sharper fear.

'I spoke to a Japanese journalist. Everything's very uncertain and of course I haven't been able to check. There was nothing he could tell me about numbers and –'

'Oh, for Christ's sake!'

'It's the *Panay*.'

The ship flashed in Sally's mind – a frozen image from which she recalled everything in an instant; the shell blasts and the fire, the upward scale of the klaxon, the last mooring being slipped and the waters churning dirty white and Hugh himself running up and down by the rail and shouting to her. What had he said? Were they now to be the last words? Peter took the dry tone of 'giving it straight'.

'An air patrol caught them halfway up to Hankow. It must have been the morning after they left here. They bombed her. She sank.'

Sally's face was hard to see in the last of the light. She was very still. She put her hands deep in her coat pockets and hunched tight as if suddenly cold. Peter continued with his professional tone but never took his eyes from her face.

'I mean as far as it could – the river's not deep enough for it to go right down. All you have to do is swim for the shore. There were casualties, though – or that's what he told me. I asked how many. I pressed him, but he didn't know.'

'Well,' said Sally.

The chain of the college gate rattled. Old Du's dry cough signalled his presence.

'Well.'

'I'm sorry.'

The gate opened a fraction. A few words of Chinese were spoken and then repeated more urgently. Old Du was summoning her in for the night. Sally glanced over at the high walls and became aware of Miss Minnie Vautrin sitting at the centre of it all. A sense of home struck her, more powerful than ever before as she broke through at last to a meaning that had always eluded her. She understood how it could overwhelm everything else, be the whole ground and foundation of a full life. From the corner of her eye she could see Peter's close attention to every move she made. England and the times had given her male habits – she strained every nerve to show no emotion and thereby set Peter into a state of confusion as to whether he might have any hopes at all or had just blundered into a ghastly, lifelong mistake.

'I expect he's fine, really. Back in Shanghai by now worrying more about you than you should be about him. I mean, if it was really a big thing this guy would have known more. Perhaps I can find out something else. I really shouldn't have . . .'

Sally remained a stone throughout this speech. Peter's words tailed off miserably. There was another impatient rattle from the gate.

'I should go.'

She pressed herself against him, held him tight, stretched

up on her toes to put her lips against the rough coldness of his cheek.

'Thank you, Peter.'

The gate closed noisily behind her. The full ritual of Du's bolting and chaining and padlocking pursued her fadingly across the grounds, signifying that she was the last to return. The smell of rice filled the air, and the smoke from ingeniously fuelled cooking fires – sticks of furniture, wax and rags, rolls of wallpaper wound tight and smouldering like peat. A line of children ran by in a hilarious chase, the plunging temperature making their breaths trail like steam from an engine. Sally stopped on the threshold of the Principal's house and turned instead to the assembly hall and its dark-windowed dormitories above. She decided she must call on Minnie before going to her bed – an exchange of Christmas experiences, however strange, would end the day pleasantly and provide the distraction she needed. She crossed to the hall and pushed through its heavy double doors into the blinding blackness of the entrance. She felt for a candle where she knew they were left at the bottom of the stairs and waited until a descending figure with her own light, showing in red lines between the fingers that guarded it, paused and passed on the fire.

Later, through the long sleepless night, she could not recall any of the evidence that seemed so clear at the time. The faces, in their dim robes of light, must somehow have signalled disaster as she edged by them on the stairway and in the corridors, though in retrospect she could not say why. Neither were the crowded dormitories, still busy with much coming and going, their doors open to a multitude of conversations shouted from room to room, their air thick with pressed female warmth, much different from what she had seen a dozen times before. Perhaps it was something within herself, her own expression reflected in others that first put the doubt in her mind. She got to the top floor, started down the corridor that led past the washrooms as the doubt became a fear, and then to the cleaners' cupboard at the end where the fear became a conviction and then a ghastly certainty confirmed by the open hatch and the stairs slid down to the floor for anyone to see. Silence came from the dark hole in the ceiling. A mechanism of cruelty turned and proved itself in her mind – that the worst always came at the worst time, and the worst time was now.

It was in this unreasoning panic that Sally stumbled up the stairs, steeled for horror, tripped on the last step, fell flat throwing her candle across the boards and making such a clatter that she nearly woke every sleeping soul in the attic. Minnie came over at once to help, but even as she supported Sally's left arm she had her finger across her lips and an urgent expression.

'Shhhhhhh.'

Sally regained her feet just in time to see the turning, mumbling girls come up to the edge of consciousness before settling down again to their dreams. She counted the dark heads just visible between pillow and coverlet as if, from such a peaceful scene, even one might have been stolen away.

'Exhausted,' explained Minnie, and then, just a little triumphantly – 'They've had a very happy day. We had goose, a good one too. Now you must tell me all about Mr Rabe and his friends.'

Sally could help it no longer. She launched herself at the older woman, buried her face against her neck and sobbed loudly. Minnie held her tightly, pulling close into herself Sally's hard, convulsed body.

'Oh, my dear. My dear.'

9

With three hours' work already done, John Rabe stood at the upstairs front window of his house, his mind and body still in bleak early light. Chang silently entered the edge of his vision and offered a small, handleless cup of green tea.

'Nothing left,' he explained. 'All gone now.'

'Thank you.'

'You work too hard, Mr Rabe. Must eat, I think.'

'No. Thank you.'

Rabe coiled long fingers about the warmth. He looked down on hands that seemed to have got away from the rest of him, to have been through twenty years more life and work than the body they were attached to. Across the stirring, shivering compound and over the top of the chained gates he looked on a quiet scene softened by a thin haze of smoke. Nanking was exhausted, consumed. There was little left to burn and few males of military age left to kill. Everything was blackened and jagged. Sections of brickwork and concrete stood here and there, remnants of buildings whose doors, roofs, floors and window frames had all been burned away like flesh from a skeleton. In the distance, the handful of selected modern buildings, the core of the new Japanese city, remained untouched. Rabe sipped his tea. He looked incuriously through a new, denser current of smoke and let his mind wander to his wife and daughters.

Out of sight, three blocks to the west, a bonfire was going well outside the Nanking Music Shop, one of the last commercial premises to attract the attention of the Japanese Army. Song sheets, books of scales and studies, half-violins for the children of diplomats and foreign businessmen, an oboe, a saxophone fed or resisted the flames according to their nature. None of them had been made in Japan; their replacements would certainly come from nowhere else. Here was the source of the smoke that did not much interest John Rabe early in the morning of 26 December 1937. He would never have recalled it had not three figures entered his view and stumbled to a halt right in front of him in the middle of the road. They were soldiers, privates he guessed, and struggling determinedly with the weight of a baby grand piano which teetered on the flimsy wheels and axle of a rickshaw. It buckled suddenly and pitched the instrument forwards so that its whole weight pressed on one leg. There was a dry crack as timber splintered and the piano came to rest right-hand down, propped at an angle of forty degrees on its two remaining limbs. Rabe watched in fascination. He had long sensed that some sort of animism must be the true religion of these invaders, a conviction that the hammer on the thumb, the mountain that obstructs the road or the rainstorm that washes it away once built are each possessed of a soul, a malicious will and agency that guides them not merely according to the laws of physics, or of chance, but with the conscious spite of an enemy. The hapless Chinese on whom the bayonet and the sabre must be practised, the petrol splashed, the earth shovelled in on their still living forms, were just a part of that imaginary jungle of resistance these men had committed themselves to carving through. A caustic need for domination burned at their insides. They sought relief from their pains, as did all men. Rabe was pleased with his theory – instead of cruelty he now saw only delusion. They must wake up from it one day, surely.

Meanwhile, in the street a piano was subverting the Empire of the Sun. Enraged by this resistance, one soldier was already tugging at its splintered leg. A few sinews still held it to the main body. The soldier twisted it with the ferocity of a crocodile on carrion and soon had it off. Now it was a club and was brought down again and again on the side and soundboard. Long full chords sounded like bells as the soldier tried to shatter the instrument with its own leg. One of his companions walked out of sight while the other, perhaps excited by these sounds, joined in the assault with the butt of his rifle. The tempo doubled, a violent syncopation thrilled them and drove them on to make an ever louder chaos of noise. The assault shifted to a weird, inspired musicianship that so seized the players Rabe could see steam rising from the backs of their shirts. Exhausted, they stood aside. Their shoulders rose and fell as they regained their breath. The piano leg changed again, briefly into a crutch this time as a skinny little Hercules leaned against it to rest one leg. The music died away slowly. The realisation that the instrument was barely damaged renewed the frenzy and this time with a little more intelligence. One soldier raised the lid of the keyboard while the other swung the club down on the keys. A series of treble chords shrieked out, hideously feminine, as a dozen keys flew up in the air and were scattered about the ground like a handful of brilliant teeth. The third soldier returned with some of the phosphorus strips that were the army's main tool for arson. Rabe watched from his window as the airtight seals were peeled away and the phosphorus was thrown into the piano's workings. The soldier, who had enjoyed neither club nor fire, now set about amusing his fellows by squatting on an imaginary piano stool and repeatedly crashing his ten fingers on to whatever keys were left. White smoke streamed from beneath the lid and then flames too as the reaction took hold. The soldier clowned on. Rabe drank the lees of his tea and laughed. He was reminded of an early caricature of Beethoven that had hung on the wall of his parents' house and entranced him as a child. In his mind he edited the scene before him, giving the soldier the fashionable frock coat, the white cravat, the crazed expression and the heath-blasted coiffure of the great romantic. Now the music seemed to be the source of the fire and the soldier its passive, consumable instrument ever on the point of being used up and disappearing altogether. For half a second the image became a reality as the sound-board collapsed over the strings and pumped out a great cloud of smoke and fire completely obscuring the soldier. He reeled back out of the fumes, trailing them after him, crying in pain as the phosphorus burned at his eyes. He stumbled about blindly until the pain diminished and he could take his hands away from his face. His companions were bored and demanded for a third time that he follow them. Rabe was alone again, looking out on a burning piano against a background of ashes.

Downstairs, he went back to worrying over rice and coal supplies, to the latest numbered digest of 'incidents' to be forwarded to the Japanese Embassy. His hands trembled over the papers on his desk. He took the two keys for the safe from their separate hiding places. He opened the safe, reconciled the Chinese currency the departing government had left them and the handful of dollars and Reichsmarks. He counted the glass ampoules of insulin, held a needle over the flame, wiped the soot from it with muslin and alcohol and eased it into a vein. From outside he could still hear the piano as, one by one, the flames overcame the strings and they gave up their tension.

A mile away in the hospital Dr Wilson awoke uncomfortably on the floor of the X-ray room. He stretched and looked about himself vaguely, noting that for another day at least the equipment had not been looted. For most of the preceding night he had been an obstetrician, being called at eleven and again at three in the morning. It was a young woman of twenty on the second occasion, very frightened and alone.

'Where's my husband? Where's my mother?' she would ask over and again through the early hours of her first labour before giving up speech altogether.

The child was very still. After several minutes he had still not breathed. A perfect boy, but all the time getting more feeble, the skin darker as the tiny body poisoned itself without the oxygen it needed. The mother too lay still and Wilson wondered if she dreaded the answer to her question, or was silently praying to be spared the burden she was so ill-equipped to carry.

The nurse – an unqualified assistant, in fact, of whom Wilson knew nothing – ran out of the room and appeared a few seconds later with a dirty metal bowl. While he was shouting at her to stop, the freezing water was already flying through the air. He remembered the glint on the thin fragments of ice as they melted and slipped off the infant's skin, now almost black beneath the miserably inadequate lighting. There was a convulsion, a moment of stunned rigidity, a gasp, and then another before that seemingly impossible volume of air was thrust back with a furious scream. The baby set up a rhythm so fast it seemed he would not be content before sucking in the whole room. His skin lightened, reddened, the tongue bright as a rose petal. The same power had woken the mother. She was trying to struggle upright, had her arms outstretched.

Wilson had finished two hours ago and now felt ill with exhaustion. He called for something hot to drink, steeled himself for an icy wash and sat down to complete his letter. He noticed the time, removed the radio from its hiding place and turned it on, just loud enough for him to hear. Only the occasional word of the Domei English service made its way through to his mind. What was being called 'the *Panay* incident' was closed. The people of Nanking continued to welcome Japanese forces, grateful for their restoration of order after recent outrages by bandits and thieves. Roosevelt's name was in there somewhere. 'Quarantine' sounded with the frequency of a slogan – his doctor's intellect fixed on the word just long enough to realise it was nothing but a metaphor. There was the usual reference to the President's polio and the moral degeneracy that surely caused it.

Wilson returned to his letter. He tried for the twentieth time to make the sentence come right in his mind. He gave up on eloquence, checked the calculation again and put down:

My Dearest,
    My baby will be six months old in four days and I have seen her for seven weeks of that time. When things are too bad I wonder what if those were to be the only . . .

He dropped the pen and held his hands to his face. He struggled not to make a noise that would be heard outside the room. He felt hot tears drop on to his palms and they raised, through the sterile mask of antiseptic, the scent of the young mother he had been with a few hours before, her blood, the creamy lochia that had wrapped her baby. His memories hounded back to his wife, his own woman, her smell, their first days fully together and that other delivery room. It was over quickly – he growled at himself, cleared the tears from his eyes, picked up the pen, scored out a line and began again.

Podshivaloff doctored himself, a mouthful of vodka easing away the familiar morning symptoms. When he had presented himself to the Safety Zone Committee and been asked how he might contribute to the cause his portfolio of exile's skills quickly filled the box and had to be carried over to the back of the page. He had been busy since then, and more diversely so than any other Westerner in the city. He already had his day planned and looked forward to a lengthy, absorbing task – it would be a day of recovery, distraction and asylum. An old diesel generator, hauled to a shed by the hospital, disintegrated hour by hour under his hands, then slowly came together again, grunted, coughed blue smoke, found a rhythm and delivered a feeble light to four wards on the first floor. Podshivaloff heard the cheer over the noise of the engine. He was happy, and because he expected nothing more, quite unmoved when the sound attracted a patrol of Japanese soldiers who wrote out a receipt for the machine and immediately stole it. In his stinking billet that night he held fast to a bundle of coats and blankets and made it grand offers. 'Yes,' replied the bundle in its maddening English accent. 'Yes, my dear. My love. In Petersburg and with the Tsar on his throne again.'

The journalists had caught a sniff of something and clustered round the hotel steps shouting questions at the liaison officer as he handed out the day's press release. What was the purpose of the troop movements around Hsiakwan? Where were the barges going to take them? Were they needed on another front, were they going down to Shanghai for leave?

'Do you think they've done a good job, sir?' shouted Peter, aware that all questions in English were futile.

He pushed forward and managed to get one of the sheets of paper. He and Delage followed their temporary friend from the *Osaka Mainichi* and begged a précis of the dozen columns of Chinese characters. Nothing new – nothing true either.

'Oh look,' said Delage, pointing at the paper over the Japanese journalist's shoulder. 'I think I am beginning to learn. This one here – it looks like a soldier bayoneting a baby. It means "honour", yes?'

The *Mainichi* man smiled weakly and bared the teeth of his excellent English.

'Tell me, Monsieur Delage – in your newspaper, are its prejudices as old as your jokes?'

Delage was already leaving. He shouted back to Peter that he would try once more to get down to the docks to see what he could learn. Peter said he would go outside the zone again – he had heard of a lake in one of the parks and wanted to check on the story.

'*Sois sage, mon ami.*'

In Ginling College a quarter of the short winter day was already over. Minnie had relented that morning and allowed the breaking up of a dozen desks for fuel. It was washday as a result – a general scene of steam and hard domestic labour, a momentary winning back of familiarity and decency. On the drying lines men's clothes hung too, like prayers at a temple.

Sally encountered Minnie when she was coming back from the gatehouse where she had just left the latest report to be passed on to the Japanese Embassy – a curt record of two rapes and an assault on a male member of staff framed in elaborate courtesy. The two women stood side by side, but found little to say. They exchanged truisms and the hope that it would not snow before moving off to their respective tasks.

'Oh,' said Sally, 'I remember now. It was something Reverend Magee said. I've even been dreaming about it, hearing it as I wake up, so I thought I should read the whole thing. I thought you would be the person to tell me where to find it.'

Sally repeated a few of Magee's words.

'Psalms,' said Minnie right away. 'Ninety-one, I think, and echoes later on.'

The old Bible study days sounded through the phrase and she had come across as more dry and scholarly than she intended.

'I suppose you expected me to say something like that.'

'It struck me, that's all. I just wanted to know.'

'It used to be one of my favourites – God as old mother hen – "He shall cover thee with his feathers, and under his wings shalt thou trust . . ." It was sweet to say that at night and curl up tight. But then, in those days I don't think I had ever been more than ten miles from home. I hate it now.'

From one such as Minnie it seemed an impossible opinion, mere rhetoric. Sally stared at her profile. She had never been paler, or more drained, or closer to defeat.

'All I wanted was to be with these people. Completely with them, but it's impossible now. Maybe it never was possible. They fall, we stand. The wing covers us, but not them. We don't even have the same enemies. How can you really know someone if you don't have the same enemies?'

From over the wall the buzz of Rabe's little swastika-spotted car could be heard. Practically the only civilian vehicle left in Nanking with any fuel, its engine had become a well-known voice. Wherever it went the Chinese waved or bowed and even the soldiers of Japan would stop what they were doing to watch it pass. Rabe had become the Safety Zone postman among so many other things, collecting reports of assaults, rapes, thefts and murders from each of the refugee camps, copying and collating them, submitting one set to the Japanese Embassy, hiding the other until the outside world was once again accessible. The engine slowed and stopped. There was time for Rabe to run up the steps of the college, collect the envelope from Old Du and run back to the car. The engine shrilly over-revved and diminished into the distance.

In the gloom of his country's embassy, the comical Mr Fukuda, Sir Harold's source of entertainment at many an evening function, moved papers here and there in a state of helpless confusion and most shameful inefficiency. From the wall behind him a photograph of a small man with weak eyes made itself felt somewhere deep in the centre of his brain. Mr Fukuda did not doubt that he wanted to do the right thing and he prayed earnestly that someone might tell him what that was. He selected a report, became lost some-where in the reading of its first few lines and then found that the ink had dried on his pen.

New Year came. The effort to look away from it, to refuse all eye contact with this beggar for attention had come to nothing. It was the Japanese Army that disposed of such matters and so there would most certainly be a New Year. It was normal and good for people to celebrate New Year, and now that everything was normal and good there must be no exceptions. Besides, their men had worked hard – they deserved a little relaxation.

Thursday saw rain, shading into wet snow in the afternoon. Its lamplit flakes signalling through Rabe's window that he must again recalculate the reserves of coal and again write to the new garrison commander to request permission to send foraging parties beyond the walls. Through the gathering dimness the flakes fell also on a meeting of sixty or so camp managers, including three of the Chinese staff from Ginling College. They shivered in the grounds of the Japanese Embassy through a laboriously translated speech on how they must celebrate New Year. The mere possession of the Nationalist flag became a capital crime and the women and tailors of the town were turned into pieceworkers stitching against the clock a thousand of the old five-barred Chinese flags and a thousand rising suns. At one o'clock on New Year's Day flags would be raised over the incombustible stones of Drum Tower, the Army of Japan would regale survivors with a musical entertainment and photographers would record the happy crowds. Cooperation with the photographers was particularly stressed. About the same time there was, as expected, the dreaded announcement of a general two days' leave for all soldiers.

There were changes in the days between Christmas and New Year. The more cheerful dispositions found some hope in them, but had to admit all the same that the barrier of December's last few drunken days was getting higher and more dangerous to cross. Hsiakwan was supposed to be a closed area, but the coolies had to be allowed to come and go to do their work. Information came with them, like seeds on their clothes, dropping in the city, spreading fast. Ships were carrying away some units, the bloodiest it was said, those who had earned their reward in Shanghai. Fresh troops were coming in and people divided on whether they could be better or worse than the departing forces. There was talk of cases of beer being unloaded, barrels of sake. A dozen coolies were found drunk and shot for stealing. A merchant-man came in, a ship of the NKK line from Shanghai, commerce on the heels of empire. Three men in clean suits and with briefcases were seen about the city in a freshly polished car. Podshivaloff caught sight of them four times in a half-hour. In the back seat one puzzled over a street map. A month out of date, it might as well have been a blank sheet of paper for all it could tell them. The Russian approached them, sympathised with their problem and cheerfully sent them off in the wrong direction. Their wives had come with them – they toured in another car, shep-herded by a stony colonel along the few streets fit to be seen. A sinister outburst of blossom-print silk and inked hair, they ran down disconcerted children, fussing them into tears with their cameras in one hand and insistent offers of sweets in the other.

Sally was quiet through these days. She had a decision to make and knew that she must make it on her own. An imagined scene from her future was troubling her – it would be many years ahead, in the strange world of 1970 or later still. There she would be, stately in her mid-fifties, worldly, unshakeable. The question would have become decent at last, or perhaps would be put to her by some young person born and bred in quite another world, tactlessly curious about ancient horrors that could never come again.

'Tell me about the people you met. Yes, and the Chinese people? And what was it like, I mean what was it really like?'

She scripted answers for her future self but never found

them convincing. In harsher moments she redirected this middle-aged, apparently isolated character, adding a nervous twitter to the voice, a compulsive diversion of the gaze from anyone before her as if all encounters had become like those between two repelling magnets.

'Oh, my dear – you mustn't ask. Is it true, do you think, that it will rain tomorrow?'

The two lives unrolled in her mind. Each had its root in this moment – here were the points in the track, they must be thrown one way or the other, changing everything that came after and cutting off all other directions. From Christmas to New Year the will to decide grew in her mind, a swelling, crystal determination about the future she refused to have. So it was that as the five-barred and the blood-spot flags were being distributed about the city, as the soldiers in the college leered at and winnowed the women in the registration line, and as John Rabe drew by hand his New Year greeting cards and carefully signed each one, Sally made her carefully crafted excuse and asked that she not be disturbed for a few hours.

From her room in the Principal's house she could still look down on the body of the rickshaw puller – he was not yet on a tourist route. The thin curtains shifted in the draught. Sally ineffectually pressed down the sash, crossed her arms and held herself tightly. She stood in her shift with the cold rippling across her skin and making it feel rough beneath her own fingers. With her breath and the steaming bowl on the table behind her a haze gradually thickened on the glass, obscuring the ash-grey scene without. She ran her fingers through it making four caligraphic strokes of clarity. Crescents of black edged her fingertips – Nanking, and its people too.

She turned to the bowl of warm water and traced her

fingers over its surface. She picked up the small brown bottle, the one she had found at the bottom of the wardrobe among the detritus of many years of guests. Two weeks ago she had peeled off the outer Chinese label and smiled to read the French beneath – not Minnie's surely. It had been mere curiosity then, but now she struggled to get every detail of the torn instructions, and the warning too. She removed the crusted, gritty screwcap and recoiled from the stinging fumes. The mirror was there before her – a human face that offered a last chance for debate, some good advice from her inverted self to forget about the whole thing. She tilted the bottle cautiously over the bowl. A viscous glistening bulged at its neck and dropped heavily into the water. Nothing happened. She upended the bottle, shaking it, rinsing its insides clean before throwing it in the waste-paper basket. She pinched her nose, shut tight her eyes against the caustic stink and plunged down into it.

It was two hours later, well into the first quarter of the night, that Old Du grumbled to himself as he struggled with the gates and shook his head as he gave advice about the folly of going out into this town of all towns, on this night of all nights. He turned the keys in the locks, reknitted his chains and thought of his grave with a keener appetite than ever – all this, and now his memory going too. Why could he not remember that woman? how did she get in? when would he have peace again?

Sally went down the steps, her scalp itching and her hair trailing the astringent scent of rocket fuel into the smoky air. She turned left along Ninghai Road and headed for the junction with Hankow. A right turn there would set her straight towards her objective. She envisaged a pause, a last and entirely reasonable chance for reflection before doing something very stupid indeed.

'I don't suppose it would do much good.'

Who said that? It sounded with all the perfect external realism of a hallucination. She turned towards the words, to her father's urbane, unconcerned voice, as incongruous and absurd as a record turning on a gramophone. She kept on walking. Her heart told her that the debate was nearing its end, somewhere deep within her, out of sight, without any conscious contribution of her own. She tracked its progress by a simple measure – the fresh thrust of adrenalin into her system every time decision came closer. She walked more quickly, now with a stage confidence. She was observed by the harsh audience of her own self. She took on her role.

Sally stopped at the next crossroads. The scene was lit by a bonfire in the middle of the road. She looked down at the broken length of broom handle and the grubby white flag attached to it. For the moment she was entirely alone, but she could hear male voices coming from beyond the bonfire, isolated shouts, laughter, a disintegrating verse of song. It helped her to contemplate not coming back. She could see her striking, unique body lying among the rest. The charisma of that image, its potency, quite charmed her and seemed so much more precious than anything else she might possibly do. She took out Rabe's red armband and slipped it over the sleeve of her coat. She practised her few phrases of German and took off her hat. She stepped out of the Safety Zone.

The celebration was in full swing – a muddle of funfair and hell, New Year and Hallowe'en, the ghost train of the twentieth century picking up speed for its journey. Sally began to doubt her senses from the start. Fear animated everything so that she had to turn constantly towards imagined movement. Burned buildings, wrecked cars, the bloated mound of a mule all stalked her. Even the dead seemed dangerous. She jumped when at last she saw living people. Two soldiers came from a lightless alley. They crossed her path and turned towards the fireglow and the singing. They hesitated at the sight of her, commented to each other, and moved on. Her charms proven, Sally also walked towards the light.

'Honk! Honk!'

Three happy adolescents in khaki stumbled past her, rolling a sake barrel. At a junction they struggled to change course, but the weight pulled them on and they ended in a giggling heap. They got up, turned the barrel in its new direction and rolled away, the last of them giving Sally a salute just before they disappeared.

Another street or two and it began to get busy. Sally was not the only one in fancy dress. Monstrous fire-eaters were part of the entertainment – an arson team on holiday with their petrol cylinders on their backs sending great yellow cones of flame into the sky or into any building nearby not yet sufficiently destroyed. Ganesha appeared. A gas platoon played the elephant god, ribbed rubber trunks swaying from their masks as they trotted by carrying a protesting corporal at shoulder height. Three Chancellors of Germany appeared, recognisable solely by their cinder moustaches and straight-legged walk. Here was a wholly unanticipated crisis. The soldiers spotted Sally and goose-stepped towards her. She froze, appalled more than anything by the absurdity of this death, so very remote from what she had envisaged. She felt inside her coat pocket and realised only then, as she held tight to her British passport, how disastrously one of her spells would cancel out the other. The Hitlers paraded in front of her and made a series of confused, Chaplinesque gestures. One of them stepped forward. Aping the jaw and chest of Mussolini he shouted, *'Ein Reich, ein Volk, ein Führer!'*

with the disconcerting precision of a mynah bird. His admiring companions stiffened and made more salutes. Sally nervously returned the gesture. Everything became impossibly funny and they ran off.

She pressed on in the direction of fire and voices, still all male save for one brief high note that stopped her momentarily like the calling of her own name. Alcohol blended with the smell of burning and with some other new element that eluded her at first. For all the fear in her belly and the rough dryness in her mouth it was definitely something edible, something that might raise an appetite. There was no shock when she recognised it as blood – a childhood memory of hunger intruded, her hand reaching upward into her mother's as she condescended a few lines of conversation with the butcher. Was it ignorance that made it such an easy place to be, habituation, or knowing unconcern about what must go on within the discreet high walls of the backyard? Was anyone ever wholly surprised by a slaughterhouse?

Sally learned the ropes of hell – her other senses quickly grasping what they needed to know. She saw, as the searcher who slowly tells oyster from stone, how readily the lifeless body camouflages itself as something that had never lived in the first place. The unfamiliar arrangements of limbs, unseen even in the sleeper, slowly revealed themselves so that she could sort man, woman and child from charred timber and twisted lengths of angle-iron. Many of the bodies were as black as these ashes. In the darkness they gave nothing back, but she learned to see these too – mere outlines, absences, figures cut out of reality leaving only a dizzying, suggestive blackness. Next came the parts. How inhuman they were, those discrete fragments of the pattern we have all been made in and for. An arm here, there a leg. Suddenly there were many, lying about some posts recently the site of sabre practice. They were so hard to see at first, the mind passed over them, the jumbled letters of a hopelessly misspelled word. Eerily they emerged, and as her awareness grew it was like movement, as if something human could be reconstituted merely by being witnessed and for ever remembered. She saw the dead everywhere now, fancying she summoned them and they were responding to her call. She went close to each one, paused by them and moved on with ceremonious care. She had to poke into everything, overturn pieces of corrugated iron (an infant under one was her reward), peer into the collapsed, smouldering houses. As her eyes adapted she realised how many she must have missed, even through the first two hundred yards of her journey. Sally returned to the main street. She walked backwards for several paces.

'I'm sorry, I'm sorry, I'm sorry.'

She moved on. Soldiers sauntered by in twos or threes, swinging oil lamps, raising them sometimes to get a look at this baffling alien. One exposed himself to her and made an amusing suggestion. A beer bottle smashed by her feet. But these were simple machines – traps fashioned for a particular quarry. Sally was too strange to trip them and they did not come near.

She was now far beyond any part of the city she had been in before. The brightest fires were still ahead, and the raucous competing instruments and the bursts of song and the strengthening smell of sake and now laughter too and the screams of women and girls and the low, wordless rhythm that began to dominate the night. The light and something about the arrangement of the buildings suggested an open space just beyond, a small park or perhaps a square of some kind. The surrounding alleyways narrowed and entangled themselves like a maze. A meniscus of corpses lay piled on either side against the walls. Sally picked her way down the narrow path between them. She could feel the adhesion of the blood beneath her feet. There was groaning from somewhere, too faint for her to be sure of its reality. A limb convulsed.

A new pattern became clear. 人 – one of the few characters she had learned – a person, a man, a woman, two people leaning together someone had told her, helping each other as they should. Sally had just laughed when she heard that – too strong a smell of the primary schoolroom by half. She trusted more to this new version, the kanji of war printed in flesh everywhere on the streets of Nanking. Soldiers' pay was what it meant now – the legs of dead women kicked apart (and a few men too). There was an artistry of rape here, an evident attention to detail in how the limbs were arranged, the throat necklaced with blood, the glinting brass jewellery of pistol rounds inserted in the nostrils or the drapery of whatever clothes remained pulled up and arranged with care to erase the human face. For them, death was not the end. Ingenious rape machines carried on the work. Here was one run through and pinned to the earth with a sharpened bamboo. A bottle raped another and there, on the corner, a golf club protruded from a mother, her left arm still about the shoulders of a silenced child.

The firelight was bright now. Sally had found her way into the square and she could feel the heat of the fires on her cheek. Silhouettes moved before the light, singly, in chaotic groups milling purposelessly this way and that, some with the exclamation mark of their long rifles always with bayonets fixed, others momentarily making patterns, black paperchains of soldiers. There was the occasional celebratory gunshot into the sky, then several in a row as a tottering captain, lassoed by his own trousers, happily emptied his

Mauser as he fell to the ground. His compatriots scattered, fearing an unfortunate accident, but cheerfully helped him to his feet again when he was no longer a danger. Firecrackers, stitched together in lengths in the Chinese manner, sparked and thrashed and filled the air with sulphur. The ground was littered with small papers – Sally scuffed through them like leaves. She picked one up, still with its soft contents. An audience assembled at once and prepared themselves for the joke. Sally unfolded the paper and picked out the mystifying object. The soldiers snickered and pressed in against her invisible protective circle. Only when Sally had fully unrolled the thick, yellowish rubber did its shape suggest its purpose. She flung it away reflexively as if it had transformed itself into a spider. The soldiers convulsed with laughter, leered, egged each other on to a further advance. Sally looked at the paper in her hand – there was a single character beneath a line drawing of a soldier charging forward, rifle and bayonet to the fore. She dropped it and walked quickly towards the circle of onlookers, forcing them to part.

At the centre of the square there was a dense crowd. Passively magnetised by some spectacle, everyone in it faced the same way towards a space where something was happening against a background of fire. Sally, protected by John Rabe's armband and the ineffably English authority of her Burberry, by the confidence with which she now moved, by her domineering six-inch advantage over everyone else there and above all by her strikingly evident ethnic irrelevance, moved through her own free space to witness this too.

Something fell away from the mood as she reached the front. The crowds who pressed from behind were animated and tense with the thrill of anticipation, but an edgy quiet fringed the arena itself. Eyes did not meet. Faces were blank, idle – the minds behind them too emptily absorbed by the spectacle. An arrangement of a dozen looted mats had been laid out on the ground in a line. On top of these, barely more animate, the bodies of a dozen young women had been carefully positioned. Sally considered whether they were dead or alive and by concentrating over a minute or two saw some slight movement from each one, sometimes only the unavoidable rise of a chest after breath could be held no longer. Immediately in front of her a portly sergeant rolled awkwardly off his victim and struggled to his feet. Sally looked down on a country girl, one who must have chosen wrongly three weeks ago and fled into the city for safety. She saw the leathered, workaday soles of her feet and the muscular shoulders of a harvester and carrier. Her thighs and belly were painted with her own blood. Beneath one breast her heart trembled against her skin, fast as a bird's. The girl's eyes seemed to lose their vacancy at the sight of Sally's un-uniformed appearance and her own incongruous splash of scarlet. A soldier moved to threaten her with the butt of his rifle, but she raised herself up on her elbows all the same. Her expression never changed and its power froze Sally in the same silent blankness. She yearned for something to be said, for a sign of any sort, a passage between them. She was on the edge of it – her chest, throat and tongue straining. 'Please' was the word in her mind – an appeal to herself, to whatever powers held her back. Please let me speak, let something be said.

Twelve more soldiers came down the line. One blocked Sally's view of the Chinese girl and began to fumble with his flies. She looked down the whole length of the line. Certainly, the scene was ludicrous, but more than that – dizzying, vitriolic, blacker than black, a mine planted deep beneath sanity itself, a boiling acrid distillate of egoism and grossness. Monsters of flesh and khaki crouched and laboured joylessly over the fruits of their victory. Sally looked up beyond the line of prostrate, mechanised forms. She could see more waiting, a dark, sinuous ribbon of men unrolling into the night. She pushed backwards against the pressure of soldiers' bodies. Some stumbled out of her way, others blocked it for a moment. Grinning faces loomed near, hands took liberties. Sally began to panic. A terrible weakness came over her and she slowed. Her vision of sacrifice returned with sudden brilliance. A disturbed idea of its beauty, its lyricism overwhelmed her reason. She stopped and looked at the soldiers and waited. That patch of ground by the country girl would be hers. The soldiers looked back, confused by the abrupt halt to the game. She tried to find their eyes, but each one looked away. A passing officer spoke to them and they returned blankly to the entertainment. The officer scrutinised her – still a young man and with mobile, solicitous features behind a most unmartial pair of spectacles. He questioned her in German. Sally remained rigid, silent. He looked at her armband, smiled very slightly and then tried French and finally English. He shrugged and they turned away from each other.

For two or three hours she wandered. Away from the fires she had only a half-moon for light and saw almost no one. The cold bit at her toes and fingers. She pulled the collar of her coat up and held its wide lapels together over her face. She crossed the railway line, walked the ghostly platforms of the deserted station. The rails made white lines in the night, narrowing to an arrowhead that pointed to Shanghai. By the broken tails and wings of aircraft she knew she was by the airfield, by the texture of its walls she knew the old Ming Palace. She crossed an open space and halted by water. The moon peered back precisely from a motionless surface. There was an unearthly perfection to the blackness that fooled the eye. The moon's image seemed not to be a reflection at all, just a still silver oval suspended from an invisible thread. Here and there forms broke the surface, the angled contact of solid and liquid catching thin lines of white light to show where they emerged. It was impossible to see what they were. Sally's mind made a story – the pond was a model ocean breached by smooth, low whaleback and sharp skerry. She found a coin in her pocket and threw it in. The moon shattered and then slowly recomposed itself. She became aware again of the cold and moved on, walking queasily for several yards over a soft carpet of discarded clothes.

Sally crossed the railway tracks again, then a broad street she could not recognise. Moments later, once again in firelight and with the occasional fleeting human shape about her, she found herself standing beside another of the Safety Zone's border flags. She moved on down the northern, curving reaches of the Shanghai Road. Boards and bamboo poles lay stacked at the sides, ready to be rebuilt into stalls in the morning. In a few days the place would be busy – loud and steamy with the business of survival. Children hawking shoes and jars of pickled plums would step over the last of the bodies, their eyes looking up and keen for barter.

Sally stopped at the first junction. Across the street was the International Club. She watched a dim light shining through a broken window on the first floor. It weakened and strengthened again as someone walked in front of it. The interference turned the light into a signal, gave it meaning. Sally went over to stand beneath it. She strained her ears to get some clue as to who was there. Not a word came down.

One of the club's double front doors lay on the pavement and the other was nowhere to be seen. The hallway was utter black and Sally considered how to find her way up by memory and touch alone to the members' lounge with its seaside pictures and chesterfield armchair. She adopted the role of a burglar, feeling her way up through the darkness and the stale smell of burning. With her fingers she read the pattern of the wallpaper. She put her feet down hesitantly, probing for debris. The stairs were concrete and silent. The door was an outline of light, an oval where the key should go. She listened for a word, a language. She bent to the keyhole, the lessons of a redundant moral training making her feel ashamed for this piece of espionage. An unfamiliar smell came to her and a drift of warmth. She put her hand on the doorknob then took it off again at once when she accidentally made a tiny noise. She listened intently for some sign that she had given herself away and prepared to bolt down the invisible stairs.

Sally was relaxing and returning her eye to the keyhole when the door opened. A man shouted incoherently and stumbled back into the room. Sally ran to the right, arms straight out to find her way in the darkness only to ram one shoulder into a wall, be spun round with the force and thrown to the floor.

'Don't move! Don't move!'

The dark outline of a man stood over her. He held a poker, first as if it were some sort of firearm, then shifting his grip rather foolishly to make it a club.

'Peter?'

Sally's body liquefied with relief. She slumped flat on the floor.

'Oh, thank God!'

Helplessly, she began to laugh.

'Get up!'

'Peter!'

'No, stay there. Don't move!'

Sally saw how the poker trembled violently and felt a renewed rush of fear herself as she heard a confusing strangeness in the voice.

The man had changed his mind again and indicated that she should stand and come into the light. He backed into the room, beckoning her forward with one hand towards the poker held in the other. Sally stood before him, smiling again now in her fawn overcoat and the forgotten swastika armband and her mannish green Tyrolean which she took off, letting the ash-blonde hair fall over charcoal eyebrows. The poker-wielder froze and leaned forward awkwardly from the waist like an amazed St Thomas or a sprinter breasting the tape. He seemed about to fall over, but it was the poker that fell loudly to the floor. Sally and Peter embraced. He held her so tightly it almost hurt. Still cold from outside, she pressed herself into the warmth of his face and neck. It was a minute before they parted. Sally wiped away tears.

'Sorry.'

Peter took the amazing hair between his fingers.

'It must look awful.'

'It's beautiful.'

'No.'

'But why?'

'I've been out.'

'What?'

'Out. Looking around.'

It was a while before she could make him understand and longer still before she could calm him down. In anger and incomprehension he talked loudly over her explanations.

'Well, I did,' said Sally at last. 'I just did, all right?'

Peter stopped. He was looking down. Sally followed his eyes and saw it for the first time. She spoke coldly.

'It's not mine.'

She took the coat off and laid it over a sofa gritty with fallen plaster. Silently, they studied the spray of blood and the single, solid arterial line near the hem where she had walked by someone who had appeared already to be dead.

'I've seen it, Peter. I've seen it all.'

Peter took her by the shoulders. He parted the blonde, peroxide-smelling hair and kissed her lightly on the forehead.

'Enough for now.'

He broke the last two legs off a chair and put them in the grate on some crumpled pages from a magazine. The scent of a match spread through the room and a fire began to grow.

'We'd better make a night of it here – you've been lucky so far.'

'Don't fuss, Peter, please.'

The familiarity of the line made him happy – he could imagine that it came from someone who had learned his habits over many years and who no longer had any real hope of changing them.

Sally looked about the members' lounge. She saw the heavy curtains drawn over the windows and the one window with curtain and rail torn down and the cracked glass through which she had seen the light. A spirit stove stood on the bar, its small blue rose of flame heating a large saucepan. Bakelite cylinders gleamed nearby and there was a little pyramid of film canisters, some empty and some still waiting their turn.

'Thought I'd do some if I could,' explained Peter. 'It's just too easy for them if they catch you with undeveloped film.'

He made a noise and mimed the unreeling of a length of celluloid to the light that would destroy it. Lengths of string had been tied up about the room. Glistening black tapes of film hung from each one. She watched as Peter emptied one of the cylinders into the saucepan, washed it out with water and then pulled out another long length of film.

'Can I help?'

'Alchemy,' said Peter. 'Initiates only. Anyway, I think I've had enough for now.'

He came to stand beside her and pinned the new strip on to its string with a hair clasp.

'I'm starving,' said Sally.

'I can help you there. Everything drinkable's gone, but I found some other stuff.'

Peter emptied the pan of fixer out the window, rinsed it once, put in what remained of the water and replaced it on the little stove. Sally took a candle from the mantelpiece, lit it and moved from strip to strip, dimly lighting the negatives from behind. Peter produced bars of chocolate, a packet of dried apricots. He polished the dust from two side plates and a pair of white porcelain cups with his sleeve. He looked up every few seconds from what he was doing.

'Don't worry about me looking,' said Sally. 'I'm immune now. It's official.'

'It's your hair,' laughed Peter. 'I can't take my eyes off it.'

'It's horrid.'

'It's magical.'

'It's novel. You'll like it less tomorrow, and then not at all.'

'Never.'

Sally moved from behind the film and caught Peter's gaze directly. They shared a moment of pleasurable guilt as if an adult had just come into the room and told them to behave.

Peter went back to his preparations. Sally examined frame after frame of miniaturised horror. The upturned human Ys were there again, shrunk to the size of a real letter on a page. There were herded groups of men tied together with ropes. A line of dark armoured cars nosed down the Chungyang Road. Then there was the little General, taking the salute and looking poignantly childish on top of his outsized chestnut charger. Then more grey Ys, the right way up this time against a sky of bright negative black – the soldiers standing on Nanking's walls with their arms upraised in triumph. Sally reviewed these familiarities quickly, stopping only at a tall dark plume, bending forward to study and at last recognise a shell splash in the water just off the wharves at Hsiakwan. Here was a moment in her war, confirmed by the electric current of emotion that ran through her. She crouched to see the lower frames, and yes – there was the ship itself, the *Panay*, churning the waters to make its run from danger.

'I could put the chocolate into the water. Would that work, do you think? Can you make cocoa like that?'

'Mmm.'

Sally held the candle closer. She looked at a melded crowd of tiny figures, a bomber's-eye view. She knew that one of them was her and that another, by the rail on the ship, must be Hugh. Impossible to say which. Irrelevant too.

'Better just to eat it as it is, I think.'

Sally moved on with her candle, lighting groups of newspaper men smiling on hotel steps, Chinese Army detachments marching in good order in their quilted uniforms, a few scenes of what she already thought of as Old Nanking – buildings unburned, cars on their wheels, people on their feet. She moved sideways to a new film and stopped at once at the distinctive horned sweep of a temple roof. And there, stiffly ranged before it was that alien line – the houndstoothed Mr Brindle, the gangling Sir Harold, Sally herself, her hand discreetly held by Hugh at her side and then Peter at the end captured by his own camera in the hands of the invisible Chinese chauffeur drifting insensibly into the last three hours of his life. Sally followed the line of the film, advancing a half-hour to the picture she knew must be there – herself and Hugh together, standing on the temple walkway, fragments of a garden just visible in the background and an interrupted kiss in the air. Peter was at her shoulder.

'You found it then?'

'Yes.'

He held out his offering – a child's first essay in cookery consisting of a geometrical arrangement of dark brown chocolate squares and the orange discs of dried apricots on a white plate.

'We must give it a name,' said Sally.

'Tepid water, madam?'

'You know just how I like it.'

Sally had stood up to take the cup. The frames of the film blurred past her as she rose, moving back a few days to three shots of Shanghai. The boastful outline of the Cathay Hotel was one and then an unexpected, fundamental form that drew her closer. Three figures smiled into the lens from the side of a pool. One was a young woman. Fair in life, her slender legs were dark on the film. At the top, a black triangle widened and spread upwards over her torso – the pale sleeve of her bathing suit with its narrow straps over her shoulders. From one of the men standing by, an arm coiled round her waist, the palm flattened on her abdomen, the tip of the middle finger pressing familiarly into her navel.

'Another Sally,' said Peter. 'I'm not sure – did you ever meet her?'

'No.'

'Sally Birnbaum. That's Tom – also a photographer. He

went off to the northern front. He'll be kicking himself for missing this – if he's still alive.'

Peter pointed to the remoter male at the end of the line.

'That's me,' he added unnecessarily. 'Sally and Tom are married.'

'She's lovely.'

'I'm sure Hugh's all right.'

'What?'

'I mean – we would have heard. If it had been a really big thing we would have heard more about it.'

Sally went to the sofa, dusted it off and sat down.

'Sorry,' said Peter.

'Don't be. It's all right, really.'

They sat together, loudly cracking the cold, brittle chocolate between their teeth and softening the leathery apricots in the warm water. The water retained a slight chemical taint.

'You're sure this isn't poisonous?' asked Sally.

'We'll find out. It's fixer – what keeps the photographs as they are. It's supposed to stop things changing. Perhaps it will work on us and we'll get slower and slower without noticing it and then just stop altogether.'

Sally thought about it and swallowed another mouthful. She spoke with the flat calm of an Alice too long in Wonderland ever to be surprised by anything again.

'We'd be here like this for ever and ever, as if we were in one of your photographs. Nothing would ever get any worse. That would be all right, wouldn't it?'

In the same tone Sally went on to describe what she had seen – the bodies, the broken aircraft, the lake of black mercury with its soft shore of clothes. 'I know,' Peter would say every few sentences, 'I know, I know.'

The sickening meal over, Sally stretched and yawned widely. She held her hands behind her head, folded her shoulder blades hard back and remembered to cover her mouth and its rows of flawless teeth only after she had finished.

'I've never been so tired.'

Peter stood up.

'I'll take the chair.'

Sally stood up too and there was a silence as they both contemplated the sofa and the bulbous armchair.

'Don't be a gentleman, Peter, please. Not now.'

Though it would comfortably accommodate two seated people, in all its other dimensions (too shallow, too short) the sofa had clearly been designed to discourage immorality.

'Besides,' pressed Sally, 'it's too cold. I know – you first and then . . .' She looked away from him and went on quickly with all the casualness she could muster: 'And then I'll go on top. My coat will be the blanket. I'm not heavy.'

Peter lay down, his head on one arm and his feet sticking out over the other. Sally hesitated, unsure of how the arrangement would work. She found herself straddling him and then, suddenly conscious of the suggestiveness of the position, she flopped forward and they both burst out laughing. She wriggled to find a way of making the two bodies fit with some compromise of comfort and decency.

'Is that too awful?'

'Not at all.'

Sally burrowed against the warmth and pulse of his neck. She began to feel very calm and soon it was difficult to think of anything at all. Peter embraced her.

'We'll fall off if we're not careful.'

His hands were on the outside of her coat.

'Put them inside. You'll get cold otherwise.'

He slid his arms under Sally's Burberry. His fingers tingled

209

on the hem of her jacket, waiting there for the first slight sign of a rebuke.

'My hands are cold.'

'I can't feel them,' said Sally. 'You must warm them up.'

She felt his fingers' light touch along the waistband of her skirt and sent out earnest, passionate prayers for them to be bold. Peter silently asked what she meant and found out, cautious, treacherous quarter-inches at a time as he traced that borderline of cloth, eased out the thin fabric of her blouse and then the soft, thick ribbing of the winter vest beneath to find the warm skin and the firm muscular ridges of her back. He felt them harden, shift and relax as Sally pressed down and nudged his head a little to one side as she found more of his neck and shoulder. She breathed steadily. Her consciousness shrank, lightened. Soon there was no part of her outside that small, humid darkness and Peter's cool handprint against her back.

Sally next opened her eyes on a muted, colourless light. It showed only the worst of everything it touched. It seemed to carry its own bleakness, an innate power to blight and hollow out the spirit. What must it be like to wake alone to such a light, shedding its dust on just such a room as this? She supposed that people did and understood for the first time how reasonable it was for them not to go on but instead to reject life's huge, cruel talent for being worse than nothing.

It took her a minute to get up. She eased the pain out of one limb after another and tried not to move her head too much as she untangled herself and got to her feet. She replaced her coat over the still sleeping Peter. At the broken window Sally folded her arms tightly against the cold and looked out on the new, chastised Nanking. The street was already filling with traders – a woman walked by, a new aristocrat of the market with chickens fluttering weakly as they hung by their feet from a pole.

Sally remembered the day belatedly – it was New Year's Day, the first of January 1938. New Year's Days from the past flitted meaninglessly through her mind – guests, meals, pretending to sleep upstairs as she listened to the adults below. She turned to look at Peter. Outside, frigid wind blew in gusts, grey with ash. Across the city the gates of Ginling College were open. Women were scrubbing the blood from the steps where Old Du had been killed at his post five hours before. The college was organising its day without Minnie. She was alone in the attic and no one went near her. She knelt on the boards, silent and still before an altar of a dozen empty beds and their torn, if still unbloodied sheets. From the International Club, Sally heard fragments of music and turned her head to hear more clearly. In the square near the foot of the ancient Drum Tower, Band Captain Tanaka's heart leapt as he pursued his vocation. His trim little feet bounced on the podium, his gloved puppet hands and his pristine baton a blur of brightness as he picked up the tempo of 'Chinatown, my Chinatown'.

10

The hygienists of war were busy. Hunchbacks with black wands patrolled the city, spraying the sterile scent of peace on anything that had once been alive. The removal of bodies began to be organised. A skeleton street map was drawn up showing the areas that were first to be made decent. A corps of battered trucks appeared and grew in number. Volunteer members of the Red Swastika Society, paid with rice, drove them or clung to the back. Commercial signage often remained on the sides of these trucks. Sally could only guess at what the characters meant – Joinery? Fresh Vegetables? Poultry? Now Japanese flags fluttered from every cab and the calves and feet of stacked corpses protruded from the back as they puttered out through Nanking's gates, heading every few minutes for the 'ten-thousand-man ditches' that had been dug at all points of the compass. It was the third or fourth day of the year that Sally opened the curtains of her little room high up in the Principal's house of Ginling College and looked down to find her Polynices gone and no monument but what she could remember and the rose-bringer and a swept darkness in the dust. Elsewhere, what could not be removed quickly enough was shovelled into side streets and alleys and guarded by soldiers. Dignitaries were escorted about the field of victory, the Japanese press corps multiplied, the odd sponsored novelist sauntered here and there, beachcombing for a little local colour for his article. Attempts to stray off the skeleton map were politely deterred. Nanking was still theatre – a Potemkin village of the living, its guards and the charred flats of its street fronts barely holding back the mounded slaughter behind.

No day passed without a building burned here or there, a handful of rapes or the bayoneting of the occasional slacker. There was general agreement that order had been restored. The garrison commander fashioned a Chinese Autonomous Government, attached the strings to its limbs and jerked it into life. A parade was ordered, fireworks distributed, the new East Asians of Nanking celebrated their freedom. Collaborators presented their credentials and were found work in the new Society for the Maintenance of Order. Some mornings a member was found with his throat cut and 'hanjian' pinned to his Western-style shirt. A reprisal would be ordered, another pit dug and filled. But the numbers were not so great any more – the orgasm was over, the will had gone and even the will to find the will. After the worst, what more can you do? The next dead collaborator was quietly added to the pile, unavenged.

From above, Chinese bombers came to destroy Nanking's airfield now it was no longer theirs. Pom-pom guns tried to shoo them away, their shells bursting into small black puffs against high, still, clay-white clouds. The encounters were watched cautiously from below – even in the absence of a Japanese patrol or a known collaborator, most faces remained expressionless. Japanese officers followed the action through field glasses before grimly hurrying back to the headquarters hotel.

'Do you think they have seen the future?'

It was John Rabe's question. It was directed at Sally as they sat together near the end of that first week in a Ginling classroom a few minutes after midnight. Their names had coincided on the rota for guard duty at the college and Sally had been pleased. The little German had arrived in a high mood. He affected great shock at the sight of her hair, but insisted on stroking it and claiming a fatherly New Year's kiss.

'I am very angry. Very angry, you know – I heard about your little adventure. What if we had lost you? That was reckless. Still, what a beautiful German you make, Sally.'

The presence of his absent daughters was suddenly real and he was forced to turn away.

'Ah, well. Ah, well. I was going to ask you something – what was it? Oh, yes – our New Year's Day concert – I didn't see you there.'

'No. I was . . . busy.'

'You missed a treasure. It almost made me feel sorry for the Japanese. They don't seem to understand anything, the poor fellows. What are they? I can't work it out – sort of patchworks, really. Made-up things, stitched together from scraps of other people's rubbish.'

Rabe soon had Sally in fits of laughter as he described the scene – a farce blended from a brass band matinée in the Munich Zoological Gardens and an American cartoon.

'I tell you, it was all I could do to contain myself. I had to say, "Johnny, you must not offend them – a thousand lives depend on your ability to stop yourself from laughing." There was a moment of extreme danger when the good Professor Smythe and I caught each other's eye. Oh, dear – that was a close-run thing.'

The memory brought more tears and a handkerchief was needed.

'Do you think we'll have a quiet night tonight?'

'Maybe.'

Rabe looked upwards and put on an expression of concentrated thought as if he had just tasted a very fine and rare wine and had been asked to identify it from memory.

'Shall we be very wicked?'

Sally responded with a quizzical, but by no means discouraging look.

'I say two incursions tonight. Six cigarettes on two incursions.'

'One,' said Sally decisively.

'You're an optimist, Miss Marsden. I like that.'

They shook hands on the wager. Rabe gathered together a few lengths of broken picture frame and some sheets of newspaper and began to set a fire in the old iron stove in the corner. He filled the silence as he worked with inconsequential observations about the weather and the most recent anecdotes of his colleagues in the Safety Zone Committee. Sally drifted, always comfortable in his presence. The fire added a little to the light and she noticed the blackboard at the back of the room. A lesson emerged from the darkness and she went closer to see. There was a skilful drawing of a baby – a well-rounded picture of health and good feeding as if copied from an advertisement. Four arrows converged on the child's body giving the impression of an infant St Sebastian. It had remained unerased since Minnie had last given her Home and Health lesson to the local girls who could not afford to pay.

'There.'

Rabe pushed forward a bowl of tea – a barely perceptible greenness in a shell of white porcelain.

'It's homeopathic tea, I think. Perhaps it will have some special effect – what do you say?'

'Thank you.'

'I think they have.'

'I'm sorry?'

'Seen the future. The better sort anyway, or those who can read, or rode on a train or went to the cinema once or twice before being conscripted. I've watched them carefully. I think it comes to them all of a sudden. That's how it was for me – although it took fifteen years. I woke up one day and understood the word "China". That was a happy moment. But for them – how hopeless it must seem. Hard to know the end already, whatever you do. Do you know what a coolie told me the other day?'

'What did he tell you?'

'It was by one of the gates. We were standing together watching the trucks take the corpses out. He came up to me, kowtowed, then smiled and said, "Farmers happy." I asked why they would be happy and he pointed to the trucks and said, "Good for fields. Good crops. China eat itself – be strong." Now what can you do with an enemy like that?'

A light snow lay outside and the tea made their breaths still more visible. Rabe had opened the window all the same so that the warning whistle might be clearly heard. Sally was content to stay silent. Rabe was quiet too for a while and an understanding grew slowly between them.

'How is she?'

'Minnie? Strong, quiet. She never gives herself a moment's peace – always working or sleeping.'

'But does she sleep?'

Sally poured more tea into the two white bowls. Rabe went on.

'It's too deliberate, I think. All this strength – it's for others, you know? Another sacrifice and then, because the first is never enough, another and then another after that. A person can make themselves sick like that.'

'She feels she made a mistake with the girls in the attic.'

'That's just stupid. It makes me angry.'

'She said perhaps they would have had a better chance if they hadn't been hidden. Some of them might have been lucky.'

'No,' said Rabe, almost shouting the word. 'They would have been taken. Every last one of them – she knows that, she can see it for herself. Only we are safe – the Christians among lions, except these lions have no taste for Christian flesh. Watch her for us, won't you?'

Sally promised.

'Closely.'

'I will.'

'No one can be that strong.'

The two friends talked on, played chess and made themselves sad as they compared thoughts of Germany and England. Rabe restored his spirits by saying more about what he would do when he got home.

'I have it all worked out, I have written the words in my head. I will take it to every town and village hall in Germany if they will have me and then show them Reverend Magee's film. I have written to Herr Hitler – again – and this time also to Herr Ribbentrop. Of course, I have not been able post the letters yet.'

Sally listened bleakly to his hopes. It was as if she had been buttonholed by some excited traveller, happy to have been released that morning from a long imprisonment. Should she tell him that he had been the more fortunate, explain how much less the world had made of its freedom than he had been able to preserve in his prison cell? It was almost a relief to her when Rabe seemed to understand.

'But will they believe it?' he asked. 'I can stand up and tell them, an honest man and as like them as two peas in a pod. And I can even show them the pictures too and still I wonder if they will believe it. People don't believe the impossible. They have to live it – as we do.'

'You can try,' said Sally blandly. 'You can always try.'

'But it is strange, is it not? And not just a theory – I have proof. I received a telegram from my employers.'

Sally sharpened and sat up straight.

'Oh yes, just this morning. It is one of the first. They say I should close the office and return to Shanghai on account of the uncertain business outlook.'

He laughed and shook his head.

'No – they will never believe.'

'You got a telegram?'

'The old press agency. It is now an Imperial Army Signal Post with a very small and very grim little man and a very large radio set. Incoming only. He wouldn't even take a bribe.'

The hours passed. There was talk, the hunt for scraps of wood for the stove, drowsing, dreaming, endless bowls of watery tea that thinned the blood until there was a tremor in the hands. Sally went out shortly before dawn to relieve herself. The clouds had cleared and a frost crusted the surface of the snow. She could feel a dry and bitter cold against her skin.

'No more snow,' she said when she went back in.

'That's always something. I meant to show you this.'

Rabe unfolded a large sheet of paper and displayed the painted Chinese characters on it to Sally.

'What does it say?'

'It's my other letter this week – from the refugees in my compound. We have a teacher there so I asked him what it meant. Apparently it says, "For Mr Rabe, with best wishes for the New Year – hundreds of millions are close to you. The refugees of your camp." I asked Chang what was really meant by hundreds of millions. He studied it closely and said, "In German mean just *Prosit Neujahr!*" This one I'll keep.'

Dawn came. Rabe took a cigarette from the table and lit it with a match. Sally picked up another and leaned over to catch the last of the flame.

'*Prosit Neujahr.*'

'*Prosit Neujahr*, my dear.'

They looked at the remaining ten cigarettes.

'Well,' said Rabe. 'We were both wrong.'

They shared out their stakes, pocketed them and parted.

A few days after that the water started to flow – weakly at first as it haemorrhaged from countless broken pipes, seeping darkly across the streets and forming black slicks of ice in the mornings. One by one the leaks were sealed and the pressure strengthened. The lights came on in patches where the transmission network had held together. Blackouts were regular and people soon learned to get their lamps and candles ready just before the evening and late-night wireless news bulletins. Registration dragged on with long queues of women and children standing all day in the cold. But the increasing number with armbands and papers began to move more freely about the city. Japanese flags spread everywhere. They disappeared one morning on the strength of a rumour that Chiang Kai-shek's armies were about to retake the city. By the end of the afternoon they were back, more numerous than before.

Before the Empire of Japan, logic bowed as abjectly as all

its other enemies. A proclamation was issued and appeared on doors and telegraph poles about the city requiring the refugees in the Safety Zone to return to those same homes the army had so energetically destroyed over the previous three weeks. Rabe in his garden, Minnie in Ginling College and the other camp leaders were besieged by petitioners begging – quite unnecessarily – not to be thrown out. A handful returned to see what was left, were duly robbed and duly raped and ran back to the Safety Zone to find more emphatic demands from the garrison commander to return to their homes and enjoy the peace his forces had provided for them. Japanese ships docked at Hsiakwan with Japanese goods for the new incinerated, co-prosperous market. The first opium shops appeared. The new masters looked on with satisfaction. Certainly, there was a special economic beauty to it when the Chinese began to rob each other so they could give even more money to their oppressors.

The attractions of an occupied capital were great, not least for the journalists who now crowded the place and jostled to satisfy the appetite for the good news back home. For Peter they were another story in themselves and an ambiguous brotherhood, ready to compare their common experiences of tyrannical editors or talk over the latest cameras and the wonder of the new wire pictures. Several liked to practise their English and would never tire of pumping him for information about the United States. What was the greatest baseball game he had seen? Was it really true that in America a poor man could own a car? Why were Americans so lazy when they could rule the world if they worked as hard as the Japanese? A journalistic Masonry drew him in – they were decent fellows who knew all about the splendours and miseries of the newspaper life. He just had to be careful not to ask what they were dispatching back to Tokyo and Osaka.

Delage fared less well with them and they did him fewer favours. There was a practical problem too – his six-foot two-inch frame was impossible to smuggle past the guards of the new *cordon sanitaire* that was supposed, in theory at least, to keep all reporters away from the outer suburbs. Peter did not look down on his new friends and was rewarded one day by being sneaked past a couple of bored privates and a well-oiled sergeant, hidden from their view by a close consort of the boys from *Asahi Shimbun*, *Tokyo Nichi Nichi* and *Yomiuri* and the modesty of a broad-brimmed hat.

Once beyond the eyes of authority the hacks split up in search of exclusives – a more heroically large heap of 'enemy' bodies or, for the photographers, at least one more artfully arranged. Or perhaps a sign of real conflict, though there were precious few of these – just a scattering of corpses near the gates still in their Kuomintang blue. Disembodied heads were at a premium and spurred the eager observers on to lush tropes on ancient family swords, their honour and edge renewed in the nation's great civilising mission.

Peter went his own way, his mind wordless and even his eye finding little new on which to use his camera. He passed through a square, quite clear of any of the signs of war apart from the burned buildings that formed its sides. A handful of Chinese stared at him. Many times he had been dragged off to witness an atrocity. Tired of these scenes now, he avoided eye contact and moved quickly on. He went as far as the airport and saw, just as Sally had described to him, the dismembered tails and wings of broken aircraft. Fresh craters dotted the landscape – wide black circles of upturned earth amid the melting, grubby snow where the Chinese had dropped their bombs, all well wide of the runway. He took a dull picture, made a note and moved on.

The wind picked up, its currents becoming visible when

it lifted vortices of ash from the ruins. Peter paused by a more recent fire, drawing in what warmth he could from the smouldering timbers. The emptiness of the scene oppressed him. Ahead, over an expanse of waste ground never yet built on, was a blank, gateless section of the walls. Behind him was the levelled plane of the old city, featureless now, a cindery rubble extending back to the concrete of the new centre. Even there, dark smoke stains streaked up from half the windows. Between the two there was only the old palace and the railway line snaking out of the ruined station and to its right, the one other structure that held the eye. Unable to recognise it, Peter walked that way and found one of the city's small parks. A painted iron fence corralled a selection of serviceable shrubs, a few trees and the stumps of some others already removed for fuel. Peter went in, past a bilingual sign forbidding dogs and the dropping of litter. At the end of the neat path an oddly Western scene confronted him. Peter had been a child in places like this – the soil extravagantly planted with inedible ornaments, the A-frame of the swings, a chute polished with use, benches to sit on, a pond for ducks and model boats at the weekend. The chains of one of the swings had been wrapped around the strut at the side holding it out of the way. Where it normally hung was a boy, his head resting on his shoulder, folded over the rope that cut into his neck. Lightly dressed, as if he had just risen from his bed, his naked feet dangled where the seat of the swing would have been. Peter went over to him and looked up at the twelve-, maybe thirteen-year-old face with the eyes still open and bright. The feet fascinated him. They were cold, but still soft. He felt the smooth skin over the top, the flesh still full and childish enough to conceal all the veins and tendons. He put his hands underneath and pressed up gently against the rough soles. He counted through the toes, letting a little earth fall from where it had gathered between them. He stepped back and took a few shots, taking care to keep the other swing in the frame, still hanging where it should. Well, at least his time hadn't been wasted. He was winding on and turning towards the pond when a voice startled him.

'He did it himself.'

It was one of the journalists who had come with him past the guard post. The man approached him, confusedly bowed and held out his hand at the same time.

'*Nihon Shimbun,*' he said curtly.

Peter shook his hand, but wouldn't look him in the face.

'*Chicago Daily News, New York Times*, anyone who'll have me.'

The man gave a quick upward nod of understanding. Peter kept his eyes on the scene around them, the swings and the pond and the strewn path even as he was aware of the other man's close attention. The Japanese indicated the hanging boy.

'Suicide.'

'You say.'

The man flinched but didn't stop unwrapping his packet of cigarettes and extending it to Peter.

'Really. Put your hand inside his shirt – he's still warm. There haven't been soldiers here for two days.'

'D'you think something drove him to it?'

The man shrugged, hardened.

'Not me.'

'Well, I'll change the caption then – "twelve-year-old suicide, cause unknown".'

The other man gave no sign of having understood.

The two journalists lit their cigarettes and stared at the pond. Small talk about the cameras they carried quickly withered. They settled to the task of photographing the pond, walking gingerly round the carpet of discarded clothes, crouching close to the surface in search of the angle that might preserve that tiny bit more of what they were seeing. Peter already knew how such experiences were water in the hands and how little even the best of photographs could preserve. He remembered how it had once seemed impossible that he might ever fall out of love with the medium – but it was a process that had long since started and was surely now in its final stages. The future for his cameras lay in the backs of closed cupboards, under the same dust that covered old musical instruments, overambitious books and a pristine set of golf clubs. The two men appeared in each other's viewfinders and there was a swift double click.

Peter went to sit on a bench. He took out one of his own cigarettes and tried to make sense of his thoughts. There was something understandable about the location. The pond was slightly sunken and the bushes about it and the gruesome innocence of the place added to its potential. In this case it was hardly necessary, but the concealment it offered must have excited them all the same. Peter recalled childhood warnings about similar places he had known in Chicago. At night they turned inside out. Muggers lay in wait and the city's hungry solitaires hunted through the bushes. Perhaps it was universal. A corner, a patch of darkness, a stand of trees were never just themselves, not under the human eye, constantly attuned to the thrilling chance for an unwitnessed act. We could all guess at the play-park rapist's ecstatic climax of self. Peter didn't know what these soldiers would go through in the future or how many would survive at all, but for those who could look back he was already sure they would remember Nanking as their freest and happiest days. He understood also that this was what Sally must have seen, what she described to him in the International Club in the early hours of New Year's morning. What was black mercury then under the moon was now a lurid brilliance under a fierce winter blue. The pond was a perfect circle of blood scarlet set on the dirty white ground of discarded underclothes Sally had felt beneath her feet. The lightless mounds that broke the surface were not the islands or whales that night allowed her to imagine but simply a shoulder, a head or the crook of a knee.

The man from the *Nihon Shimbun* was standing beside him again. He became agitated as he prepared to speak. Peter stared at him discouragingly. The Japanese nodded at the scarlet pond and then looked at Peter's camera, at his pockets.

'Colour film?'

'What?'

He half turned towards the pond.

'You have colour film?'

Sally did look after Minnie, though neither of them ever admitted it. The attic was shut up and the storeroom door that led to it locked. Being orphans, so far as anyone could tell, the girls that had slept there were not much mourned by the refugees in the college. Whatever their fate, it could not be exceptional and it could not be helped. A surface brutality held Minnie together.

'Well, that's that,' she said. 'I'll do what I can and not what I can't.'

An angry glare at Sally invited her contradiction and defied it at the same time. A guarded 'Of course' was all she would say.

Minnie put the storeroom key in the drawer of her desk in the Principal's house. She knew she would go up there again, but not until she wasn't needed anywhere else. Four hours of sleep a night became her rule rather than five.

'Fewer dreams,' as she explained it to Sally. 'And more work to do in any case.'

New battles helped her – the hiding of rice from the puppet government that came searching for its own means to power, and then a dangerous stand-off with the garrison commander who had declared the college dormitories free and his intention to station troops on the campus. From the early hours of that morning, Minnie moved her forces with martial cunning and precision. On inspection every living space was found already to be hopelessly overcrowded. Near the gates on his way out, the officer squinted suspiciously at his opponent. He cocked an ear to his nervous inter-preter, asked him to repeat the words and then left without finding any reply to Minnie's insistence that she could not, in any case, permit his troops to be stationed in her college for reasons that he, and every mother in Japan, would understand only too well.

Sally adjusted her day to spend more time with Minnie. Inspections were made together and in the evenings they shivered under the same lamp, updating the accounts of supplies and recording the latest violations. Sally knew how the inefficiency of it irked the older woman, but she was never sent away to do something else, however useful it might have been. And so long as there was no hint that Minnie had needs, that she might share a little of the common frailty, Sally was allowed to stay.

Outside, the clear-up went on. Concentrically, the bodies were removed in an expanding ring of sanitation that moved out gradually towards the walls. The dogs took whatever was left. Then the dogs disappeared too and for a few days there was meat again in the market. The city took on the appearance of having been struck by a purely natural disaster. The scene astonished even the new troops being brought up steadily from the coast. Marched in from their disembarkation points in Hsiakwan, they couldn't help but look about themselves. Distracted, they were forced to skip every few paces to slot back into their rhythm. The relieved units sauntered past them in the other direction with a look of proud contempt in their eyes. The brotherhood was already forming and these latecomers would never be part of it.

The Yangtze became nearly as busy as before, and from the midst of its traffic the USS *Oahu* nosed into port. A gleaming Buick was lowered gently on to the dockside and three well-dressed men got in. They drove down Chung Shan Street before taking a right to press through the mêlée of Shanghai Road and finally pull up before the American Embassy where a crowd had already assembled to view the miraculous arrival. A flag was raised and the building entered. The fragmentary remains of the American and Japanese diplomatic seals were removed from its doors and of the two hundred Chinese who claimed to have been on the staff, the most credible six were re-employed. As soon as she heard, Sally ran all the way there. She found Peter and Professor Smythe too, registering their survival. With their help she persuaded the new Consul to send a naval radiogram from the *Oahu* to Shanghai and onward to London so that her parents should know they still had a daughter.

The Germans came next, much to the satisfaction of Rabe and Kröger. Another flag signified another set of witnesses and the city seemed to relax a little more as the lights went on in the looted wreck of the German Embassy. A commandeered bottle of champagne reconsecrated the mission and Rabe went home that night with a pocket full of letters from his wife in Shanghai and his children now back in Munich.

He had agreed warmly to the proposal for a joint German-American reception for all the foreigners in the city and the Japanese diplomatic staff.

'Just to make sure they know we are here,' explained Dr Rosen, the new ambassador. 'To say those things that can't be said any other way.'

Rabe was back in his favourite role of shepherd and promised to deliver every member of the guest list, even the increasingly disgruntled Delage and a sober Podshivaloff. In the event, Sally would not be part of this reception but it was, all the same, to keep the appointment that she ran down the stairs towards Minnie's study in mid-January, her skin still tingling from the cold wash and a fresh coat of cologne. She knocked on the door and opened it, as had become her habit, without hesitation.

'Oh, sorry.'

'It's all right,' said Minnie. 'Come in.'

Minnie was sitting at her desk. A young Japanese officer stood in front of her in the attitude of a delinquent school-boy. He spoke again in the rapid brusqueness in which they were all trained, but bowing at the same time and adding a plea in English at the end.

'Do you know how overcrowded we are?'

The young man looked baffled.

'Fuel to find, mouths to feed,' emphasised Minnie, making the universal gesture when he still didn't seem to under-stand. He bowed more deeply and with shaking hands began to rifle his pockets producing a little occupation currency, a silver pocket watch and a gold ring he unwrapped from a handkerchief.

'No, no!'

Minnie pushed them firmly back across the desk. The soldier turned to look at the two Chinese girls watching from the far corner. Sisters by their appearance, one seventeen the other maybe a year and a half younger. He pointed at the older girl, took a step towards her and stopped. He stared at her for a moment and then something in him seemed to break as he turned back to Minnie and began an impassioned and increasingly tearful speech in Japanese. She stiffened with embarrassment as she found the young man at her feet, pressing his forehead against the carpet and continuing to emit an increasingly incoherent stream of noise. The sight of a submission due, in Minnie's mind, to no human master, angered and upset her. She leaned forward to touch him on the shoulder. As he seemed not to notice, she hooked a stout finger under the collar of his uniform and pulled him sharply upwards. She pointed at the chair which the young Lieutenant Ando reached just in time.

'But why?' Minnie insisted on asking him.

'Posted away. Sent back to Shanghai.'

'Why won't they be safe?'

'You know why,' shouted back Ando, immediately following with another elaborate apology.

Minnie leaned towards him and demanded with a relentlessness close to cruelty, 'But I want you to tell me. If I have to take them in, tell me why.'

Lieutenant Ando looked down and twisted his hands in his lap. With every ten seconds that passed another year peeled away from him. At the end, it was a miserable, tear-stained eight-year-old who gasped in a convulsive breath and sobbed, 'Don't know!'

'Get out.'

The Lieutenant, his Chinese lover and her little sister all stood up together.

'No,' said Minnie. 'You two stay. You, get out.'

The Lieutenant reversed out of the room. Sally moved to the window to watch him running down the steps and then across the college grounds, a shrinking figure in khaki weaving in and out of the refugees, faster and faster towards the gates, as light as if his own life had just been saved.

Even in the midwinter cold a sheen of sweat was on Minnie's face. She fanned herself with a missionary pamphlet.

'I shouldn't have done that.'

'Why not?' asked Sally. But she needed to calm herself too and took out a cigarette.

The two Chinese girls kept their heads down, but looked slyly upwards at Minnie wondering, perhaps, whether their protector had done them a good turn or not. Minnie summoned one of the Service Corps and gave instructions for Ginling's two new citizens to be found some food, some work to do and a space to sleep. They picked up their bundles and trooped silently out of the room.

It was the oddness of the phrase that Sally remembered, heightened by the daily plainness with which Minnie offered it to her. She was checking herself in the mirror to make sure she was presentable for the reception. Quickly satisfied, she shuffled herself into her second coat and while buttoning it looked up at Sally with a smile.

'That was from God.'

Any number of bitter rejections rose at once in Sally's mind. She took her place before the mirror and said nothing.

'Ready?'

'Yes.'

'Such a waste of time.'

The two women went to the door of the study. They opened it to find a man standing there in his spotless

Crombie coat, a mirror polish on his shoes and his hat in his hand. The other was raised to knock on the door. The man considered both the possibilities before him. Failing to find exactly what he was expecting, he addressed the space between them in the dismaying accent of England that Sally had not heard for a month.

'Sally Jane Marsden?'

The car passed the junction with the Qixia Temple road. After another few minutes its tyres quietened as they reached the metalled surface of the new highway. It accelerated south-eastwards towards Shanghai. Deliverance or expulsion? Her heart was heavy. There was an awkwardness ahead and something very like a desertion behind. Fields and burned villages unspooled past the window. Mr Primrose-Browne, Second Secretary of the Shanghai legation, turned from where he sat in the front passenger seat.

'We should get in an hour or so after nightfall, not bad really. Oh, I'm afraid they made rather a beast of themselves a couple of miles further on. It's on the left. I'll let you know when it's coming up.'

'Don't be such a bloody fool.'

The muscles in Mr Primrose-Browne's face went dead. He did not speak to Sally again until bidding her goodnight as she walked up the steps of the Cathay Hotel.

An hour before, it had been a colleague of his at Minnie's door while others raised a Union Jack over the embassy roof and went to present their credentials to the garrison commander.

'You got our message?' he had asked.

'I did not.'

'Sorry,' said the man. 'It's all a bit of a shambles at the

moment. It's like this — the Japs are talking about freedom of movement for neutrals, but just between ourselves we think it's a bit of a story. We have one car over that's going back to Shanghai today under diplomatic protection. You can go back in that or God knows when. Half an hour all right with you?'

'I'm staying,' said Sally.

'No you're not,' said Minnie, already seizing her by one arm and propelling her up the stairs towards her suitcase and her few possessions. A few minutes later she stood in the street outside the college, dressed in her one preserved suit of clothes as if a month of history had never been, tearful with unnameable emotions as she accepted a folded sheet of paper and a kiss from Minnie.

'I'll always be here,' said Minnie. 'But just in case, here's my brother's address in Illinois.'

'Give my love to everyone. Tell Cola not to drink too much and tell Herr Rabe not to work too hard. Tell them all I'm sorry for abandoning them.'

'I certainly shan't tell them that.'

'Look,' said Sally, 'I can come to the reception, say goodbye to them all in person. It'll only . . .'

Minnie cut the plan off firmly.

'And if they go without you? If you're still stuck here and something happens — after you could have been safe? It's not as if you planned to be here, Sally, is it?'

'I don't want to be safe.'

'Childish nonsense. I'll come with you to the embassy. Come on.'

'It's all right.'

Sally would have preferred more resistance. The image she had of herself required the grand gesture, the observance of the true proprieties at all costs, especially dangerous ones.

Instead, she was consenting to be bundled out of Nanking as passively and chaotically as she had got into it in the first place. A flicker of self-regard made her hesitate, only for it to be followed by the thought of her half-hour and the pressing question of how much of it had already passed. Easier to go like this. Better for Peter, too. That was the way – call it a sacrifice.

'No, it's all right. I'll go.'

Sally made her way through the throng of the Shanghai Road and then down wide Chung Shan Street to where the British Embassy stood in sight of the ancient Y Chang Gate. She dawdled, toying with the idea of being late, of arriving just in time to see the car depart and turning back with blameless relief. The Service Corps girl Minnie sent ran as fast as she could. It was because of her message that Sally arrived to find Rabe's little car already there, Rabe himself and Peter standing beside it. Rabe embraced her and planted a fatherly kiss on her forehead.

'Remember our plan, won't you? Tell everyone what you've seen. We can still change the world. Will you post this for me in Shanghai?'

Rabe withdrew discreetly to sit in his car. Primrose-Browne intruded, drily stated his name, and held out his hand for Sally's suitcase. She gave it to him and he put it in the back of the sweeping, assertive diplomatic vehicle, instructing the driver to start the engine at the same time. Peter came forward. For a moment he kept his hands in his pockets and looked down. A sudden fearful sadness ran through Sally. She hooked two fingers behind one of the big buttons on his coat and pulled him gently towards her. Her eyes filled as she heard him say, 'I didn't know if you'd want me to be here.'

'Don't be silly.'

They embraced tightly, Peter feeling the promise of a woman somewhere beneath the thick layers of winter clothing.

'I'm being deported,' said Sally. 'Half an hour or nothing.'

'Good. I hate you being here.'

He decided to make it sound like business.

'I'll be out in a few days myself. They can't keep us here for ever, not with the diplomats back. Anyway, I've got cables to send, pictures to sell. I can't do that from here. Look, I wonder if . . .'

Behind them Primrose-Browne had opened the passenger door of the car. He paced and glanced crudely at his watch. Something instinctively worrying caught his eye and he edged closer to get a better look. A slight frown appeared as he saw the American take four rolls of film from his pocket and hand them over to a British subject.

'Of course,' Sally was saying. 'Of course – so long as you promise to take them back. You'll have to come and find me now, won't you?'

The diplomat walked up to them and once again performed the checking of the watch.

'Look, I'm sorry,' he said, 'I really am, but we are pressed for time.'

Sally and Peter regarded him as if from an enormous distance.

'Poor man,' said Sally. 'Have you noticed?'

'What?'

'There's something wrong with him. There'll be something wrong with everyone now – except us. Be careful, won't you?'

'I will.'

Sally got into the car. Dully, muffled by the glass of the closing door, she heard Peter say 'See you soon' and watched him raise a hand in valediction. At once the car began to move. Sally waved a brief, ordinary wave and looked ahead. The interior of the car was familiar, its smell even more so and she had to hold herself steady as a wave of nausea washed through her. In less than a minute they were slowing at the exit checkpoint. The soldiers bent down to study the three figures in the car then waved them on without ever bringing them to a halt. There was the blinding darkness of the tunnel and the flash of brightness at the other end as Sally left Nanking, unscathed.

Primrose-Browne remembered his private business. He took the letter from his inside jacket pocket and turned to face Sally. Best to get the embarrassment over with.

'Mr Jerrold wanted to be here. The service has rules about that sort of thing – personal and professional, you know? It just wasn't possible.'

For half an hour Sally held the envelope in her hand. She felt its expensive texture beneath her fingers and the outline of the red, letterpress crown on the back. She watched the countryside pass, alternately devastated and untouched. She rudely silenced Primrose-Browne and then, as they passed on the left acre after acre of burial pits with their coolie gangs hard at work and their big fires, made out of homes and carts, burning to keep the soldiers warm, she tore open the envelope. She looked generally at the two sheets, turning them over to examine the back, automatically checking the signature at the end, hazily registering the familiarity of the hand. She looked up and confronted the chauffeur's eyes in the rear-view mirror, forcing them back to the road.

Dearest Darling Sally,
   Until a few days ago I could not even be certain if you were still alive. How can I tell you how horrible

235

it has been? I have had my own adventures and have so much to tell you. For now, all I want in the world is . . .

Sally folded the letter and returned it to the envelope. She laid her head back and closed her eyes.

11

Through a portière behind the bar in the Mandarin Lounge the clack of bones could be heard as waiters whiled away the afternoon with game after game of mahjong. Business had fallen off a little, but it suited Sally who had come intensely to need that enriched, social loneliness to be found only in sparsely populated cafés and restaurants with tables set for one. She had established herself in half a dozen such places, diluting her custom between them so that no single set of coffee drinkers, newspaper readers or chess players would become too familiar and force her to move on. There was time spent with Hugh, of course, but the crisis had been good for him (his own phrase), and though their conversation had never been so direct it was understood that Sally should make no demands that might hold him back. When there was an opportunity for them to advance together Sally was happy to make her contribution. This particular day would be the most important of all and her immaculate appearance fully honoured the occasion.

A cocktail piano sighed lovelessly in the corner. The

player, a Singapore Chinese, was a man Sally had never seen detached from his instrument. A black cap of shellac hair was bonded to age-proof ceramic skin. A great consoler of solitary ladies, he offered precisely uniform smiles at regular intervals which only added to the impression that he could be nothing more than an extension to an elaborate pianola. At that moment he was giving particular attention to Sally as a result of a misunderstanding. His mechanism had already favoured her with two or three smiles and he could only believe that it was because of these that she had moved closer. Sally pretended to read her book, but turned her ear to the other three people in the lounge. She wished the pianist would play more quietly, or not at all. She had seen in the newspaper the other day a little piece under the headline POETS TO TOUR WAR and suspected that these were the men and that the third, with notebook, must be a journalist following up for another paper. One had straight fair hair which was a little too long for him and he kept sweeping out of his eyes with a studied curve of forearm and hand. His darker, neater companion sat quietly by, content to let the fair-haired man speak for both of them. They had the look and sound of English public schoolboys. Sally listened to them with a confusion of irritation and nostalgia.

The journalist made a note and asked if they had found it hard not to join the fighting for the Republicans along with so many of their friends. The poet coolly dismissed the provocation.

'Not really. I'm a poet of realism – the futile gesture has never had any charm for me. I make the contribution I am best able to make. Like yourself, no doubt.'

His more taciturn companion raised his head and his eyes met with Sally's. He smiled disinterestedly. Sally responded but quickly looked back down at her book. *Der Vater ist böse;*

Der Apfel ist schlecht – how was it possible for language to be so dreary? She fanned forward through a hundred pages of exercises and tried to raise some ambition to understand the incomprehensible sentences there. Once again, the lust for self-improvement sensibly withered and she stifled a yawn. Perhaps she should try engines again, or radios.

'We're very interested in slums,' the dark companion was saying. 'Could you tell us what the best way to see them would be? I want to be able to say what the effect has been. Nothing much seems to have changed here.'

Sally could only see the journalist from behind and regretted that his expression was hidden from her. He tore a sheet from his notebook and handed it over.

'A couple of chaps I know – they can help. But I wouldn't go on your own. You gents will be off to the front, no doubt, with the rest of the war correspondents?'

The poet confirmed this, mentioned their letters of introduction to the Kuomintang command and talked of his keenness to see the war. A shadow fell over Sally and the weight of a hand rested lightly on her hair. Hugh bent down to kiss her and took a seat opposite, blocking her view of the other three men.

'You look wonderful.'

'Thank you.'

It worried her a little to see on his face that genuine happiness and pride she seemed to bring him these last few weeks. Nevertheless, it pleased her still to be inspected by a man. She could feel the deeper, automatic part of herself respond to Hugh's gaze – the series of tiny choreographed movements of a female on display. At least she would be wanted, and so many had to settle for less.

'Just perfect.'

She smiled back at him spontaneously. Hugh leaned

forward and lifted up her book to look at its title. He made a sour face.

'Good heavens – are you training to be a spy?'

'But my dear,' said Sally brightly, 'why do you think I pay such close attention to everything you say?'

Hugh's face clouded and Sally laughed. She had already teased him about being far too literal-minded to make a good diplomat. That mistake had led to a whole evening of sulking. She put her hand on his.

'Don't be silly.'

'Oh, I don't mind, but there'll be some people this afternoon who don't have much of a sense of humour. You will be careful, won't you?'

'Don't worry. I'll be note-perfect. You'll be proud of me.'

'It's not just social, you know. It is rather important.'

'Don't fuss.'

'Sorry.'

Behind them the journalist stood up, pocketed his notebook, shook hands and left. The men of letters paid their bill and prepared to follow him. Hugh looked at his watch.

'We're fine for time. We could have a drink here if you like?'

'I'm all right. We can be a little early, can't we? "O for doors to be open and an invite with golden edges / To dine with Lord Lobcock and Count Asthma on the platinum benches."'

'I'm sorry?'

'It's Auden – that's him, isn't it?'

They stood outside the hotel. Hugh creased his face up against the bright spring sunshine as he watched the poet and his friend get into a taxi and be driven away. He signalled for the embassy car which slunk up to the steps like a dog.

'You know what they are, don't you?'

'Perhaps they'll be at the garden party?' said Sally. 'We could have given them a lift there.'

Hugh put his hand on Sally's waist, let it slip down to the hard edge of her hipbone as he guided her into the car.

'They will not be there.'

The car pulled out into the dense stream of traffic. Sally had been back in Shanghai for several weeks. Her first assumption on returning – that an urgent flight should be made from Asia as soon as possible – met with with various obstructions and confusions and subtle dilutions of the will. For one thing, a number of steamer services had been cancelled and cabins on those that remained were rare and costly and might require dealing with people one should not deal with. For a formidable sum of money one could fly from Hong Kong to Penang and then hop one's way up the globe in an Empire Flying Boat all the way to London. She considered it briefly, but could find no sufficiently pressing reason for such an extravagance. The idea of flying back clarified the wintry England to which she would be so abruptly returned. Neither the season, nor the country attracted. Besides, Shanghai was at peace. The Japanese Army had long since finished its business in the native city and had settled to a steady occupation. Through fresh barbed wire and past the new sandbag blockhouses controlling the roads and bridges of the international areas, Sally could often glimpse the movement of familiar uniforms. Their aircraft flew overhead three times a day and their ships rode at anchor in the wide Whangpoo, jostling for space with the men-of-war of a dozen other nations. Within the wire, French gendarmes and British colonial police directed an unchanged life.

'I'm half packed,' said Sally.

'I've started too. Are you looking forward to it?'

'I've bought five novels and I'm going to do absolutely nothing but sit in my deck-lounger and read them and sleep, and perhaps make fun of the other passengers and have a martini every day at five, or more likely two martinis, all the way to Southampton.'

Sally looked out on a city enjoying the warm early spring of south China. The car nosed towards the French concession where the new British Ambassador's private villa awaited them and two hundred others. Sally let her mind drift cautiously over the events of the last few weeks. It had been hard at times, but it was easier now to see her disappointments as what they really were – the lessons of a more worldly and unambitious wisdom, a sort of reawakening to the requirements of a long life of peace. She stretched out her right hand and pressed it down gently on top of Hugh's. After all, what was love if it was not also endurance?

The car turned to the right. They passed the Florida Club. Sally had known it whole and had enjoyed the enticingly deplorable stories about its upstairs rooms. Now there was a V of sky cut deep into its concrete layers where a stray bomb had fallen. There had been jokes (all apocryphal) about the newspaper coverage – 'an uncertain quantity of casualties believed to comprise an equal number of ladies and gentlemen whose names we are not at liberty to divulge'. To which the response would always be 'an equal number? Now that I don't believe!' The ground and first floors had a bright, cosmetic freshness and a temporary banner sign hung above the purple doorway – BUSINESS AS USUAL, HERB WARD'S ORCHESTRA, SERVICE MEN WELCOME, CHARMING DANCE HOSTESSES. There and at the Metropole Garden, the Majestic, the Grand and the Palais Café the undefeatable danced on.

The club passed out of view. A minute later the car swung

out to make the wide curve into the driveway of the Ambassador's villa.

'Here we are.'

Hugh swallowed and checked his collar and his tie knot and the lie of his jacket in the vanity mirror. He smiled nervously at Sally.

'It'll be fun – and then the sea and martinis.'

Servants with white tunics and yellow stripes on their trouser seams walked the car to a halt. They reached out with white-gloved hands and balletically opened the doors.

Across a lurid, wintery twilight and then two hours more of sleepy, humming darkness the car pressed on to leave, at last, all trees and dry paddies behind as it nosed sluggishly through the outer labyrinth of Shanghai. The scent of the Chinese city acted on her memory as acutely as smelling salts. There was little she could see through the dark car window – it was through the fan heater that the city came – men and women, their warmth, their food, their excrement, their tobacco and opium, their trades and their sweat. Here was where she had imagined spies and been followed and watched shops being wrecked and dolls burned. Here also was where the Japanese Army had fought for control street by street while she enjoyed Nanking's last weeks of peace. Sally pressed her forehead to the window, cupped her hands around her eyes to see better into the darkness. Bicycle lamps glimmered, golden rectangles appeared as doors slid open, a noodle shop was brightly lit and a woman ran to get under its steamy canopy as the rain started. Where shells and fire had made gaps in the houses there were already ingenious replacements patched together from debris. The car stopped at the concession boundary. Cold air and a few needle spots of rain gusted in as Primrose-Browne wound down the window and showed a document to a British corporal. The barrier was raised and they were admitted to the fragile, invisible glasshouse that sustained the West. Headlights stared out everywhere, dazzling Sally as they turned across her path. A burst of jazz was briefly loud. Car horns argued over the night. Bright letters and images floated in the darkness and flashed out in green, pink and orange the attractions of movies, dance orchestras, girls. The rain thickened, pearled the window and greased the roads where all the colours mingled and destroyed themselves. Sally could make little of the scene until the car slowed without warning and she saw the wide sweep of the Cathay's steps and a bellboy running down them, struggling with a vast, monogrammed umbrella. A moment of panic tripped her heart. Was Hugh one of those figures standing near the door? What had been arranged? She had been disinclined to speak another word to Primrose-Browne and it was too late now he was standing by the car with her suitcase in hand. They went up the steps together. The door revolved, its daily polished brass and the cut edges of its many panes of glass glinting like a lighthouse as it pumped the warmth and scent of the Cathay out into the night.

'There's a room for you, of course. Just give your name, everything has been explained.'

The bellboy took the suitcase and made for the door. Sally hesitated. No one else noticed them. Primrose-Browne spoke again.

'Mr Jerrold couldn't know when we would be getting in. I can tell him right away.'

'It's late,' said Sally. 'Don't wake him.'

Inside she wrote her name in the book and blankly accepted a key and a thick sheaf of letters and telegrams. It unnerved her that 'everything had been explained' and she feared any expression of concern, spoken or even in the eyes. She followed her suitcase across the lobby, fixed on the middle distance, ready to repel any acquaintance that ill luck might put in her way. The sudden heat of the hotel made her sweat. The last six weeks of hard work and camp hygiene were not acceptable here. She was aware of her own strong smell as she stood in the lift and smiled wearily at the bellboy who took on a look of disciplined concentration as he tried so hard to pretend he had not noticed. At the room she had no money to give. She apologised and promised to see him the next day. He smiled his contempt and bowed out.

Sally was alone. She threw the letters down and looked about herself – narrow bed with bulging pillow in its starched white pillowcase above tight, cool sheets folded over and a flesh-coloured quilted satin coverlet; a table beside with glass-shaded lamp clumsily reaching for art nouveau; an armchair in the corner, wardrobe, writing desk and chair by the window behind which coiled the bulky iron pipework that filled the room with an arid heat. Muffled traffic noises strengthened as she tugged up the window sash and drew the curtains which bellied out over the cool night breeze. After a month of living without heat it became suddenly urgent for her to take her clothes off. She kicked her shoes noisily against the wall and quickly shed layer after layer, tucking her underwear under the bottom of the pile where she would not have to look at it. Another door led off. Even anticipating it made her happy and when she threw the light switch and saw the porcelain and the chrome and the glass and the heavy taps over the deep, pristine bath she experienced a leap of simple joy. She opened the taps and sat naked on the bed watching the steam drift from the bathroom as she sorted through the letters and the telegrams from London.

She put them aside. The water stung her cold feet. Over a minute she edged into its heat. She held her nose, crooked her knees and slipped under the surface, her hair floating up in a dark-centred golden circle. She rested her heels on either side of the taps and half floated, contemplating the crescents of dirt beneath her toenails, composing the words of the cable to her parents and the instructions she would give the night porter about her appointment with the hairdresser tomorrow and the two bananas and hot milk and glass of brandy and the latest English newspaper they should send up. She drained the bath, swilled away the thick grey scum, refilled it. As she waited she regarded her hazy image in the mirror. She ran the fingers of both hands through her hair, put all her weight on one leg and bent the other until only the toes rested lightly on the floor. She turned until she could just see herself with a sideways look. Perceptibly thinner than before and with the quirky, alien blondness above black delta and the untended darkness beneath her raised arms, the image had the excitement of a stranger. Her mind briefly narrated an encounter in a Turkish bath – conception faltered at the next scene and she drifted back to herself. She posed for her own entertainment, making herself a languishing odalisque, a self-regarding Venus, an Edo courtesan, a Pre-Raphaelite priestess by an incense-clouded altar. She knew she was perfect and would never be more so – here was the crisis of evanescent beauty and she would never have more to give. A powerful self-desire stirred. Not even by a full day had the burdens of work, cold, dirt and fear been lifted and here she was, the stronger power, more impatient and demanding than ever after her month of denial. Sally placed folded, prayerful hands between her legs and stared hard at the mirror in a fierce satire of modesty. She closed her eyes and pressed two fingers gently inwards.

Is that how it was? Where was Peter that moment, what would she say to Hugh tomorrow? There was a light tap on the door. Sally looked warily from the bathroom and noticed two shadows beneath the door where feet blocked the light from the corridor. The feet shifted and the tap was repeated, though no louder than before. Sally cautiously retreated and slipped into her bath for the second time.

'Just plain black? Black like mine?'

'Like mine,' said Sally. 'The way it really is.'

She inclined her head and let Mariarosa lay on professional hands.

'It's nice to be able to change your mind. I always say it's what hair's for – making mistakes and then putting them right again. I'd dye people's skins if I could – or bleach them, and everything in between, whatever they wanted and then they could just come back and change it and no one would ever know what they were really like underneath. Now that would be a good business. I'd be a rich lady if I could do that. That would be nice.'

Sally's chair rotated, pivoted and her head was guided gently backwards until cold porcelain made contact with her neck. She spent an hour and a half in Mariarosa's company, under her touch, while her little crucifix swung above her eyes like a hypnotist's watch. She learned about her two children and about her husband, unseen for five years. Sometimes she wept for him, sometimes she had nightmares about him coming back. She prayed for him every night and made his daughters do likewise. She heard all about Manila, its beauties and its claims on Mariarosa's heart, how she worked hard to get back there next year, always next year. Questions came back the other way and Sally told her story to abundant sympathy and wonder. She slipped easily on to Peter and Hugh, stopping herself only when the thought of the meeting began to disturb (she looked at the clock on the wall and made an anxious calculation). Mariarosa calmed her and Sally did not want to waste the last few minutes. She shut her eyes as a hot electric wind whipped through her hair and made her scalp tingle.

'A man's like a house my mother always told me – somewhere to lay your head at night, something solid to come back to at the end of the day. You don't want a wanderer – only come back to nothing sooner or later and what's the use of that?'

Mariarosa applied the last touches of her craft and reached for the mirror.

'There – your old self again, madam.'

A less changed face looked back.

'Perfect. Thank you.'

The note that had been slipped beneath her door had, of course, been from Hugh. With one of her own she had written about tiredness and put him off from an early-morning meeting. Now, at eleven o'clock, she faced an edgy half-hour trying to envisage what this meeting would be like. She replayed scenarios in her mind, prepared responses, worried fruitlessly at the ethics of love. She had asked him to come to her room, reasoning that the opportunity to wait before opening the door would give her a vital last moment for self-composure. In the event she arrived a few minutes late and had only the walk down the corridor to where he was waiting.

'Hello, Hugh.'

The greeting startled him, but as he turned quickly towards her his face broke into a wide and then a slightly quavering smile. They embraced and he spoke her name in a new way. His arms tightened around her and then, momentarily, she felt his weight increase as if she was supporting him. She drew back.

'Wait.'

Sally fumbled in her bag for the key and they both went in. In the room they stared at each other and made small, uncertain movements within their own isolated spaces. Neither knew this role and before many seconds had passed it seemed as if even the flowers in Hugh's hand had forgotten their lines.

'How are you?'

'Let me take those.'

Sally took the flowers, removed the dried arrangement from the vase on the writing desk and replaced them with the lilies.

'They're beautiful. Thank you.'

Hugh took her in his arms again and through his chest and the texture and scent of his jacket against her cheek she heard his voice.

'I thought you were dead. We got some reports – we knew what was happening. One day I was certain you were dead and nothing could shake the idea. There was no reason for it, but for days I was certain. I can't . . .'

The memory of it forced him to stop. He kissed her on the cheek, the brow, he stroked her hair.

'I'm fine.'

'Really?'

'Yes.'

'Completely?'

There must be a long and complicated answer to this question, a changing answer revisited over the years.

'Yes,' said Sally. 'I really am completely fine.'

She became aware of the light pressure of the bed pressing against her calves. Her body effected an almost violent change in her emotions. Was it outrageous, or just inevitable, or right? The questions faded in favour of a sense of timeliness and decent, natural necessity. Now was surely the moment and afterwards everything would be clear. Sally issued her invitation – a nuzzle, a slight bend of the knees, an eighteenth of an inch incline towards the bed. Abruptly, she found herself sitting on it as Hugh retired in confusion to the armchair and blew his nose on a dazzling handkerchief.

'So much to catch up on,' he said.

'Yes.'

'Shall we have something downstairs?'

They were alone in the sunny, glasshouse warmth of the lounge. Sally ordered hot chocolate and a glass of brandy.

'Peter?' asked Hugh.

'In clover. Well, I shouldn't say that, but you know what I mean. Anyway, he's all right.'

'I always liked Peter.'

The waiter came and poured the coffee and the chocolate. He put the glass of brandy by Hugh who waited until they were alone again before moving it to Sally's side of the table.

'It's become a habit,' he observed.

'They go well together.'

She knew she ought to ask about Sir Harold but held back from what she expected to be talk of death and a merely embarrassing expression of regret.

'I think everyone you knew in Nanking is still alive. They've all been frightfully lucky, really. The Japs are promising to let them out soon, but I suppose you know more about that than I do.'

Sally drank her brandy as Hugh talked about the war. She watched a corner of her head in a gilt-framed mirror as she meticulously worked over the tactics of a hypothetical adultery.

'So Peter could be back here soon,' she said. 'He says he'll get out as soon as he can. He has a lot of business to do here.'

'He's a good man. Sir Harold's all right.'

'Oh, yes?'

'They got the bullet out and say he'll make a full recovery.'

'That's wonderful,' said Sally a little flatly. She suggested that she must go to visit him and was relieved to hear that he had been packed off to Malaya for some recuperation before being recalled to London.

'There'll be a new man soon and they're going to keep the embassy in Shanghai now – no more Nanking, not that it will affect me.'

'Well, that's something.'

The inanity of her comment almost made Sally wince. A silence grew and threatened to become dangerous. Hugh made a run at it but was deterred at the last moment. His half-open mouth tried to disguise itself as a smile and then hid behind a coffee cup. Sally resorted to the only solution she could think of.

'Tell me about your adventures – the *Panay* and getting back here. It must have been awful.'

She listened to how the planes came and Hugh and the others could do nothing but keep out of the way as the crew went to action stations – a pointless machine gun puttering up into the evening sky and the whole boat weaving across the wide sweep of the river as the bombs came down. Hugh still didn't remember the hit, but coming to on deck he found blood on his face and the grit of shattered glass between his teeth. His ears rang and the chaos around him was muffled and remote. He thought really that he had been pushed into the river by a crew member. If only for reasons of style it became a jump in the retelling and then an athletic swim for the shore, the coldness of the water, the exhausting drag of a full set of winter clothes. The survivors shivered on the banks, crouched among reeds as Japanese motor launches raked the sinking *Panay* and her lifeboats with machine guns. More bombs fell. Junks were shattered and in the quietness afterwards Hugh heard the screams of dying Chinese coming faintly across the water. A storekeeper was dead and the captain of a merchantman travelling with them and the Italian journalist Sandri whom he had seen stumbling from the wardroom, holding the hopeless wound in his belly and proclaiming his own death. She heard of hours of walking, of buying beds at the first village and breaking them up to make stretchers, of the donkey for the wounded American diplomat, their relief at reaching the first telephone and the ensuing confusion before they were finally taken on board the USS *Oahu* and HMS *Bee* and brought back down the river to Shanghai, escorted by two unapologetic Japanese gunboats.

Hugh wandered on in self-absorbed detail about the diplomatic correspondence between Washington, London and Tokyo. Sally made attentive noises but went her own way, encountering a problem that had been building since earlier in the morning when the hotel confirmed that private cables could still not be sent to Nanking. They could be sent through the embassy, but only with Hugh's help. She puzzled over what she could ask Hugh to send to Peter. She became physically uncomfortable with the effort, but still it defied solution. She resolved it by believing that Peter would be in Shanghai before the end of the week. She listened vaguely to Hugh winding up his story. He was handsome – durable too. Had she ever been more confused, less capable of decision?

'. . . of course that was a pack of lies, but everyone just agreeed to ignore it in the end and it all came to nothing.

Wars have been started for less. Sir Harold's come out all right – there's been a vote of thanks for his efforts in the House and an ex gratia payment. I saw a copy of a note from the Cabinet Secretary – "The Prime Minister considered that some value should be put on the life of a British Ambassador." Five thousand pounds, apparently. By the way, I shouldn't have told you that.'

He smiled, then looked at his watch.

'Well,' said Sally, 'it's been ghastly for you and I'm sorry. You've been a very brave boy.'

She leaned forward to kiss him on the cheek.

'Not really,' said Hugh. 'Do you remember when the boat pulled away from Hsiakwan?'

'Yes.'

'And you were left behind?'

'I remember.'

'When I looked back all I could see was fire – just where you had been. It's not brave when you don't care any more.'

Time passed. The days ticked down to the date on her liner tickets when the *Brittanicus* would take her and Hugh (a decorous ten cabins apart) back to England. The preservation of their original plans seemed a sort of triumph, a gesture of imperturbability against everything that had conspired to knock them off course. Emotionally too, it reassured. Sally was making a choice and she felt more confident when the external world arranged its symbols to back her up. At the very least the sailing schedule of the Peninsular and Oriental Steamship Company did not contradict her heart – another featherweight drifting down on one side of the balance. A flurry of cables to and from London eventually persuaded her parents that she was alive and unharmed. Slower, longer letters followed. There was always a notice in the papers — US AND EUROPEAN MAIL DUE TODAY — and she would queue in the central post office. There were remonstrations from her mother, stern orders to survive for her sake, and one from her father she kept in a special place — apologies and a rare profession of love.

Peter did not come. A telegram was sent at the first opportunity, but it explained nothing. Hugh was constantly attentive. There were flowers and gifts, some of them expensive. She never spent an evening or a weekend alone. She pondered flirtatiousness, infatuation, the conspiracies of circumstance and emotion — a night on a plaster-dusted sofa, trapped in a half-ruined building, danger all around, warmth and safety in the arms of a handsome adventurer. It was enjoyable enough to be the heroine of a bad novel for a week or two, but later, when neither was still right for the part and the youthful story rolled brutally on — what then? She thought of her parents. The way they lived the quiet flatness of their lives took on the qualities of virtue. Whether she had grown in Nanking or been broken by it she was not sure, but to have some idea of where and what she would be in five years, or in ten, now seemed very precious. There were understandings too and a tiredness that made her reluctant to break anything, even something so frail as an understanding.

Her days were her own. She dipped cautiously into the old social life. Margery Berkshire was briefly reputed to have exited in fire and glory in the Florida Club bombing.

'We thought she should get a VC,' an old socialite told her one lunchtime. 'For Venus!'

There was no truth in it, of course, and it was Margery's own predatory cry that stopped Sally one morning as she crossed the lobby of the hotel. She found herself at a charity party that afternoon. She listened to speeches and gave for

Chinese war orphans. Later, at the Cathay, she locked her door, wept and ignored the phone. She was happier alone after that. She learned the bars and cafés of the city and would sit until early evening, looking out through glass half obscured with signage in English, French, Russian, Hebrew and Chinese. She idled with the papers – MAJESTIC – HAND GRENADE THREAT DISPERSES DANCERS; WAR NOT TO AFFECT OLYMPIC GAMES IN 1940, SAYS JAPAN; UKRAINIAN PREMIER TAKES OWN LIFE; A DOG'S HEALTH CANNOT BE DETERMINED BY THE TEMPERATURE OF ITS NOSE; FOREIGNER MAY HAVE CHOLERA; SHELL FALLS AT FEET OF BEAUTY – BATHING-CONTEST WINNER CHEATS DEATH; SEE HUMPHREY BOGART IN 'LIFE IN THE RAW VS. MAN-MADE LAW' PUNCHTASTIC THRILLODRAMA!; PSYCHIC – THE MOST RELIABLE EVER TO VISIT CHINA. IF MADAME HELEN PIPER CANNOT SEE YOUR DESTINY IN THE CRYSTAL BALL NO FEE WILL BE TAKEN; GERMAN JOURNALIST KILLED IN DUEL TO UPHOLD HONOUR – CAUSE OF DISPUTE UNKNOWN; IMPERIAL ARMY SHEATHES BAYONETS IN HARMONIOUS NANKING.

Dark, solitary and distracting, the city's numerous cinemas also gave Sally what she needed. She sat through many a thinly attended matinée as Marlene Dietrich slunk danger-ously through *The Garden of Allah*, Paderewski played in *Moonlight Sonata* and Cagney held the line in *G-Men*. The Paramount News would follow and *Popeye the Sailor Man* would send them on their way. They were places for meet-ings. Several times young men, and the not so young, greeted her with hopeful warmth and tried out their opening phrases. The films played on her imagination. Alternative lives became clearer, the supposed costs of transgression as unreal as the pictures on the screen. She drank with one of these men in a café nearby – coffee and the cognac Hugh would later smell on her breath. She didn't pause in her anecdote when she felt the touch beneath the table. Calling it an experiment, an objectively curious enquiry as to how far things would go, she did nothing to stop the tentative move to the inside of her leg, nor the courteously slow upward advance, halted only by the gentlest of pressures as she moved her thighs together.

'I have a flat nearby.'

Sally looked down and stirred the lees of her coffee. He was an Englishman. A banker, he said.

'We could be very happy for a few hours.'

Sally explained, not entirely clearly, her situation and apologised for wasting his time. They talked on for a few minutes and parted in civilised regret. Everything she had been told about such men appeared not to be true. She returned sadly to the hotel, jostled by the first of Shanghai's nightbirds – sing-song girls with snaky, hot-curled hair; bath-house boys leaning by anonymous doorways as they trawled the crowds with smiles; optimists queuing by the blue posters for lottery tickets, soldiers and sailors urgent on short passes; taxi dancers hurrying to clubs for another night's hire.

She wrote to Minnie and Rabe and spent as much money as she dared filling boxes with jam and tins of butter and chocolate and aspirin and sulphanilamide and a few phials of insulin she extracted at last from a reluctant pharmacist. She took Peter's films to be developed. The Chinese assistant examined her intently when she went to collect them. She asked if they had made an extra copy for themselves. He denied it nervously and fumbled with the money.

'Don't you think you should?' asked Sally. 'I can leave them with you for another day.'

The young man confessed. As she left, a Japanese soldier on leave stepped back smartly from the doorway. Just a handsome, shy boy – bowing and solemn-faced, just as he had been before his elementary-school teachers less than a decade before.

Sally wandered to another part of the city, in need of somewhere strange. She sat outside in the cool, bright day having, as was so often the case in Shanghai, crossed half the world in a quarter-mile. Polish, Russian and German filled the air. The latter, familiar accents made her think of Rabe as she watched the Jews gather for synagogue. She remembered his Christmas dinner, now settled in her mind as a half-funny, half-sad blend of Peace Conference and child's tea party. Obedient to her promise, she composed her letter to Mr Chamberlain. It never sounded right – something too high-flown about the rhetoric, a desperate reliance on the power of words themselves precisely because there was nothing else to rely on. She felt it would make the reader laugh, that a civil servant would shake his head in world-weary despair and direct it on to a pile of earnest school-girl exercises distilled from the latest editions of the Left Book Club.

Sally looked through the photographs, unmoved except at finding herself among the dead.

On the stage Sid's Cathay Syncopators were hitting their stride. Smoke hung in the air – Virginia and Egyptian – and the lights were low and sunset red. Sally watched the waiter's back as he negotiated the tables. She picked up the gin and it he had left by her hand. Hugh was in a high mood. He opened the silver square of his cigarette case and held it out to her.

'I saw Peter today.'

Orange and yellow circles of light ran around the bell of the trumpet. Its high, human cry took on the same colour. Sally looked into its dark centre as the metal seemed to extend and flatten like clay in a potter's hands. She stuck her chin out to hold the end of her Chesterfield over Hugh's lighter.

'Really?'

'He seems well. Got out without any problems in the end.'

'So you had a chat with him?'

'Yes, for quite a while. He was asking about you. I said I would be seeing you this evening and he sends his regards.'

Sally guessed (or perhaps hoped) that some tiny detail had been lost in the translation. She wondered what this conversation could have contained – how to go fishing in these waters?

'So, did he tell you about Nanking?'

'Didn't want to talk about that much and I thought it best not to ask.'

An ample black woman stepped up to the microphone. From an octave below she followed the trumpet. She closed her eyes, produced a tear on the upbeat, surged upwards to meet and then overwhelm the note as it became a word. Sally concentrated hard on the singer's face, diminishing Hugh's presence to a shadowy profile far to her left. She wouldn't turn to check, but she felt sure he was examining her. She became edgy, as physically uncomfortable as if she were being intruded upon by a stranger. Then he was close enough for her to feel his heat. She heard his voice beneath the song – cautious and tightly measured.

'He has some letters for you. I think he said he was staying at the press club.'

The cabaret was good. It rescued the evening which ended with a kiss on the steps of the Cathay. Sally took her key and the folded sheet of paper from the night porter. In the overheated room she threw off her clothes, letting them drop here and there about the floor. She stood naked by the window, dimly backlit by the bedside lamp, high enough for discretion's sake, perhaps just visible as a blessing for a late-night walker on the Bund below. She sat on the bed and opened the note to find, in Peter's handwriting, a time and a place.

They talked in a Russian café – sweet, scented tea in glasses and dripping honey cakes to be eaten cube by cube with miniature forks. Avatars of Lenin and Trotsky huddled and laughed in a corner. They established that both were well. They commented on the weather, the tea and the news from Spain in that morning's paper. There were no European fatalities to report from Nanking. Sally handed over the photographs.

'Hugh said you had some letters.'

'I thought I had.'

'Well, we'll just have to make some up. So you had quite a talk, Hugh tells me. A chance meeting?'

'Not exactly – he knew I was here. It's easy for him to know who's coming and going.'

'How long?'

Peter offered a cigarettte, lit them both with a match. The waiter came with an ashtray, took away the plates and poured more tea.

'Ten days,' said Peter. 'You didn't know I was here?'

Sally began to give up on the game and let the tone of her voice rise.

'How was I supposed to? Ask a policeman, ask Hugh perhaps – is that it?'

'He did tell you.'

'In his own time – or did you come to an arrangement between yourselves? Have you sorted things out, who's going to get what?'

The Russians raised their heads. Sally glared back and made Peter laugh when she demanded, 'Need a translation?' Only the mention of a policeman had interested them and they turned back to themselves.

'Well at least I don't embarrass you, Peter. Just think how Hugh would be suffering now.'

'No, Sally. You don't embarrass me.'

Rain started. They looked out as rickshaw coolies paused to hood their vehicles before pulling on. Enraged drivers set up a fanfare of car horns.

'I saw you about a week ago,' said Peter. 'I was going to the hotel.'

Sally was miserable and angry with everything.

'Perhaps I should go blonde again – would that help? Tell me what men want, Peter.'

'I followed you. You were with Hugh.'

The rain strengthened. A couple ran into the café, shaking drops from mackintoshes. As the light failed the window became a mirror. Sally looked through a faint image of her own face on to a dreary scene that could, with so few changes, be London or Paris.

'I don't know. I just don't know. Take me to the pictures – tomorrow.'

In the heated, afternoon darkness over the next few weeks they sat together as Laurel and Hardy sang of the Lonesome Pine, as Jerry and Lucy sneered and snapped at each other only to learn in the end of *The Awful Truth* about their love, as Snow White woke to Prince Charming's kiss. From time to time they spoke a little about Nanking, though only to each other. Peter sold a few of his pictures – a statuesque General Matsui inspecting the victors from his charger, the old walls fringed with the silhouettes of soldiers, arms raised in banzai salute. The others were of no interest. He took work on the society pages to make ends meet – Mr Hugh Jerrold and his young friend Miss Sally Marsden of Hertfordshire at the Jockey Club Benevolent Dance. But it was Sally and Peter who saw the picture first as they read the morning papers together in Café de la Paix.

'You are wicked, Peter. You've made me look fat – you're trying to put him off.'

'*Au contraire*, my dear. I have made you the talk of Shanghai. I shall never have you now.'

As friends they made a joke romance for themselves, sharpened by the joke poignancy of Sally's future with another man. Together they had learned the eroticism of violence, and together too they learned the suddenness of its withdrawal as soon as the source of its dangerous energies was shut off. Sally always let Hugh know when she had seen Peter. He would be pleased and say how important it was for her not to get bored during the day. He was eager not to be a jealous man and understood also how the slightest thrill of the clandestine could rekindle whatever might have happened in Nanking, whatever Peter had not wanted to tell him. His virtues remained clearly on display and when, in those sudden, unbidden moments of clarity, Sally saw the frighteningly long future set out before her all at once, they seemed to be even more worth holding on to.

The early southern spring began to take hold. Postal services to Nanking became more reliable and she corresponded with Minnie and John Rabe. The situation was not getting worse – except for the murder of collaborators. There was a flurry in the British community as the new man arrived from London. The date was set for the garden party at which he would entertain all those who mattered in Shanghai. Tremulous with excitement, Margery Berkshire went about describing it to all who would listen as 'an event of the first order'. Certainly, it would be the first of its kind since the invasion itself. It fell a few days short of the departure of the *Brittanicus* and thus promised a restoration and an ending at once. An anxiety worried at Hugh – an impediment, a social uncertainty as sharp as grit in his shoe. What would Sally be at such an event? In a cinema, an ill-lit nightclub and indeed in broad daylight at a less formal event there was no difficulty. But he was conscious of how much he had already been indulged. The new man from London would come as a London man, not as a Shanghai man understanding Shanghai ways, and it would be a shame for Hugh if he were to stumble at the last. These calculations nerved him for the task and he managed it at last one Sunday morning with a stammer and a circumlocution of such utter opacity that it spoke of great things for his future in the Foreign Office. Sally understood only when a tiny box appeared – blue shagreen, brass button catch, black velvet and white silk within. Hugh took out the ring – white gold, a diamond in a pentagon of sapphires. He took Sally's hand and she straightened her fingers to receive it. An announcement appeared in the papers the next day.

Hugh's mind was rested, Sally's too. It was, surely, as part of this new clarity that she should accept an invitation from Peter to meet him early in the botanical gardens on the day of the garden party.

'It'll be a tiring day,' he had argued. 'You need to make a good start to it. There's nothing better than a walk in the gardens and early is best.'

Save for the gardeners they were alone. A discreet mist collected thickly in the hollows. The glasshouses were unlocked just for them and they walked through a Victorian bubble of permanent summer.

'So you won't be with us this afternoon?'

'That's right – strictly no press, not even men with cameras and stepladders peeking over the wall. A private function.'

'Well, I shall tell you all about it, then you can have a

scoop and they can run around wondering where you got it from.'

'Most undiplomatic.'

'You protect your sources, don't you?'

'To the death.'

Arms brushed together as they left the glasshouse. They walked hand in hand over lawns shaded by vast cedars, down paths by formal beds. The first narcissi were in bloom. Magnolias were brilliant – extravagant, gaslit chandeliers of petals. By the grotto, bronze children sheltered from an unceasing monsoon beneath a bronze umbrella. Fresh green spears sprouted from near their feet, already beginning to unfold leaves the size of elephants' ears. Peter suddenly spoke.

'You're doing the right thing.'

He would not look at her and when she asked him if it was a question or a statement the silence was long.

'It's a statement,' he said at last. 'It's what I believe – best for both of us. We'd have been fools otherwise, don't you think?'

They wandered on – now in China, now passing a geometric bed straight from a Manchester municipal park. A statue moved, becoming an old man at his morning exercises. Peter's reassurance didn't come and he persisted.

'I mean, to try to make a life on – what? On a moment.'

Sally squeezed his hand until he felt the hard ridge of the ring. They drifted towards the exit where the traffic was already building on Avenue Joffre.

'Yes,' said Sally. 'Of course it's right. The cobbler should stick to his last, isn't that what they say?'

They stood together on the threshold. Peter put his hands about her waist and turned her towards him. They looked each other in the eye for the first time that morning.

'Don't misunderstand, Sally, please. All I want is to be able to say I never did you any harm, that I never held you back or made you unhappy for some reason of my own.'

From behind her back he signalled to a taxi. When she turned it had already stopped and the door was open as if conjured there just for her, to hasten the parting. She got into it without speaking another word. It took her to the Cathay where she bathed and breakfasted in her room, thought of nothing through the long, painstaking preparation, finally approving herself in the mirror, going down to wait in the lounge, flirting with the pianist, spying on poets, being kissed and adored by Hugh and driven through the city until the uniformed servants stood by and she and Hugh walked together over the freshly raked gravel towards the beflagged portico of Number One House.

What was left of that afternoon on the lawn? Little enough, to be sure, that first night when Sally lay alone in her room at the Cathay amid a litter of suitcases – the telephone a burning ordeal, too hot by far for her to lift, however passionately she prayed for it to ring. The end was still there, but only the end – the ninety-nine other hundredths hidden behind its magnesium flash. What did they matter now, a handful of cut threads? She sensed their presence, preserved behind the glare, and how they would emerge again over the coming days and years.

Sir Algernon Farquhar-Starr, still a little dazed by his good fortune, greeted his guests assiduously, meeting every one himself on the sound reasoning that he could not yet be sure which were important and which could be safely ignored. He fluently received the French, but with such uncompromisingly English vowels that he set their teeth on edge. He did better with the numerous Germans, diplomatic and commercial, and inspired the Japanese with gratitude for managing a few words of their language at all. The representatives of Chiang Kai-shek had already suggested to half a dozen journalists that they had been snubbed in their own country and now did their best to make this true by deliberately arriving late. The Italians felt that they had received less than their due. A Korean industrialist was obliged to leave after being mistaken for a Chinese and a servant had to stand between the two consuls from the two Spains to prevent an even greater embarrassment. It was a solid start and Sir Algernon appeared to have inspired the contempt only of his own kind.

'What does he think he is doing standing there all that time? He might at least have ignored the Italians,' Sally overheard from a congested Englishman gesturing vigorously with a canapé. 'I mean, you have to decide – do you want an ambassador or a cinema commissionaire? That last chap was just the ticket.'

The woman who could only be his wife stood by. She smiled a wan apology towards Sally as she echolessly absorbed his rhetoric – this day, as every day, for the last forty years. A further gust of indignation sent a flake of pastry fluttering from her husband's beard.

'It's all going so well,' Lady Farquhar-Starr was heard to say, the strain making her features sharp and five years older than they really were. Sally observed her from a distance and recited silently that her own future would only be what she made it. She took a glass of champagne from a table.

For some, even hell is heaven, and there indeed was Margery Berkshire enjoying once again the heights of existence that, only a few months before, had threatened never to come again. She incised her way through the now considerable crowd, sustained above the literal firmament on a bow wave of caustic bons mots.

'At least they've kept the hyphen, that's always something.

I had a soft spot for Sir Harold, you know. And he for me, if truth be told.'

A passer-by let out a derisive hack of laughter.

A moment later an elderly, rotund and baffled German with a Hindenburg moustache found himself looking down at this strange woman and wondering why she was addressing him and what she could possibly be saying.

'I wonder if the FO has been wise,' she speculated loudly. 'My grandmother had a dog called Farquhar and we children had to take him to the park. Well, we became quite reluctant after a while. He would always misbehave and what can you do? There are some names not fit to be shouted out in a public place. Ah, *Entschuldigung bitte!* I've just seen someone I do want to talk to.'

Sally watched her cross to the far side of the lawn where an iron fence marked the start of the long grass and the river bank beyond. She accosted this person to whom she did want to talk and he seemed very pleased. She hooked her arm through his and they moved regally among the other guests. A word or two of the man's voice came to Sally and completed the memory she was struggling to make clear. Here again was that anonymous conversationalist from one of her first encounters with the Shanghai beau monde; the traducer of Lady Berkshire's authenticity, his mind magnetised by her wealth, the fabled squalor of its origins and the prospect of getting close to it.

The presence at Sally's elbow, which she had been trying hard to ignore for the last two minutes, finally spoke up. This self-possessed and rather striking man in his middle thirties smiled with worldly indulgence on Margery Berkshire and her companion. Sally tried to identify the very slight accent in his excellent English, but in the end couldn't even guess at his nationality.

'You know Mrs Berkshire?'

He asked the question as if it were some sort of subtle joke that only the two of them would understand.

'Don't tell me you want an introduction,' said Sally.

'There is no vacancy there, I think.' He indicated the man on Margery's arm. 'She already has her *parasite du jour.*'

Infected by everything around her, Sally spoke in someone else's voice.

'I'm sorry, I think you want someone to admire your wit and I can't help you there.'

The man apologised suavely and withdrew, leaving Sally miserably alone. She placed her empty glass on a passing salver and picked up another. She could feel the alcohol pulsing heavily against her brain and the beginings of a gentle sea swell beneath her feet. She reviewed the tables, bowed beneath their elaborate extravagance of food, but could find no appetite. With a jaded eye she watched the Seaforth Highlanders play their instruments. Dressed for half a century ago and a little prematurely in their summer tunics, they gave the impression of a flock of cockatiels blown down on to some Surrey garden by a centennial storm. Behind them, the awesome lead-grey bulk of HMS *Birmingham* slid silently by on the oily stillness of the river. Sally swallowed champagne like water, discreetly belched out its bubbles into the warm spring afternoon and began to indulge the feeling that some invisible hand was favouring her by nudging the last pieces of a puzzle into place.

For the first hour Hugh and Sally had been together, though she had been forewarned that she might at some time have to do her own socialising.

'These things can become a bit of a working lunch' was how Hugh had put it. 'You don't mind, do you? You know plenty of people here.'

It was easy at first. Congratulations took up the first minute or two (everyone had seen the announcement in the paper) and then, with women, there was the admiring of the ring and the questions about arrangements. A dozen times they admitted that nothing had yet been done and a dozen times they gratefully accepted the advice to start at once as there was always too much to do and always a rush at the end. With men Sally needed only to smile when they told Hugh what a good job he had done in making an honest woman of her.

Sir Algernon and Lady Farquhar-Starr were charmed by these handsome ghosts of their younger selves.

'You've got a good thing here, Hugh, I must say. What could I have done without my Frances? No man gets far in the service without a good wife and a good solid hobby. One would go mad without them. Arc you interested in pipes, Hugh?'

'Oh, don't be silly, Algie – of course he isn't.'

Sir Algernon seemed genuinely crestfallen. For three decades Lady Farquhar-Starr's glassy contempt for his life's one enduring and wholly absorbing passion had caused him constant pain. He put on a manful expression and gave nothing away as his wife briefed Sally on her future. He looked about himself and shifted his feet as the need to slip away and dust his racks became all-important.

'My dear,' his wife confided to Sally, 'you must reconcile yourself to marrying the service as well as the man. Allow just a little space for this mistress and then say, "No further!" and all will be well. Isn't that right, Algie? Oh, where is he now?'

A man from the Hong Kong and Shanghai Bank whispered in Hugh's ear – he had to go and Sally was cast off to drift her own way through the guests. She nodded distantly to

Primrose-Brown who, even though he had found himself becalmed at the same time, was unwilling to cross the grass to talk to her. A group of German, French and Chinese industrialists briefly took her in. A salacious review of the latest scandal was coming to an end. It was the high fashion of crime in Shanghai and threatened to knock the opium business down to second place for the first time in a century – the abduction of women by Chinese gangsters, their herding on to railway trucks in the middle of the night and sale to Japanese military brothels in the interior. Everyone was talking about it. The police knew nothing. There was even said to be a film on the way – an American policeman on holiday and a kung-fu master were going to sort it all out. They turned to business, the Germans quickly forming an impassioned bloc furious with their own government.

'Why after all this time does Berlin suddenly fall in love with Japan? For twenty years I've done business in China and never had an enemy. Now I have to apologise for being a German every day. My oldest friends are very kind, but do they renew their orders? No – they have their pride.'

'It's the same for me,' said another. 'I shall have to sell up by the end of the year if things don't improve.'

'I tell them I'm an Austrian,' said the third.

'Do they know the difference?'

'It needs some explaining, but it helps in the end.'

The Frenchman looked bored as he followed the passage of a shapely female form across the grass. The Chinese owner of an armature winding concern smiled compassionately at these foreigners and considered his own future with assurance.

'You must know John Rabe,' blurted Sally a little too suddenly, perhaps.

The Germans looked blank.

'Siemens? In Nanking?'

'They're not in Nanking now, are they?' one asked of another.

'Well, I thought they'd shut down – what does he do?'

A gentle crescendo of social laughter saved her from further difficulty. They looked over to the neighbouring group. There was the Japanese Ambassador, the First and Second Secretaries and a uniformed military attaché. Sir Algernon and Hugh completed the circle. Briefly, the Japanese spoke among themselves. The rhythm and tone of their language came to Sally and fell on her like a shadow.

'They think they're going to win,' said the man by her side. 'That's why they're doing it.'

The Chinaman smiled. The ruined Germans shook their heads.

'Madness.'

Sally drifted on, scooping up a pink gin and staring at strangers until they looked away. She developed a theory that it was proper to be drunk in such company and another glass of champagne confirmed it. A man put his hand on her elbow and she found Mr Brindle, sleek with success from his latest trip, delighted by her engagement, delighted by her survival. He summoned some friends so they could hear his tales of danger and death on the Nanking Road confirmed.

'Here she is,' he brayed. 'Here's the young lady I was telling you about, the very same.'

He continued to talk as Sally walked serenely away. People were looking at her and she did nothing to discourage them. They seemed to have become players and she the unique member of their audience. The one who had paid (a little guiltily, no doubt), and ducked under a low beam to some dingy freak show in a nameless quarter. Here was Margery again, clinging to another captive's arm.

'But what will they call her then – assuming, of course, they're going to be here for any length of time? Lady F? But I thought we had some of those already!'

Sally exchanged a more sympathetic acknowledgement, but did not stop. As if an adjustment had been made to some small but crucial wheel in the instrument of her mind, everything became quieter and more distant. For all she cared or was aware of, she might be spying on these people from the other side of the river. Faces became interesting only because of their resemblances – hints of Minnie, John and Peter appeared everywhere. Others hinted at Delage or Podshivaloff (how happy she would have been to find him just then), a servant must be Chang. She scrutinised people closely, as if she must know them well. When they were about to speak to her she moved away in disappointment. Hugh signalled for her to join them and she did so, just as the Seaforth Highlanders changed their tune and everyone agreed to ignore the remote and disordered percussion underneath.

Sally was introduced to the Japanese delegation as Hugh's fiancée. There was an outbreak of delight at making her acquaintance and much bowing. Sally opened hostilities immediately by presenting her hand to each man and keeping it there through their hesitations until they were forced to accede to this Western gesture. She held their eyes from an equal height and advanced charmingly on the military attaché.

'But I think we've met before, do you remember?'

Sir Algernon spotted a fellow pipe enthusiast and made his apologies. The attaché gave a nervous eyes right in the direction of his ambassador, as if in hope of some telegraphed instructions.

'I don't think so, madam.'

'Oh yes, but I'm sure. It was in Nanking – have you been there recently?'

He cast a more frankly pleading look towards his superiors, and then shook his head.

'Your brother perhaps?' Sally persisted. 'You have a twin? I remember it clearly – he was . . . Well, let's leave that for now.'

Hugh was pressing her arm in panic, but the Japanese seemed genuinely not to have understood. Ten semiquaver beats of a machine gun sounded weakly from across the river. Here and there watches were consulted and excuses made. Margery's excited tones cut through the hubbub. The Ambassador of Japan was unperturbed.

'You are going home soon, Mr Jerrold tells me. Have you enjoyed your time in China?'

'Very much so,' said Sally. 'The people are so civilised. They have such – how shall I put it? – endurance.'

The delegation sighed with relief. They warmly agreed on the qualities of Chinese civilisation. While a man who had begun to use the word 'guerrillas' too loudly was led away, the Ambassador built up to a rhetorical declaration of love.

'That is what you must explain at home, Miss Marsden. How much Japan loves China, how much it is our privilege to help her. What else could make us shoulder this great burden if not love?'

The shots sounded again – a short, swift run and the new, individual pulses of a higher calibre weapon. The Ambassador waved them away.

'Our own troops. Target practice, that's all.'

Sally felt sick and unsteady. The Ambassador was smiling at her. He seemed to be enjoying her company. Elsewhere, a sly collective shift in the direction of the front courtyard continued. Servants were summoned and sent out into the road to marshal the chauffeurs.

'Love?' said Sally.

'Have you travelled in Japan?' he asked her.

'No.'

'I hope you will. Things are very different there. One would say it is another world. And yet in thirty years' time China will be just like Japan. There will be hardly any difference at all. That will be our great gift to China – the way good parents gift their virtues to their children, at any cost.'

With a half-educated ear Sally detected the approach of aero-engines. Together with the military attaché she looked up and southwards, but nothing could be seen. Only Margery and her gentleman friend headed for the source of the noise, walking down the lawn towards the fence and the river. Sally watched as her foot found an unevenness in the grass and she stumbled briefly against his arm. The Seaforth Highlanders packed away their instruments. From the road there came the sounds of engines starting and the wheels of limousines crunching the gravel.

'If I might be allowed an impertinence,' said the Ambassador, 'you will have children, Miss Marsden. They will carry all your hopes and they will grow up strong and honourable under such fine parents. Sometimes they will make mistakes and you will correct them just as Japan corrects China. So you see – it is love.'

'I was in Nanking.'

The Ambassador smiled and nodded.

'Ah, yes. I hear it is a very beautiful city.'

She took a step towards him and felt Hugh's hand tight around her wrist.

'No, you don't understand. I was in Nanking. I was there.'

'And in the future,' said the Ambassador, 'it will be even more beautiful.'

The engines were louder. They had the steady tone of a

direct approach. There was more firing from the far side of the river and the Japanese spoke among themselves. The aircraft appeared – four in a tight diamond formation. There was a sudden crescendo of target practice. Margery, a hundred yards distant, was cut out darkly against the bright surface of the river. She waved and hooted at the departing guests.

'See how they run. From this . . .' She raised her arms up against the blue in a gesture Sally knew well. '. . . this caviar!'

The planes surged on and the futile gunfire died away. It was over, save for one last wasteful, meaningless rattle. People were looking away when an engine raced on full throttle. The last plane pitched upwards and climbed almost vertically into the sky. The noise became still more shrill as it passed the perpendicular, slowed and turned upside down. It rushed downwards before pulling up again with sickening violence to make another perfect circle. The sound of clapping came from the end of the lawn. Margery danced and shouted.

'Well done. Oh, well done. Bravo!'

The plane looped faster and faster. White streamed from its wing tips into the moist air. Six times it went round, drawing a huge white zero against the blue. At the height of the seventh circle the engine fainted. The plane tipped sideways. The nose turned down before the engine found its rhythm again. The crippled pilot, convulsed against his own controls, flew faster than any falling stone into the blank steel of the river and was fabulously changed to a fountain. Spray hissed down on to the water. Momentarily, a dark tail could be seen through the haze – an absurd whale until it too dived out of sight.

The others had gone and now only Hugh, Sally and the attaché stood together in a line. Margery, forced to abandon her belief in an aerobatic display, cheerfully changed the object of her excitement. She whistled with a hooligan's skill, cupped her hands around her mouth and bellowed congratulations across the river.

'Bull's-eye!'

The attaché saluted and turned to follow the rest of his delegation. Hugh slipped an arm around Sally's waist. He smoothed a lock of hair from her temple and kissed her there.

'Are you all right?'

She said nothing. Hugh took a deep breath.

'Well, one to remember, I suppose. Come on – I think we can go now.'

Thirty guests milled in the front courtyard waiting for their cars. Everyone was smoking or laughing. The gunfire over, they began to relax. There was a jam in the road outside and ineffectual attempts by embassy servants to unsnarl it. Every minute a car would get in and collect three or four people before trying to push its way out again.

'I'll just have a word with Sir Algernon.'

Sally found herself alone. Her vision swam and she put her head down to clear it. She squinted along the unfocused side of her nose and saw how pale she had become. Nausea and excitement tangled in her stomach. She watched the Japanese delegation's car pull slowly round the courtyard and come to a halt in front of the portico. The four men got in, the Ambassador making himself comfortable by the open window. He was smiling, leaning out to complete his good-byes. Nothing more was needed. She was walking very fast, in the hold of a sudden triggered impulse, if no longer to dominate life (that childish ambition had quite gone now), at least to mark it, to leave unforgettably that welted, scarlet double crescent where the teeth had caught and all but met clean through the flesh of experience itself. Here was one to remember. She bent down by the car window – so certain now. Everyone could see that something was wrong. But she went further, so much further and they could hardly understand the sharp, animal breath and that tiny pause in the middle as Sally caught at the gathered saliva in her mouth and threw it out with all her strength.

Sally took her hand from the telephone – sober now and not a new person after all. Courage was a strange thing. Circumstance made it for the moment, as singular as a key to fit one lock once only. And after the transfiguration, the falling back and the old self again, the dog at one's heels, only less acceptable for having been so nearly eluded. Why did no one call? She got another glass of water from the bathroom. She failed again to shut off the seized radiator valve and pushed the window open a few more inches. She was hungry but believed the room-service staff must be talking about her and so would not call. She drank and looked down on the glittering curve of the Bund. A pattern of high stacked lights showed where the bank was, steadily sinking into the silt beneath (so everyone said) such was the tonnage of gold in its vaults. She packed a few more things in a suitcase, closed it, opened it again, sat down on the bed. Everyone must know. Peter must know. Wasn't he curious, even if it was just professionally? She looked again at the telephone, but no effort of will would make it ring. She thought of her parents and of the morning's newspapers. She had to fight harder not to cry. It was all nonsense, it would all pass and life was long.

Half an hour of vigorous packing steadied her nerves and when she heard the knock on her door she was ready to admit that none of it mattered quite as much as she had thought. She hesitated all the same, considering the option of remaining silent. There was another tap and a purposeful clearing of the throat she immediately recognised. Her name was spoken quietly through the door. She opened it and found Hugh looking pale, disordered and dramatically miserable. He mumbled something.

'Hugh?'

He swallowed and seemed to feel some pain when he met her eyes.

'I'm sorry. I . . . Look, I'm just so sorry. I really . . .'

Sally didn't like it, but she didn't deny it either — as she felt again how his weakness strengthened her so instantly, as if it was what she had most needed.

'Hugh, what's wrong? Come in.'

He sat on the bed, fumbled uncertainly inside his jacket then pressed his palms on his knees. Sally began her own apologies but stopped when Hugh held up his hand.

'I've chosen you. That's what I came here to say. Maybe it won't work now — I'll understand. But I chose you anyway, whether I can have you or not.'

He took out a folded sheet of paper and laid it on the bed.

'I've resigned.'

12

C lothes, blankets, a towel or two and the coverlet with its embroidered insignia lay about the floor rucked into the contours of rough water. The bed stood in the middle, a white solidity, an atoll in the 4 a.m. gloom just big enough for the saving of two souls. The stillness and heaviness of the air and the engine's calm bass note sounding through the steel might cast a spell of reverence on any watcher. In cryptic darkness the figures could be funerary, a carved lid inscribed around the edges with the names and virtues of the dust within. These ones moved. One plucked away the last sheet and let it slide to the floor. They embraced more closely and their voices sounded wordlessly in sleep. The incense was theirs, and the moisture too that clouded the porthole glass and collected at the bottom of its bright brass frame, dropping dew on a spray of everlasting blooms.

Sally stirred and ran a hand over her lover – she examined and learned the hard bone in the centre of the chest, the ridges of the ribs on either side, the strange firmness of the pectoral muscles and the softer, darker skin of the nipples as small and pointless as a child's. She wriggled down to lie on his abdomen. It became hard as he shifted his position, softened again as he relaxed and seemed, by his breathing, to be still asleep. Her second finger fitted his navel with a perfection that could not, she thought, possibly be coincidence. She pressed gently inwards till the ring of skin reached the first joint. She moved it to and fro until a rumble came from above and she withdrew. Just below, a ventral line of hair began. With her eye so close Sally could see each short black bristle as it was pressed against the skin by her fingertip and sprang up again as she moved down. The edge of her hand reached the thick fringe of pubic hair and the base of the penis. Small now, fat and soft in its nest, she gathered it in her hand and stroked her thumb along its length. Another hand came down. Sally pushed it away.

'No. It's mine.'

She curled the hair around her little finger, made tight coils on either side and neatly arranged the penis between them.

'There,' she said. 'You should be David.'

'Mmm.'

She took the tip between her fingers and held it up. She stretched, then allowed to fold back the concertina of skin around the shaft, somehow endearingly excessive like a bloodhound's face. She let go and watched it flop on to his thigh. She picked it up again. Let go again. It sustained itself for a moment then wobbled and fell back, landing softly against her nose. She closed her eyes and breathed in deeply – herself, mostly.

He stroked her neck and shoulders as she dreamed. Was this how lovers lived every day, was it possible for this to be normal? And if so, how could such a vast secret be kept, held back until each one discovered it for themselves, if ever? Perhaps that was the only way – what is unspeakable must be lived. Life had been marble, bronze, paint – a yawn and a sly distraction in Miss Hattendon's art appreciation class. An hour she had spent on Michelangelo, the carving of the head, the feet, the exquisite hands, much talk of Florentine republicanism – what was wrong with the woman? There had been cruel laughter before the end. In China, meanings had become themselves, swelling off the page and the canvas into rounded life. First at night in Nanking, lethal, blood-ied, and now again so sweetly. It was as if Sally had only read her life, but now 'apple' on a page would merge, grow and green before being plucked clean off and eaten.

Her thoughts turned more cautious, playing on the few real marriages of which she had any knowledge, her parents' first and foremost. How soon had it gone wrong for them? When, how, why – was the fatality of love inherent or was there some trick to dodge it? Were there Ulysses of love who always got through in the end, outsmarting all the monsters? Sally thought she might be one. Anyway, they hadn't started as she was starting, not one of them. She was sure of that.

Her ear flat on his belly, she listened to the constant chat-ter of intestines doing their work. He moved his hand down her spine. Vertebrae were counted, and the dimples at the small of her back gently searched. A finger found the little lump of tail bone and slid along the curve of buttocks and firmly between them into the heat and the thickness. Sally moved – saying yes. She must have everything now, give everything. Modesty was love's vice of vices. He stroked the back of her thighs, eased two fingers between them and made his own claim with a sudden inward pressure. Sally opened her eyes, arched her back to push herself more firmly against him. Double in her crossed vision, the penis rose, faltered short of the vertical before slumping back to bump softly against her nose. They moved apart, exhausted and not a little sore.

Sally got up and began to scuff through the clothes, throwing the male items towards the bed.

'Come on,' she ordered. 'Sunrise!'

Hugh's apology that night after the garden party had been long, sometimes bordering on the tearful, sometimes on the poetic. It became general, an apology for himself and a passionate plea that he should still be acceptable to Sally. There was new language and a new refining heat that drained him and left little at the end. Too astonished by this different and stirringly novel man, Sally said little. She had expected another scene – a melodrama with herself as collapsed supplicant on a background of Victorian carpet. And so there was relief as well as surprise and even a certain low delight at the thought of her own wickedness going unpunished. Hugh at last fell silent, head down, the fingers of both hands combing through damp hair.

'I don't know,' he said wearily, shaking his head. 'I just don't know.'

Sally went to sit beside him. She kissed his cheek, put an arm around his head and held him close.

'I'm the one who should be sorry,' she said. 'It was awful, and silly too. Pointless. Embarrassing. Just not me at all.'

An abasement contest seemed in prospect and Hugh was determined to win from the outset.

'Don't apologise. Never apologise for that, please. I was insensitive, stupid . . .'

Sally got up from the bed as a sign that they should not start all over again. Hugh looked up at her. He seemed bedraggled, rained on and the moment was not entirely to his advantage.

'Can you forgive me?'

Sally shrugged and said, 'Yes, of course,' casually enough to cause him another needle-stab of pain. She was aware of her harshness at that moment, but there had been something in Hugh's appeal that justified it. She cared much less about her own life than before, and for Hugh now to so dramatise his own existence and its link with hers was a luxury in lean times. Hugh pondered the tone of that trivial 'Yes'. Perhaps the whole thing was just another misunderstanding.

It was 2 a.m. and both were at the end of their strength. They stood together by the door. They embraced – more tightly as the seconds passed.

'I thought I'd lost you,' said Hugh.

He was about to ask if he should go, just as Sally was about to say he didn't have to.

'Well,' said one.

'Well,' replied the other.

'Tomorrow, then?'

'Yes.'

Sally woke at ten, as restored as if she had slept for a week. She had just showered and chosen her outfit for the day when the shipping courier came. She held back the two cases she would live out of for the next few days while he, chatty with the latest news, filled in labels, pasted them to the other cases and carted them off down the corridor. It was the perfect start and everything that morning filled her with energy and the excitement of change. In the lobby she happily met the bellboy's admiring, complicit smile as she slid her key over the marble counter and took the thick wad of messages. She looked through them quickly and found what she had been hoping for. A passing waiter stopped and bowed. On the steps the commissionaires raised their caps.

The newsboy ran forward with copies of every English-language paper but would take no money. Sally made her way to her rendezvous along a familiar route, past the salute of the fruit seller and the rank of shoeshiners who sent word along their line, paused in their work and looked up as she went by. Angled spring sun caught every edge of glass, metal, tramline and shined shoe in the city. Sally wore the sun – earned gold on head and shoulders. At the café the waiters could not agree, and so all three came to take her order and stare at the beautiful stranger who, if the rumours were true, had so dramatically become one of them.

The bowl of *café crème* worked quickly on the after-effects of yesterday's alcohol. Sally looked through the messages – there were brief notes from journalists with telephone numbers attached, two visiting cards (one just a line of kanji characters) with their corners turned down in high Proustian outrage letting her know where she would never be welcome again, and a confused letter from Margery. Margot, as she had now become, had declared herself French and wrote a few lines of passionate, if ungrammatical, support in her new *langue maternelle*. There was a PS and a girlish, exuberant arrow in the bottom right-hand corner. Sally followed it to the other side of the sheet where she found an invitation to a Marianne party – 'bare breasts only, my dear, for peace and freedom'. The letter ended with a couplet from *Coriolanus* and a breathless clutch of exclamation marks. Margery at least had been entertained. Sally returned the letter to its envelope and dropped the visiting cards in the ashtray. She checked her watch and turned to the newspapers. In the American- and British-controlled papers there was a word or two of code to confirm what everyone already knew – a moment of awkwardness, an unfortunate embarrassment. In another she bridled at talk of a young Englishwoman and too much wine, though she would have accepted it humbly the night before. Where Japan held a majority of the shares the event had been an unparalleled success which had finally put to rest those unhappy feelings caused by the misunderstanding over the machine-gunned Ambassador. She had a friend in the *New China Nation*, but one who made her smile with his talk of passion and idealism and injustices that could no longer be borne. Tiredness and drink had been, no doubt, part of the story too. Peter sat down opposite.

'Reading your reviews – how are you?'

'I'm well,' said Sally. 'In fact, I'm very well.'

'You got my note, then?'

'I did, and all these – look. I'm famous.'

Peter fanned through the messages then poked at the visiting cards in the ashtray. Sally smiled.

'So old-fashioned, don't you think? So stuffy.'

She accepted a cigarette and Peter lit them both. The honour guard of waiters appeared, curious to see what company she kept. They took his order and retreated with backward glances.

'Peter, what is going on?'

'Have you read the Chinese papers?'

'No – and don't pretend you have either.'

'A friend tells me what's in them. Oh, and there's a photograph too.'

'And how did that get there?'

Peter shrugged.

'I was careless. I left some things around the Press Club and it seems as if one of them went missing.'

Sally gave a sceptical frown.

'Don't worry – it's a good one. Look.'

He handed over a folded newspaper and there she was – a generous three-inch by three-and-a-half close-up framed by Chinese characters, bold down one side where the headline ran.

'What does it say?'

'You're a hero.'

'And the details?'

'I can't remember the details.'

Sally looked at some of the other pages – two illustrated advertisements and her own photograph were the only things she could understand.

'Keep it,' said Peter. 'You can frame it and hang it on the wall at home. You'll be able to make up any story you like.'

Talk of home resounded between them and when the conversation started again it was in another key.

'Hugh's resigned.'

Peter was solemn and silent for so long Sally prompted him.

'Did you know?'

'Not exactly. I called the embassy this morning – newsman habits – and got Primrose-Browne. He was cagey and not very polite. I made some suggestions and all he would say was "it's a bit of a grey area" and then the phone went dead. Has he really done it?'

'He came to the Cathay last night, that's when he told me. He'd already done it – he'd left the letter at the embassy but had a copy with him.'

'Ah,' said Peter.

Eyes met. Peter's hint of doubt irritated Sally intensely and she let it show. He looked out into the street.

'What did it say? If you don't mind . . .'

'I won't tell you. I'll never tell anyone. It was all quite a scene – for three hours or so we talked before –'

Shouting and blaring erupted from the street as car and rickshaw narrowly avoided a collision. Peter leaned closer.

'I'm sorry?'

'Before he left. We went over everything. He was apologising to me. I wasn't expecting that. In fact, I didn't really expect any of it. Hugh isn't just what he seems, you know.'

Peter held up his hands defensively.

'I'm his friend, Sally. You don't have to tell me.'

'He . . .'

Sally hesitated and looked upwards as she concentrated on the phrase in her mind. Was it right? Could it be taken the wrong way? Alternatives failed to come and she had to say something.

'He sort of rose to the occasion really – in his own Hughish way. That's where he is now – at the embassy finishing off. Well, he would be anyway of course. Three days and then we weigh anchor or whatever one does. It's like we're on the run – fun really.'

'Where to?'

It was Sally's turn to shrug and make a diffident wave with her cigarette.

'Somewhere else. Only I wish it was somewhere else, not boring old England. That's why I wanted to come to China – not because of China, but because of England. Perhaps we'll jump ship in Hong Kong. Hugh will grow a beard and we'll plant coffee in the Philippines, fish for pearls off Surabaya, beachcomb and dream in a little bay on Santa Isabel, our last shreds of clothes having worn away to nothing years before.'

'You've been reading the map.'

'I used to as a girl. Nothing dealt with a wet Sunday afternoon in Hertfordshire better than a map. Did you know there are *Iles du désappointement*? For a while I didn't know what it meant and that was where I most wanted to go. Then when I found out I thought it must be a trick.

They really were the most wonderful places in the world and the people who had found them and named them just wanted to keep them for themselves.'

'They're all *Iles du désappointement*.'

'Are you sure – can't you be too worldly, Peter?'

'Isn't it too late for being unworldly? You've been to China, Sally, and so have I. You've seen it and I know what you've seen.'

'But it doesn't all have to be like this, does it? Not every-where.'

She watched the traffic in the street and an awkwardness lengthened. The unspoken broke the surface and they both understood. Sally stayed silent as her chest tightened and her eyes filled. As she looked down heavy, sunny drops splashed on to her skirt, darkening the cloth as they soaked into it. Peter was searching his pockets, but she found her own handkerchief first.

'I'm sorry. Why now, after all this? Minnie would not approve. She'd find me a job to do and then I'd be fine. I was never bored in Nanking, Peter. Never less bored in all my life and that's what frightens me now. What if that was the height? I just couldn't bear that.'

She sniffed and wiped her eyes decisively.

'I'm talking nonsense. Ignore me. I'm meeting Hugh at three. He's finished then and we have two days to get all our last-minute things done. Be my good friend for the next few hours.'

They walked – the waiters looking after them (one with newspaper in hand), before turning to pick relics from the table, crestfallen at the sight of money. Sally and Peter talked of the future, but so vaguely that it made her laugh and say they were no better than a pair of fairground fortune-tellers.

'I see travel,' said Peter, 'and much change.'

'So you're off too, then? Where this time?'

'Where the story is.'

'Wherever the world takes you?'

'Yes.'

'That's nice.'

They ambled on, looking in shop windows, cautious and tense with desire as they calculated each new and long-separated question in the game.

'We must go into the Chinese city,' said Sally suddenly.

Peter started with an objection.

'No, we must. One last time. Anyway, I have to buy some things – souvenirs. I'll have to go back with something or they'll think I've never been here.'

So they queued at one of the crossings until waved through by British soldiers. Thirty yards on Sally got what, in part, she had come for – the awakening flush of fear, the primitive ripple in the small, fine hairs at the back of her neck as she once again stood close to Japanese soldiers. They finished searching a peddlar and motioned Sally and Peter forward. Sulky and frozen-faced their mood was not improved by the sight of an American and a British passport. An unnecessary amount of time was taken leafing through the pages. They stared at Sally particularly, at the photograph in her passport, at her face again. There was a conversation before the documents were handed back and they were allowed to pass.

Around the edges of the International Settlement there was a vigorous fringe of recovery as if fed by some invisible nutrient that leaked from its borders. Sally and Peter soon reached the end of it and saw the familiar acreage of destruction beyond. Here and there, isolated in rubble and ash, small factories had survived or been quickly reconstructed. Smoke came from chimneys as the Chinese within worked hard for East Asian co-prosperity.

Near the boundary there were plenty of shops and stalls. Ginger jars, soapstone buddhas, carved discs of green and white jade and miniature lacquered chests of drawers abounded. Prices were low and the shopkeepers eager. Sally inspected the merchandise carefully, rejecting anything with the war cry 'Made in Japan' on its base. She was determined to take no money back across the border and was soon weighed down with parcels. In the last shop she exchanged her watch for five yards of silk.

'It's too much,' said Peter.

'It doesn't matter.'

The shopkeeper ground the case on a touchstone and went outside to check the results in daylight before agreeing. It was by the suitably traditional structure of his shop that she piled her purchases on the pavement and demanded to be photographed.

'Come on, it's what they expect. I can't manage a dead tiger, so this will just have to do instead.'

She posed sportingly with one hand on top of the pile. They were near the Japanese checkpoint and Sally could feel herself playing up to their curiosity.

'And together. We must have one together.'

In a high mood, Sally had Peter's camera out of his hands before he knew it and was pressing it on a passer-by. She began simultaneously to speak and mime instructions, but the man seemed to know what to do and took up a suitable position. He looked through the viewfinder and then raised his head again and moved his hands together. Sally and Peter squeezed into closer contact. Their photographer took his responsibilities seriously and in the twenty seconds or so he spent finalising his composition their smiles became a little strained as the implication of parting crept over both of them. The shutter click ended their difficulties.

They recrossed the border. The Japanese, perhaps having made use of the field telephone sitting on the sandbag wall of their position, nodded politely and declined to look again at their passports. The British soldiers took up a quarter-hour of their time searching Sally's packages and questioning Peter about what sort of things he liked to photograph.

'What time is it?'

Peter looked at his watch and told her.

'Too soon. You're not busy, Peter, are you? Not really?'

A taxi was summoned, loaded with purchases and sent off to deliver them to the Cathay.

'I shall have to buy another suitcase now.'

They wandered aimlesly through streets, a park, a market, blessed by weather more like May than mid-March. It was in the Avenue Roi Albert in the French concession that they passed the open doors of the Lumière. The timing was right, and the darkness and the prospect of the last two hours together without the need for speech. They bought tickets and sat with half a dozen others in an auditorium the size of a drawing room. An outdated French newsreel flickered by – something arcane about new labour laws in Paris, a selection of colonial footnotes. The main feature started and there was Bob Conway, gentleman and adventurer, the future Foreign Secretary of England, making the most of his innate authority as he rescued the last few Westerners from an advancing swarm of savage Chinese rebels. Their plane, hijacked, took them to the furthest point from civilisation and the isolated, mystifying humanity of Shangri-La. Philosophy for the common man – what to do? Stay for a century or two in the Valley of the Blue Moon, tight-sealed like a seed of all goods, abstract and concrete, waiting to open on to an outside world clean at last only because it is empty, or leave at once – fight, suffer and quite possibly die?

The lights came on. Sally and Peter sat on alone as a young woman collected litter from between the seats.

'Had you seen it before?' Sally asked.

'No.'

'I don't think it was quite what I expected. It can't be an accident, can it?'

'What can't?'

'Usually nothing means anything very much – or not in my life. Then it flips and everything seems to mean something special. It must come from within, don't you think? Things are really the same, it's just that you see them differently. I want it always to be like that.'

In the foyer, by a clock that showed she was already late, Sally wrote on a scrap of paper.

'Do you already have this? I can't remember.'

She put down an address and a telephone number. She paused and then added the name of a ship and the day and hour of its departure – and the cabin number.

'There – I've seen it in your hand. You've no excuse now. I'm of the short and simple school when it comes to goodbyes. Keep safe, Peter. Be yourself.'

Sally walked out into the brilliance of the street, turned to the left and was gone.

Two and a half days remained. The excitement of their imminent departure and the calming absorption of small tasks made them easy. Last letters were written and enclosed in last parcels of jars and tins to Nanking. Sally included her address in England and imposed on every recipient the heaviest obligation to write to her there. She cabled her parents to confirm her departure and projected day of arrival at Southampton. The last packing was done and she accompanied Hugh on his own rather dutiful souvenir shopping trip. A selection of acceptable gifts was made — the artefacts of a diluted half-China that her craftsmen had made just for Hugh, as they had for his ancestors these last three hundred years. In the last shop he gave instructions for their delivery to the embassy.

'Well — that's that. Now we're free.'

They enjoyed the weekday city in the hours that Hugh had always been deprived of before. Sally was an excellent guide and was proud to show how much she had learned. Acquaintances, by sight at least, acknowledged her in Russian cafés, Chinese tea houses and a Jewish restaurant where they lunched. Hugh was admiring and inwardly a little angry with himself as he felt a twinge of resentment at how thick and rounded was this other life to which he was only now being admitted.

'I've been neglecting you,' he told her on the afternoon of their last full day.

'Not at all,' said Sally. 'I like cities. I like wandering.'

Sally's future was clearer now — events had seen to that and she enjoyed the calm of having things taken out of her hands. She took Hugh's arm as they walked in the botanic garden. The weather was fine, the surroundings just strange enough and the prospect of an English summer enticing where it had once appalled. Acceptance was a pleasure in itself — its ease ran through and heightened everything she saw and felt. Mere chance was in abeyance for both of them — for a moment, at least, the dice were taking their side and it was not hard to believe they deserved it. Under their happy influence Sir Algernon Farquhar-Starr had telephoned Hugh early on the morning after the garden party. He shouted and banged the table, exploiting to the utmost the opportunity for a magnanimous drama. Strange indeed, but he had once been young, he had once felt strongly and more simply about things.

'Jerrold? Some bloody fool has left a letter on my desk, but I'm damned if I'm going to open it. Be here at eleven.'

Sir Algernon had no children of his own – or not real ones. His imaginary offspring, Victoria (six) and Hector, an everlasting four-year-old, were such discreet creatures that not even his wife had any idea of their existence. His favourite scenes with them involved the dispensing of humane wisdom and the pardoning of great crimes. Hugh bore little resemblance to these fantasies, it was true, but he was young and had clearly been foolish. There was tea at eleven, and much fondling of a favourite pipe as Sir Algernon waxed lyrical on pragmatism, worldliness and the higher morality.

'So you see, young Jerrold,' he concluded, 'while I can have no knowledge of what is in this letter, I feel strongly that I ought not to read it.'

The offending letter was pushed across the desk. Hugh received it sheepishly. He noticed how the flap had been picked at and crudely reglued as he slipped it into his pocket. Sir Algernon escorted him to the door.

'By the way – damn fine turn of phrase. It'll come in useful, I'm sure.'

With three telephone calls Peter did what he could to square the press. Hugh's gesture was stifled in the womb. Sally was relieved and called it nonsense when he said he should have insisted for her sake. Walking in the garden late on their last afternoon, Hugh was buoyed by the knowledge that he had at least the potential for nobility.

The day of departure started early. Hugh dispatched his baggage from the embassy and came to meet her at the Cathay. They breakfasted almost alone. Shanghai freighted them with one final story – a distant champagne pop accounting for Chou Sing-chi, one-time general, entrepreneur, new friend of Japan and servant of many masters as he arrived for a confidential meeting. As they left there was still some disorder about the front steps. The staff looked concerned, but Sally stepped nonchalantly over the pale rosé of watered blood as she got into the taxi.

Boarding dragged but cabins, once found, were acceptable and the *Brittanicus* looked like a pleasant enough home for the next three weeks. Sally and Hugh explored eagerly. They looked down on tugs as they pulled and nudged the liner out into the channel. Shanghai began to slip away. A crowd gathered on one side to get a closer look at the new sensation – the vast, shark-snouted threat of the *Gneisenau* taking a break from its sea trials to pay a courtesy visit to China. Tree-trunk guns poked in all directions and the red, swastika-hearted ensign at the stern was just held by the breeze. Sally thought of how proud Herr Rabe would have been.

'Ah well – homeward-bound.'

'We're on the first officer's table this evening,' said Hugh.

Leaning over a rail, looking down on the busier decks below, Sally saw a face and coolly moved on. They rested that afternoon. Sally went over the passenger list in her cabin. She found her own name and checked that it was correctly numbered. She lay still for two hours of dreamy, if exacting self-dissection. Was she cold, was she cruel? Did she care either way? Had she been made like this or was it bred in the bone? Would it do to leave everything to chance and then say it was no fault of hers? Whatever happened it could be nothing more than a tale of individuals – which was as much as to say a tale of nothing, or as near to nothing as made no odds. Here she had changed, and knew it. Before, in all her favourite stories singleness magnified. Now it atomised. She listened to the tread of fellow passengers in the gangway outside. One slowed and stopped. A man swore at finding himself on the wrong deck and moved on. Sally got up, rearranged the silk flowers on the writing table and began to prepare for the evening.

They ate well and the conversation was diverting. The familiar process began of testing, selecting and rejecting companions for the voyage. Later, groups coagulated in the first-class smoking lounge and began to feel comfortable with each other. Language defined most of them with only a few accented contrarians out of their place. Sally and Hugh, arm in arm, made a slow tour of the room. Under the dominance of English she heard almost every European language she could identify and some she couldn't. A badminton doubles was agreed for the next day. Hugh found a like mind and got involved in discussing the situation. Sally, tired, found a good vantage point and sat down to spectate. She idled through the last of the Shanghai papers on the table before her — FÜHRER ENTERS HOMELAND — RAPE OF AUSTRIA; 'PROTECTIVE CUSTODY' FOR NEWSPAPER EDITORS; 'WAR WON' — FRANCO'S CONFIDENCE; SOCIALITE 'UNWELL' AT FRENCH CONSULATE; THIGH BONE OF PEKING MAN FOUND — NEW PROOF OF CANNIBALISM. She let them drop as the voices around her blended into a single half-familiar and ancient harmony. The West was going home. And the money too — Sally looked up, a dozen other heads moving with hers as cyclamen Schiaparelli rustled by. Hugh came to sit beside her. They talked inconsequentially. Sally, tight within, covered her mouth and yawned widely.

'Shall we turn in?' suggested Hugh.

At her cabin door there was hesitation and a short, word-less debate. Sally offered her cheek and looked away over his shoulder.

'Well then,' said Hugh. 'Until tomorrow.'

'Goodnight.'

She did not turn on the light, but paced in the darkness and tried to breathe out the stifling tension. She found a wrap by touch and went out to the promenade deck. From around a moon just short of full the clouds thinned showing, for no more than a minute, a perfect aureole before clearing altogether. Shadows became sharp in the bleaching light. Sally leaned on the rail and looked out on a calm, speckled sea. She was good at conjuring faces, always had been. She knew well how this quirk of mind had its fashions – one would predominate for a while, catching at every slenderest resemblance before fading, then vanishing entirely. Perhaps always a sceptic of love, the last few months had confirmed her views. Love was an overheated, celluloid thing – a sort of emotional boasting when we all knew really that lovers can be replaced and that the inconstant heart always heals. It was too weak to do anything else. The Romantics had a style, but no truth. Dying was simpler than they allowed – one does it literally or not at all. No one really dies of a broken heart, still less of boredom as she had once believed. No one is driven out of the slaughterhouse in a gleaming, diplomatic limousine, not a scratch on their skin, without leaving something behind. Sally had left a great deal behind, but regretted nothing. She contemplated her future with indifference.

The air turned chill and she went inside. A steward made way for her – a man of many voyages, he smiled generously.

'Goodnight, madam.'

'Goodnight.'

Had it proved nothing but a fantasy she would not have been surprised. When she turned the last corner to find him there she approached him calmly and happily, taking her key from her evening bag to accept what had surely always been inevitable. All decisions had been made, all things said. They did not speak until five hours later when Sally threw his trousers at him and ordered a walk in the dawn.

They had the afterdeck to themselves. They moved two recliners together and sat down side by side to wait for the sun. Red shaded to yellow and they began to feel the warmth on their faces.

'It's tough on Hugh.'

Sally thought of him still sleeping below and of the scene that must soon follow. The pain would be great. She would inflict it.

'We must tell him at once. No skulking. No shame.'

'Yes.'

'I would have married him, Peter. Perhaps I would even have stayed. I would have loved the children and perhaps, just now and again, another man.'

Peter looked across at her. The richly coloured dawn light was on her face. Sally laid her head back and closed her eyes against it. He believed her when she told him with a smile that she was dangerous now and that she would promise only honesty.

'If I sleep with another man, Peter, I'll tell you but I'm done with lies. Let there be pain and then recovery and moving on, but no lies.'

'There it is.'

She looked up and opened her eyes to see the first direct brilliance of the sun. The point lengthened then thickened into a clear segment. She stared at it until half the disc was above the horizon and she was forced to look away, its shape staying with her, a shimmering montage over everything else.

'Hugh won't even hate us. He'll try – poor thing. He'll find reasons for hating us but they'll never really catch fire. They just don't with some people.'

'We can get a flat in town,' said Peter. 'There'll be no trouble getting work.'

The sudden return to the prosaic pleased Sally. Some part, at least, of their future became clearer. The flat swam into view. She decorated it, then populated it with the right friends and the right books and magazines. It was noisy and busy and there was never time. Uniforms hung from the hooks behind the doors and in the beds there was blind love behind the splinter-taped windows and the blackout curtains.

'It's going to be all right, isn't it?'

The sun lifted from the horizon like a balloon. The silhouette of the stern rails moved across its face as the helmsman read his compass and turned more fully to the west.